MW01169481

From Then to Now
A Treasure Lost in Time

From Then to Now
A Treasure Lost in Time

Jon Scallion

Library of Congress Control Number: 2018911213
ISBN: Hardcover 978-1-9845-5411-6
Softcover 978-1-9845-5410-9
eBook 978-1-9845-5409-3

This is a work of fiction. Names, characters, places and incidents either are the product of the author's imagination or are used fictitiously, and any resemblance to any actual persons, living or dead, events, or locales is entirely coincidental.

Print information available on the last page.

Rev. date: 09/19/2018

To order additional copies of this book, contact:
Xlibris
1-888-795-4274
www.Xlibris.com
Orders@Xlibris.com
783366

CHAPTER 1

As I walked into the room, a chill raced through my body while the stillness in the air magnified the absence of sound. Across the room I saw the morning rays of sunlight shimmering in a crimson pool and a pale figure lying in the center. It looked like she was asleep, Snow White waiting for her Prince Charming. But there would be no Prince Charming today; the evil queen was now the fairest of them all.

The scene wasn't new to me, but this time something wrenched in my stomach. I have seen worse that had little or no effect on me, but this was different. I knew her, only briefly; still I knew her.

She was in her late twenties with red hair that now blended with the scarlet loch that caressed her and accentuated her ivory skin. She was a vision of loveliness that didn't deserve to be left for the vultures to pick over with insensitive abandonment. Still the vultures would have to come, pictures taken, the body probed, prodded, and talk that proved the insensitivity of man, but although I knew what was to come, I still knew what had to be done. I've been in this business long enough to know not to get caught in the middle unless it couldn't be helped.

I called Lieutenant Mike Cavanaugh on my cellular and told him where I was and what to expect. Mike and I have known each other since the dawn of man, or so it seemed.

After high school, we enlisted in the army, which led to becoming police officers when we were discharged. We served in the same precinct, but I left after five years. Mike remained and moved up the ladder. I was unable to sit back and watch the criminal go free and the victims put bars on their homes, so I gave it up to pursue a career of private law enforcement. I wanted to be able to get the job done without all the bureaucratic red tape and not have to wipe the nose of the bad guy.

With a few minutes to spare while waiting for the police, I looked around. On a table next to the window was what appeared to be a suicide note. It said, "I can't get these visions out of my mind. I know this will let me truly find myself."

I didn't have time to dwell on the note, although I found it to be strange that it wasn't signed. This woman wasn't one to leave a note unfinished; everything to her had to be done properly or not at all, and besides that, I didn't feel this kid was the type to do the Dutch. I left the note for the police to investigate. If I needed any information about it, Mike would let me have it.

As I continued to look around, I saw books on the floor, on shelves, chairs, everywhere. They were all about reincarnation, the afterlife, and spiritual guidance. My guess would be a hundred or so, including magazines, neatly set about, some opened as if she was researching on something. It looked as if she was competing with the local public library or getting ready to open her own shop. All was neat, orderly, and categorized. I wouldn't have expected less.

I remembered her talking of past lives, mainly hers; this is what got me involved with her in the first place. I let her talk. I didn't want to lose a potential client, strange or otherwise; besides times haven't been the best. Anything was better than nothing, so I thought at the time.

On top of a small stack of books sitting on the mantle over the fireplace was an address book. I picked it up and started thumbing through it. Under "C," I was drawn to a list titled "Club Members." In bold print at the top was the name "Dr. Jonah Hyde." Now that's a name. He was probably born on Friday the thirteenth at the stroke of midnight in what was the worst storm of the century and delivered by a midwife with a crooked nose, wart, and her own boiling caldron all within a circle of fire.

I shook my head thinking this wasn't the time for this type of speculation. I took the book, and as I slipped it into my coat pocket, I was drawn to her face as she lay there motionless. There was a haunting hint of disbelief across her face, almost asking how this could have happened. I wanted to close her eyes but didn't want to dirty the scene for the investigation. As I looked on, I noticed the phone partially under her neck as if dropped when she fell, her wrists turned up, her hands open, reaching out like one would do if examining their palms. The cuts were straight, not jagged or punctured as I have seen on many a suicide victim. Stranger yet, I thought, was the absence of an instrument that could have made these wounds.

My thoughts were interrupted by the sounds of sirens. The boys like to hear themselves or just wanted to scare away the cats as they drove here because there wasn't any other reason to make all that noise to get here now.

As the sirens fell silent, you could hear the patter of flat feet and doors banging shut. "The Keystone Cops" have arrived.

The door opened and Mike walked into the room with the usual circus, after all the sirens led the parade.

Attached to Mike's side was Detective Sergeant Peter Callahan. I often thought of them as Siamese twins. I figured it was better than picturing him as a mole on Mike's ass, and I didn't want to go there.

Callahan was with us at the academy. Our views differed from the start. Callahan went by the book. I figured that was why he always wore that stern, furrowed brow expression. I was sure he had a manual for the proper procedure to wipe himself after using the toilet. Pete should have been an English Bobbie because he sure looked the part right out of the old movies.

Pete started, "Well, as I live and breathe, it's Captain Avenger."

I bowed gracefully, my arm in a gesture indicating that the "Bird of Paradise should fly up his . . ." I don't dislike Callahan. He is a thorough investigator, but he was born without a humorous bone in his body. He made a pie in the face seem like a hanging offense. Slapstick comics roll over in their graves when he comes around. In short, he wasn't any fun to work with, and God knows in this business you need humor to make it through the day.

I greeted Mike. He had a grip of steel, and when we shook hands, it became a contest of strength, but being adults we would smile and let go. Mike was into physical fitness, weights, and the like. Women would stop and watch "him" walk by. He enjoys it, but it drives his wife crazy. Not that she's the jealous type; it's just that he likes to rub it in.

I'm not ready for a walker just yet, but I don't feel you need to punish your body to feel good.

"I see you still haven't been able to find a surgeon capable of freeing you from your evil twin," I said with a hint of a smile.

Mike put on his usual frown, glanced at Callahan and back at me, and said, "You two should join a comedy group."

I interrupted, "Callahan would have to change his name to Gracie."

Mike continued as he rolled his eyes and shook his head. "Let's get this over with. Tell me how you managed to be here this time. It seems that if there isn't a body lying around, you wouldn't be around."

"I'm Captain Avenger, right, Callahan?" He just looked and grunted.

"Okay, knock off the bullshit. What happened?" Mike asked, agitated with the bantering between Callahan and me.

"I received a call around six this morning. I knew the voice, normally soft, always confident, but this time it was low, frantic, and without patience. She was gasping pleas of help. I got up and rushed over here. I was too late."

"This is Shannan McCready. She hired me to . . . you will enjoy this. Find out who she was in eighteen twenty-six," Callahan interrupted, "from Captain Avenger to Ghost Chaser! Impressive resume Falco."

"Callahan, is that humor seeping from your jowls?"

He raised one eyebrow and didn't say any more. I often think he was a direct descendant of the infamous "Inspector Lestrade" as described in the Adventures of Sherlock Holmes. Must be that Bobbie thing again.

"She was a client," I said as I was interrupted.

"Over here, Mike, look at this." Callahan was calling from the table by the window. He was holding the note in his gloved hand, offering it to Mike. He continued, "It looks like a closed case. This is a suicide note."

Mike took the note, looked at me, and asked, "I suppose you saw this already?"

"Yes," I answered.

"You didn't want to tell us . . . why?" he asked.

"I knew you would find it since it was right out in the open; however, I think you may want to rethink suicide," I replied as I started toward the door.

"Where are you going, Falco?" Callahan asked.

"You don't need me here. I'm sure you can muddle through on your own."

"I wouldn't doubt that he has some of the evidence in his pockets," Callahan said to Mike.

Although it was true, I couldn't let it pass. "Callahan, I didn't know you cared that much to want to strip-search me. After all, that latex glove does make you look like a proctologist wannabe," I said sarcastically, watching the veins in his neck flare and his face flush as he held himself back. I was sure he was going to explode.

Mike headed off the fireworks. "Why don't you just leave, Vince, and we'll get to work." He held out his hand in a halting motion to Callahan.

"If you need me later, Mike, you know where I'll be. If I'm not, have Callahan look for me in the shadows." I looked at Callahan with a smile and a wink as I watched him grind his teeth and give me a cold steel gaze.

As I was walking out the front door, there was the usual fanfare of "concerned citizens" and most of the local TV news vans with—and I say this with reservation—reporters. I have yet to see an accurate reporting of a crime scene from any of them.

Across the street separating two of these vans was a cab. I noticed a man sitting in the back seat staring over the edge of the half-opened window reminding me of the old drawing that said, "Kilroy was Here." He had a slender face sprouting a Freudian beard and round wire-framed glasses with eyes like you see in portraits that follow you wherever you go. He saw me watching him then tapped the driver on the shoulder and drove off.

I noted the cab's number out of habit and walked away not answering any questions being fired at me from the gaggle of reporters trying to see why the "circus was in town." I often think that if they didn't have police scanners, they would be sitting around doing needlepoint and gossiping.

CHAPTER 2

It was a warm October day, sun shining, white billowy clouds aimlessly floating in a bright blue sky, and Halloween decorations dotting the area. It seemed everything was all right with the world, but not for Shannan McCready.

I was up since six and needed a caffeinated beverage, steaming hot, to get my body regulated. I needed a coffee fix.

I stopped at Lilly's Café. It was one of those greasy spoons with atmosphere that attracted a certain kind of clientele to which I was privileged.

Lilly was six feet something, weighed in at two eighty or so, shaved head, and three days' growth on his face. He wrestled in his prime but stopped after he fractured his neck. He liked to cook, so he opened this place. His specialty was cooking everything with lard, of this I was sure. Fat-free wasn't a phrase Lilly knew.

I sat at the counter. Lilly was at the far end wearing what I would swear was the only apron he owned. and it still had remnants of the first meal he cooked. Most people frame their first dollar. He held on to the first meal he served, well, preserved on his apron. Maybe he should have it bronzed to put in the Greasy Spoon Hall of Fame.

"What'll ya have, Falco?" he bellowed from the grill.

"Coffee with a little inspiration." Lilly poured the coffee and slipped it under the counter as he added the inspiration. He sat it down, looked at me, and said, "You look like you lost your best friend."

"Close—it was my client. She wanted to see her next life," I said, half joking and half sincere.

Lilly picked up on the sincere part. I didn't think he had it in him.

"What happened or don't you want to talk about it?" he asked.

I told him what happened. A faint glimmer appeared in his eyes. I could actually see a thought forming. Then he spoke.

"You know, Vince, about two, maybe three years ago, I was down South visiting some friends and there was a scandal in the town. It was a small town, didn't take much to get everyone going. Here it wouldn't even be noticed. Anyway, two women did the same thing side-by-side, you know, suicide. The strange part was that both of them belonged to some religious group that believed they were reincarnated. The scandal part was the group leader, Swami something or other. I don't remember the name. Anyway, he vanished the same night the girls were last seen alive. Not to mention that one of the girls was the daughter of the preacher. The local paper said it was some kind of cult thing. They really went after the rest of the group, never could prove anything, and never found the swami." Lilly hesitated, his face expressing deep thought, then he continued.

"Some real nut cases out there. I guess you see them all," he said, shaking his head.

"Yeah, Lilly, some real nut cases," I said with a sigh as I got up and put the money on the counter to pay for the coffee.

"It's on me, Vince," Lilly said as he pushed it back toward me.

"Thanks," I replied as I walked away.

CHAPTER 3

I was back in my office, staring out the window, and looking down on the main street, not noticing the hustle and bustle of the city as I thought about the events of the day.

I wondered how many other people were looking at or even thinking of their past lives before this life. I know I never gave it any thought before, but it sure was haunting me today.

I heard a beep, beep, then it registered. My recorder wanted to tell me something. I pushed the button. The mechanical man that lives inside my phone announced in his best voice, "You have one message in box number one. Wednesday 3:30 p.m.," then the message came on. "This is . . . this . . .," and click went the receiver. Whoever it was hung up.

As I looked away from the phone, I noticed that I had Shannan's file on my desk and remembered the first time we talked. It was late in the afternoon, around four or four thirty, and the phone rang, startling me, I had thought it was rebelling against me since it hadn't rang for days.

"Hello." I always wait to see who is on the other end before admitting to be me.

"Is this Falco Investigations?" she asked.

"Yes, may I help you?" I said in my best receptionist voice.

"I need to talk to someone about doing some investigative work for me. Is there someone available?" she asked, her voice warm, sensual, and confident. You could say, sophisticated.

It was getting late and I did want to continue doing absolutely nothing. I relented and said, "Yes, who are you and what can I do for you?"

She replied, "My name is Shannan McCready I . . . I would like to have . . .," she hesitated.

I interjected, "Someone followed?"

"No!" she said, somewhat startled. "I need to discuss my situation in person." Her voice was confident but had some underlying tones. I knew this voice: it always meant big bucks and right now I could use some.

"Let me check my schedule." I didn't want to seem too anxious. I continued after a brief moment of rubbing some papers together over the phone. "I can see you tomorrow at 10:00 a.m."

"Could we please meet this afternoon after five? I realize this is short notice, but it is important to me," she said it almost as a command, yet I could hear a plea in her voice.

"Okay, I'll wait here until six." I didn't want to tell her I would be in all night.

"Thank you, and who should I ask for?"

"Falco," I said as we both hung up.

The sun was setting, leaving the office in shadows. I like this time of day. I left the lights off just for the ambience, put my feet up on the desk, leaned back in my chair, and clasped my hands behind my head. I let my mind wander while I waited for my client.

There was a knock on the door, bringing me back to the real world. I glanced at my watch. It was 6:00 p.m., I must have dropped off to la-la land. I got up and opened the door.

In front of me stood the vision of an angel. The light from the hall outlined her image. Her red hair glistened as if on fire while her face shown of smooth white ivory with eyes that shined. Words struggled to escape from my lips.

She broke the trance. "Mr. Falco?"

"Yes, please come in," I said in my best nonchalant manner as I reached over to the switch on the wall and turned on the lights.

"Please have a seat," I offered as I sat behind my desk.

She had a graceful motion as she moved to the chair in front of me and in a very elegant fashion sank into the soft leather cushion of the chair. "How may I help you, Miss McCready?" What she told me was a story out of Poe.

"I'm not sure where I should start, so I'll begin with the most recent event," she said.

"I had arrived at Paragon, that's where I work, and as usual went into the elevator. Everything seemed all right, but as the doors opened to the floor I work on, the air felt still and there was an unnerving quiet, yet I heard a soft, almost strangled, cry for help. I seemed to be floating as I stepped out of the elevator, looking for the person behind the voice.

"The floor is normally filled with people scurrying to their cubicles and offices, but this time it was empty. Everything was black and white, dim like you would see in a smoke-filled room and moving in slow motion. It seemed like a dream."

She hesitated for a moment, the look of stern concentration on her face as she searched for the words to describe her experience.

"As I moved down the hall, a woman crossed in front of me, turning her head as she slowly ran past. The lace from her gown fluttering likes wings behind her. She was screaming in a mournfully slow drawn-out tone, then . . . silence." She continued, "I didn't remember anything else at this point. I found myself at my desk with some of my co-workers standing beside me asking if I was all right and telling someone to get me some water. I was lost for words, I didn't know what to say so didn't tell them anything.

"I didn't feel ill, only confused. I managed to make it through the rest of the day although it left me in an unsettled state because it seemed so real and I felt that it wasn't over. I have seen this in my dreams on more than one occasion, and I'm not sure of what it means except that I feel it has something to do with my last life."

Knock me over with a feather, I thought, then blurted out, "Last life?" She sat back in the chair and gave me a look that indicated that she hadn't prepared me for this bombshell.

"I'm sorry, Mr. Falco."

I interrupted, "Just call me Falco."

"Fal . . . co," the words struggled from her lips.

I enjoyed watching her toss proper etiquette out the window. Her mother taught her well. She had grace, charm, and elegance that could be found in the forties but lost ever since. I couldn't help but think this was one classy dame out of the forties living in the nineties and not more than twenty-seven years old.

She continued, "If I sound a little crazy, please forgive me. I believe in reincarnation and I know who I was in my last life, but not how I died. I feel as if these dreams have something to do with my death then. If I could find this out, maybe the dreams will go away," she said, holding her head in an aristocratic manner as she spoke.

"I do realize that this sounds eccentric, but if you would help me, I would be forever grateful."

That pleading tone in her voice could have made Genghis Khan a house pet.

After she was done with her story, all I could think was "She sure knew how to break a mood." I glanced over at the calendar to see if there was a full moon tonight and if my next appointment was going to be the Wolfman wondering who he really was.

Maybe, just maybe, some of my friends, and I use the term lightly, came up with this Halloween prank, I thought as I asked her, "What do you want me to do?"

"My name was Elizabeth Anne Barrett and I lived in North Carolina. I don't know much more at this time. I only found this out a few weeks ago. I was hypnotized and regressed to the year 1826. I became agitated and had to be brought back before any more information could be had. I'm not ready to do that again. It was a very emotional experience. So I would like you to find out what you can about Elizabeth Anne Barrett."

I'm not sure, but I think my face said this was going to cost big bucks. She reached across my desk and handed me an envelope. It was thick and full. I would count it later.

"It is worth it to me whatever the expense, Mister, I mean, Falco. If there isn't enough there, please let me know."

I knew she couldn't leave out the mister without a struggle. I got up to show her out as I said, "This is fine for now; I'll get back with you."

At the door she half turned, her eyes pleading, her moist lips parted slightly as she spoke. "Thank you . . . Falco."

I closed the door behind her and just stood there wondering what just happened. I must have left the real world and stepped into the Twilight Zone. Was Rod Serling down the hall?

A cold chill washed across my face as the phone rang, bringing me back to reality. I let it ring, waiting for the machine to take the message.

After what seemed forever, it came on. "You have reached the office of Falco Investigations. Sorry, but I'm out of the office at this time. Please leave your name, number, and a brief message, and I will get back to you. Thank you for calling." I was going to replace the message with one of those crazy ditties but haven't gotten around to it yet.

The voice was the same as the one that hung up earlier.

"This is Samantha Richards. I want to talk with you about Shannan McCready. Please call me. I'll be home all evening." Repeating her number three times.

I let it go. I wasn't ready to discuss Shannan with anyone. I didn't know a Samantha from any of the media so why bother. It would keep.

I have had some cases, what to many would be considered strange, but this one is at the top and considered very strange. I never figured myself as Ghost Hunter. All I could think of was where is Casper when you need him.

CHAPTER 4

I tossed and turned all night and now that there was a glimmer of light shining through the window, I figured I might as well get up and at it.

This McCready thing was still eating at me. Something was missing, and I had to find out what it was.

I picked up the phone and called Mike. I wanted to see Shannan's apartment once more without any hassle, and he could arrange it.

"Hello." A low, sleepy, sexy voice answered. It was Mike's better half.

"Marcie, did I wake you?" I said, knowing that at this hour what else would the sane be doing.

"No, Vince, I was just getting in from an all-nighter," she said in a sassy tone. "If you want Mike, you missed him so call him at the station. Good night, Falco." She hung up.

It was only 6:30 a.m. He didn't have to be in the office until eight. I wondered why he left so early.

I put on the coffee and got dressed while I gave Mike a chance to get to the station. Then I called his direct line. "Hello, Sergeant Baxter here," the voice on the other end of the line said.

"Baxter, Falco, I need to talk to Cavanaugh."

"He's not here, Falco. He said if you called, you could find him at the scene."

"What scene?" I asked with the answer in the back of my head.

"The McCready place, thought you knew," he replied.

I grabbed my coat; the address book fell out of the pocket. I had forgotten about it.

I quickly thumbed through it out of habit and the same page jumped out at me "C" for "Club Members" and Dr. Jonah Hyde at the top.

It must have been an exclusive club, I thought, because the list was small—only six names, not including Shannan. The list started with Jonah Hyde, no number, followed by Mary Ornsworth, Patricia Smith, Anne Foxmore, JoAnne Morely, and Beverly Washington. They all had phone numbers. I put it back in my pocket and left.

When I arrived at the apartment, cops were all over the place. I wondered why Mike was back here. He normally had Callahan handle the little details to clean up a case.

I found Mike. "What's up?" I asked.

Mike looked up at me and said, "Well, good morning to you too."

Callahan broke in as he crossed the room, breaking his neck to get close to Mike and me before we said anything he wouldn't be able to hear. "What time did you arrive here yesterday, Falco?"

I didn't have time to answer when Mike told him to look around and he would talk to me. Callahan closed his notebook and dropped his head, but his eyes were still drilling me as he turned and walked away.

"Well, are you going to tell me what's going on or let Callahan get out the rubber hose first?" I said irately, my annoyance more with Callahan's advance than with Mike.

"We received the autopsy report. They found a small puncture wound at the base of the skull. She was drugged. The medical examiner said this put her out while her wrists were slit. She wasn't supposed to wake up, but she did. That must have been when she called you."

"With that much of a blood loss, it's a wonder that she was able to call you. She must have been in a horrific state," Mike said, jaw tight, shaking his head.

The words hit me hard. I could imagine the torment that went through this kid when she came to. I could still hear her voice pleading for help. What kind of person would do something like this. Monster wasn't the right name for this individual.

"Tell me everything, Vince," Mike asked.

"There isn't any more to say that I haven't told you already. Let me think about it and I'll get back to you," I said as I started walking toward the door.

I turned back to Mike as I was leaving and said, "Mike, okay if I come back after you're done? I would like to look around for myself."

Callahan turned and said, "What exactly are you looking for, Falco, that you don't want us to see?"

"I just don't want to upset anything before you're done doing it yourself," I answered sarcastically.

"I don't like the idea of him messing with the scene before we have something solid," Callahan said to Mike.

"Pete, I don't think Vince is going to walk off with anything. He has always cooperated with us."

"Okay, Vince, let me know when," Mike said as a matter of fact.

I gave Callahan a snide smile and a wink as I walked out.

When I left the apartment, it was as if I stepped back in time. The weather, the sights in the neighborhood, and that bearded fellow, but this time without a cab. He was sitting behind the wheel of a Mercedes, black on black; very nice, I thought, although it didn't quite fit the neighborhood but why not flaunt it if you have it. I knew he never left the car. It still had wheels on it.

Don't misread this location. It is a very good neighborhood, but it is surrounded by other-than-desirable sights, sounds, and clubs, to put it nicely.

The area is something of a historical cultural center. It has its own security, but things still happen.

I started toward the Benz when he took notice and drove off.

The air was crisp and cold; I wasn't going to chase after him. I figured he would be back and I would be waiting for him.

As I walked to my car, thoughts kept rolling in my head. I had a feeling this would be more than just a simple homicide; robbery didn't appear to be a motive, and if it were, then why the knockout drug and the wrist slashing?

Who wanted her dead and why? Who was this Freudian type that keeps popping up? And why was he here at this hour of the morning? I just let it go for now.

Questions, questions. That's all I had. What I needed was answers.

I hurried back to my office, I wanted to talk to this Samantha Richards before Mike found out about her. I know I said I would give everything to Mike that I had, but I didn't say when.

CHAPTER 5

When I walked into my office, my machine was beeping like a smoke detector. I was sure it had gone over the edge; it must have received another message. Two in two days is obviously too much for it. I may have to shoot it.

I pushed the button then it spoke: "Mr. Falco, this is Samantha Richards. I must speak to you. It is most urgent. Please call me at Paragon Studios. I'll be here until 5:00 p.m."

The next five messages also were from her. I guess she wants to see me as much as I want to see her.

I dialed the number and listened to it ring and ring. I was just about to hang up when a voice came on.

"Good morning. Paragon Studios, how may I direct your call?"

"Samantha Richards, please," I acknowledged.

"One moment, please," she repeated as she stretched out her "please," sounding more like "poleeeese."

"Hello, Samantha speaking." The voice was very pleasant and alluring, but phone voices can be deceiving, "How may I help you?" she asked.

I thought, By being as beautiful and seductive as your voice, then I answered, "This is Falco. You've called a few times. Sorry it took so long to get back to you. Your message said you wanted to talk about Shannan McCready."

"Yes . . ." There was a hesitation in her voice then she continued, "Not on the phone.

Can you meet me for lunch, about eleven thirty?"

I looked at my watch. It was 10:25a.m.. I figured why not. "Where would you like to meet, Miss Richards?" I said in my most charming voice.

"Do you know where Lilly's Cafe is?" she said unashamedly.

I thought, Lilly's—he has two patrons: this female gastronomist and me. "Yes, as a matter of fact I do."

"I'll see you there. Good-bye." She hung up.

Lilly's was only twenty minutes if I walked so I had time to get there and put my thoughts together before she arrived and still be able to make a quick stop on the way.

I grabbed my coat, walked out to the hall, locked the door, and turned to leave when there in front of me was Mrs. Luce. Sarah Luce was in her midforties with a body that made twenty-year-olds sit up and take notice. She had dishwater blonde hair, blue eyes, and always dressed in fashions that revealed her feminine wares.

Perhaps I should say the widow Sarah Luce, since her husband died of a heart attack. He was seventy-two. They had been married six months. Now she was my landlady.

"Vince, I haven't seen you for some time. You still look good," she said as she rubbed her hands across my chest.

"Sarah, how nice to see you, all of you," I said as I stepped back, admiring her body from head to toe.

"I know this isn't the right place to discuss the rent. Perhaps we can go inside and . . . get a little more comfortable before we discuss it," she said as she started rubbing my chest again with her eyes telling a story of desire.

I reached into my pocket and pulled out a wad and counted out the twelve hundred I owed and handed it to her. I didn't want to seem ungrateful for the offer since I've paid the rent before her way and may have to again.

"I was getting ready to get it to you. Glad you showed up, Sarah, but I really have to go. I have a client waiting. Perhaps we can get together later," I said as I held her close and kissed her good-bye.

"Okay, Vince, but you better call me soon," she said as I walked down the hall, leaving her standing at my door.

CHAPTER 6

I walked into Lilly's seeing the usual handful of customers seated at the booths, two occupying the counter, and Lilly wearing his "Mel's Dinner" costume of an off-white T-shirt, white bib apron with the day's menu fully displayed non-verbally, and a stocking cap for this festive holiday season, Halloween. He should have wrestled in this outfit. I could see it now. He would have been even more impressive as he stepped into the ring in this cook's outfit wheeling a spatula. He was an impressive figure in his day: a big black man with shaved head and painted face of blue and red, but boy would I have paid to see him in the ring like this.

Lilly looked up and yelled out a greeting. "Falco, I reserved the back booth for you and Sam."

I must have looked dumbfounded; Lilly smiled and said, "Sam called, said she wanted a quiet place for you two. Way to go, Falco," he said as he gave me two thumbs-up.

I sat down facing the door, wanting to ask Lilly who this Samantha Richards was, but he was busy so I didn't bother. I just waited.

I didn't have to wait long. The door opened and in walked this vision of loveliness. She looked to Lilly, he pointed toward me, and she walked my way.

She walked like a model, had auburn hair, red moist lips slightly parted, eyes that glimmered like green pools half looking at you with a shy yet mischievous stare. As she approached me, she reached to greet me and said, "Mr. Falco, I'm Samantha Richards."

"Falco, just plain Falco," I said as I reached out for her hand.

She sat across from me in the booth. "What can I do for you, Miss Richards?" I asked, to get things started.

"Falco, you can call me Sam," she said and continued. "Shannan told me she hired you to check into her past, so I thought you would be the one to help me prove that she didn't commit suicide."

"How do you know it was suicide?" I asked.

"I called her when she didn't come to the office. She always called if she wasn't going to be in. A police officer answered the phone and told me she was dead. I couldn't believe what I heard, so I left work and went to her house. One of the news teams told me it was a suicide."

"The police officer told you, on the phone, no questions asked, that she was dead?" I asked knowing that it wouldn't have happened like that on Cavanaugh's team.

"No, I was given to an Officer Callahan. He asked who I was and what my relationship to Shannan was. By then I was frantic and pleaded for information about her. Another police officer came to the phone. I think he said his name was Mike. He told me she was dead and said he would like to talk to me so I gave him a number I could be reached at."

"If he told you she was dead, why did you go there?" I questioned.

"He wouldn't tell me what happened. I was pretty shaken by this time and had to find out more."

"Did you talk to anyone else at Shannan's place?" I queried.

"No, I wasn't able to talk to anyone except a Channel 3 news reporter. I went home and that's when I thought of what she had told me of you. So I called your office."

"You hung up?" I said, more as a question than a statement.

"Yes, I couldn't get it together," she said in a low sad voice, tears beginning to well in her eyes.

"Shannan wasn't the type of person to commit suicide. I want that known." Her eyes glared with fury as she commanded me in unspoken words to exonerate her friend.

I stared into those green pools wondering what was going to happen when I told her of the latest find. Her eyes looking back, searching to see what I was really about.

Would I find the answers she wanted or just say forget it?

I put down my cup and started to reach across the table when she sat back in her eat. I didn't want to push it so I just spoke out and waited for a reaction.

"Sam, it wasn't suicide. She was murdered." The words barely out of my mouth as she was fighting to hold back her tears.

I moved to her side of the booth and put my arms around her. For some reason women need this, and I really wanted to hold her. She held back the tears, looked up at me, and gave a half smile as if to say thank you. She felt good pressed against me. I didn't want to let go, but I didn't want this to get personal. It was the wrong time, wrong place, wrong reason.

She picked a napkin and wiped the tears from her eyes as she asked, "How do you know?"

"The officer you talked to, Mike, is a friend of mine. He told me what they had found in the autopsy." I told her what had happened.

"She never harmed anyone in her life. Why would someone hurt her like that? Why? Shannan didn't use drugs, she didn't smoke, she always helped people. She was a good kid," she said as she tried to hold back any outburst of wet emotion. "What are you going to do?" she said, staring up at me.

"Nothing, the police are handling it," I said, knowing I couldn't stay out of it.

"We have to find her killer. You can't ignore this as if you haven't an interest in it. Shannan gave you ten thousand dollars to help her. You owe it to her." Her voice making me feel like a heel if I refused.

"What do you mean we have to find her killer?" I asked.

"I'm going to help. After all, who knew her better? So where do we start?" she asked.

"I'll get back to you. I have a few things to settle before I start this one."

I was saved from being more committal as Lilly approached the booth.

"You guys aren't eating. What's the matter, Falco make you lose your appetite?"

Sam looked at him, half smiled, and said, "No, I'm not hungry right now."

"You look upset, Sam, what's this guy been saying?" Lilly looking at me in the way a father would look at a would-be suitor picking up his daughter for a date.

Sam reached over and put her arms around him and started the waterworks. "Shannan was murdered," she blurted out between sobs.

Lilly looked surprised, sad, and angry all at the same time.

"Falco, this the client you told me about yesterday? The one you said was suicide?" he asked.

"Yes, but it turned out to be murder. How do you know her?" I asked.

"I knew her from when she was a kid. Her father and I are best friends. He called me from Florida, left a message that he was coming up and would see me then. I tried to get hold of him, but he left by then. Now I know what he wanted.

"I want the killer, Falco, I want him, and you gotta get him." His voice was right out of the wrestlers' best intimidating voice manual. People turned and stared at us after his outburst.

I'm no slouch when it comes to holding up my end in a fight, but right now I wouldn't want to say anything to upset Lilly more than he was.

"You get him, Falco . . . you get him," Lilly repeated.

I got up and said my goodbyes, leaving them there to comfort each other.

It sure is a small world after all, just like the song says. Never would have been able to match Shannan with Lilly, not at all. Beauty and the beast, without a doubt. I was heading back to my office when the phone rang.

"Vince, Mike, I need your statement. When are you coming down?"

"If you don't mind, Mike I'd like to check a few things first. I may have more for you then," I said, trying to avoid going there. "Make it today, Vince," he commanded.

"Sure, okay, see you later."

It was getting more and more complicated. Lilly knowing the family and this Richards dame. What was next, I wondered?

CHAPTER 7

It was 5:00 p.m. The sun was starting to set; I figured the police had to be gone from Shannan's place by now so I headed over there.

The door was locked, but that never kept me out. I used my special key and then like magic it opened.

I didn't know what the police had found, but I was sure it wasn't what I was looking for even though I didn't know what I was looking for. I figured if Shannan had such a belief in reincarnation, then she would have kept a journal or something. I started looking around.

It was obvious that the cleanup crew hadn't arrived yet by the stain that was clearly visible on the carpet, outlined by the line drawing of Shannan as she had lain during the investigation.

I wasn't there more than five minutes when I heard someone at the door. I went over to the door and stood to the wall side of the door, ready to repel the door on the person entering.

As soon as the door opened, I reached out and grabbed the intruder, wrapping my arms around the upper body of this person to fling him to the ground, only finding that the intruder was soft, smelled awfully good, and let out a squeal. The air rushed out of my lungs as an elbow met my solar plexus, forcing me to open my arms. I reacted instantly blocking the second attack and started to strike back when I noticed it was Samantha. We recognized each other at about the same time.

"What the hell are you doing here?" I asked as I tried to catch my breath, still feeling the blow she executed.

She looked at me with a sparkle in her eyes and a smile on her face that would melt Antarctica and said jokingly, "What's the matter? Big boy can't hit a girl?"

I just looked at her with an expression that said, Try me. She continued since I didn't reply to her quip.

"I called her parents. They arrived shortly after you left Lilly's. They asked me to get some of her things. They didn't feel ready to come here."

"Now what are you doing here and how did you get in?" she asked.

"You didn't get permission to enter. This is still a crime scene, and you could get in trouble, you know?" I said as a matter of fact. She just looked at me with those big green eyes and smiled mischievously.

I felt differently about her helping me after our short encounter and told her what I was looking for.

"Yes, she did keep a journal. In fact it goes back to when we were in college. I was working on my master's. She was an undergrad, but we hit it off instantly. I became her big sister and best friend.

"They should be under the drawer next to the computer. She was always afraid someone would grab them by mistake and copy over them," she said as she headed for the bedroom.

"Wait," I called after her, "if she kept journals since college, they couldn't all fit under one drawer."

"No, she kept them on disks in a fireproof box under the drawer in the nightstand next to the bed," she replied.

"She planned on putting this life and her last together in a novel when she had all the pieces. Don't you ever wonder who you were and what you did before this life, Falco?" she said earnestly.

"Don't tell me you subscribe to the McCready library of reincarnation?" I said, testing.

"Falco, you're not a believer? Do you think we are here for this brief moment in time and then gone, poof, no more? What do you think makes this world go on? There is a reason for everything in this universe, and the plan of survival is to use the life energy force eternal!"

I interrupted, "What is this life energy force eternal? What plan? The one to over populate this planet? The next thing you are going to tell me is that we keep planet hopping as we fill them up. Now, don't tell me, let me guess, you were the Queen of Sheba, right?" I said sarcastically.

"As a matter of fact I was: In Ra Tu, the high priestess of the temple of Isis," she said in a regal manner. "And the life force eternal is what we are. You could say it was our souls. We travel from plane to plane to raise our level of consciousness to . . . well . . ., to reach nirvana on a cosmic level."

I looked at her with one of those "you're crazy" stares, her eyes blazed, her mouth was half open in disbelief that I would think she was crazy and if she could, she would have spit fire.

She said in a very discerning tone, "If you were right and we just ended after a few years, then why even try to make order of chaos? Why have laws, rules, government, if it doesn't matter?"

I wasn't ready for a philosophical debate on reincarnation at this time or in the near future if I could help it.

"Let's get the disks and get out of here," I said, hoping she would drop the debate. She turned, bent down, and pulled out the case. Then she stood up, turned, and shoved the box at me, almost making me lose my balance. I think she was mad, but I didn't say anything.

"Where are we going to look at them? We need a computer."

From her tone of voice, I would think she believed I live in the Stone Age, still counting on my fingers and drawing pictures on my cave wall. Well, maybe the picture part is true. After all, what else can you do in a public restroom?

"I have computer," I said in my best prehistoric grunt. She put her hands on her hips, laid back her head, smiled, and said, "Okay, truce, and if we can't get in the disk, what then?"

I dwelled on that smile for what seemed an eternity. She looked at me quizzically. I knew I had better move on. "I know people who can get into anything," I said as I turned to leave.

She was on my heels as she said, "I'll ride with you. I came in a cab."

Things were looking up, I thought, as we headed to my car.

Outside the night air was cold, stars filled the sky, the moon was near full and shone brightly. This time of year a moon like this brings visions of witches on brooms riding across its face.

Sam took hold of my arm and pulled in close. I could feel her shiver and said, “A little cold?” She just held on tighter, looked up with those eyes that could make a sane man crazy, and said in a voice low and sensual, “Not now.”

CHAPTER 8

On the way to my office, I told her about "Freud" hanging around Shannan's place. She didn't know anyone that fit the description.

I parked in my usual spot half a block down from the building. I turned to open the door and nearly had a cardiac as a big grinning baboon stood at my door.

"Callahan! I take back all the things I ever thought of you. Well, maybe not everything. I see you happened upon a sense of humor as sick as it is." My chest still pounding as I built his ego.

He grinned even bigger. "Mike wants to see you . . . now!" he said with a smile you see on kids after they get their siblings in trouble.

"I was just going to pick up everything and head over to his place," I lied.

"You won't have to. He's waiting for you in your office." The grin grew again. Pretty soon he was going to lose his face.

I turned to Sam, "Don't mention the disks. In fact, let me do the talking."

We got out of the car. I could see Callahan eye Sam and the look on his face said it all. How could a guy like me be with a woman like this.

Mike was sitting behind my desk when we walked in. I took notice to the scowl on his face and thought it would be to my best interest to open the conversation.

"You look good sitting there. I told you, you should join me and have an honest job," I said jokingly to frost over what I knew was coming.

"You're not funny anymore, Falco," he replied.

I knew he was pissed, but when Mike calls me Falco, not Vince, it's more than pissed.

"I said I would be down to see you later; it just wasn't later yet. Besides, I told you everything yesterday. I'm sure Callahan took down everything I said word for word."

"I went on the limb for you again, and as usual I got the shaft. You were at the house tonight. I got a call about prowlers. The black and white got there too late. I want to know why you were at the house; I want to know everything, Falco, everything. Start talking and don't stop until I'm happy."

Mike was definitely upset. Every word out of his mouth came from behind clenched teeth.

I looked over to Callahan. He was in his glory. The look on his face said it all. I didn't answer Mike. Instead I introduced Sam.

Mike commented quickly, "Miss Richards, I left a message at your office and your home. Our conversation on the phone led me to believe that Miss McCready was a close friend of yours. I would hope you will be able to open this case up for us, but first I want to hear what he has to say," he said as he pointed at me.

We just looked at each other then I started, "Mike, I guess you're just getting too old for this job. Your memory seems to be failing. I'll talk slowly so you can get it all down." I was a little pissed from his behavior and let him know it.

"Keep it up and I'll take you downtown," he said as he bolted upright, pointing his finger at me.

"I don't think you really want to push it that far, do you, Mike?" I said, holding back my fury.

Callahan, knowing our history, spoke up before we both said something we would regret later. "Vince, just tell us again how you knew the girl, please."

I told them how Shannan became my client and of the call I received from her the morning of her death. I didn't give any details of the "Club," Dr. Hyde, or the journals.

Mike asked, "What have you found out about her, it may help?"

"I went to North Carolina, checked records in the Capitol, and came up with an Elizabeth Anne Barrette. There were many Barrets, B-A-R-R-E-T, and Barrettes, B-A-R-R-E-T-T-E. There were only two Elizabeth Anne, both were spelled B-A-R-R¬-E-T-T-E. One died in 1972, the other in 1826. I went for the older woman," I said with a smile.

"The older Barrette was from Chowan County. I went to the county courthouse and checked the records. It seems the family was well-to-do in their time. I was directed to the plantation by the clerk who also was a member of the Historical Society, and she told me they were trying to get the state to give them the plantation for restoration and show.

"When I finally got to the plantation, I was somewhat let down. It had gone to ruin. You could still see the Georgian-style architectural design and make out what was once gracious gardens, a tree-lined drive to the house with remnants of billeting for slaves, a barn, or stable, and some outline of what could have been a drying house for tobacco or peanuts.

"In the back off to the side of the house surrounded by magnolia, pecan, and sycamore trees was an overgrown graveyard, the monuments, half sunken, cracked, and tipped over, showed signs of the years past. In all there were twelve weathered tombstones. One of which had written on it, 'TO YE GREAT SORROW OF YE FATHER AND YE MOTHER, LIE HERE WITHIN YE MORTAL REMAINS OF ELIZABETH ANNE BARRETTE TAKEN FROM THIS LIFE TO ANOTHER. MAY GOD REST HER SOUL.' Beneath the inscription were the dates, Sept. 14, 1800, Nov. 9, 1826.

"I went back to the county clerk. She isn't a woman you would forget. She was close to five feet two, had strawberry blonde hair, deep blue eyes that smiled with excitement when she talked. She had that smooth Southern belle accent that held you to her every word. I told her I was researching the Barrettes and would appreciate any information she might have.

"She said the Historical Society was putting together an information package on the family for their presentation to the state and would get me a copy as soon as it was ready. That was three weeks ago. I've called her since. It still isn't ready.

"That's where it all stands to date. Shannan was looking forward to the information and believed she was Elizabeth Anne Barrette. Ironically enough, if she was, then she beat her old life by a year."

I could see Mike had little use for the information I gave him, but he seemed satisfied that I gave him what I had. I didn't feel bad about holding back some of the things I had. It didn't come together yet. I needed names, something more tangible than a hunch before I gave him any more. Besides I still didn't like the way he came on to me.

Sam didn't have anything for him, just the reincarnation thing, and mentioned that Shannan belonged to some group that researched reincarnates. She had no idea who would want to harm her, let alone kill her.

"If you think of anything else, call me and let me decide if it helps or not," Mike said as he got up from behind my desk.

As he approached the door, he turned, looked at me, and said, "Pal, you're always there for the good ones so find out what's going on . . . real soon. I'd like to close this one up before the media comes up with another serial killer idea." He walked out with Callahan trailing behind.

Sam looked at me and said, "He seems like a very nice guy, so what was all that macho chest pounding about between you two?"

"Yeah, he's all right," I said, dropping it there.

"Maybe we should take the disks somewhere else. Knowing Mike like I do, I wouldn't doubt if he has someone watching outside," I said as I looked outside, watching movement in the shadows across the street.

"We can go to my place," she said as she started to put on her coat. "By the way, you mentioned Chowan County. Strange thing, but we had two friends that lived there and we used to go there on weekends from school," she added.

"Where is the Barrette plantation located in the county?" she asked.

I must have had a strange look on my face from the way she was looking at me, but something started thumping in the back of my head. I was having all kinds of questions running through with no answers and now Sam added this whopper. What has Chowan County have to do with all of this?

"Somewhere around Edenton. I could get there easily from the directions, but to tell you exactly, forget it," I said, answering her question.

As we left the office, I spotted the tail sitting in a blue Crown Vic. He was trying to disappear as he slipped down in his seat. He was facing in the opposite direction. We stopped at my car, got the disks, and headed to the corner. Sam looked a little puzzled until I let her know what was going on.

When we reached the corner, I looked back, seeing him make a U-turn. I pulled out the cellular and called a cab. He was heading north so we crossed the street and headed south. There was a corner drugstore open, so we went inside waiting for the cab.

The cab arrived a few minutes later. We jumped in and I said to the driver, "There's a twenty in it for you if you lose the blue Crown Vic that will be behind you in a second."

"No problem, mister," he answered as he pushed the pedal to the floor.

We circled the area for a few minutes, making sure he was gone, then got out at my car and headed to Sam's.

CHAPTER 9

It was a third-floor two-bedroom apartment, well-kept and adorned with pictures, knickknacks, and other country craft items. The furniture was early available, two steps above orange crate, but well-kept.

"Excuse the mess, but I wasn't looking to have company," she said as she started straightening a newspaper on the coffee table. I couldn't see a mess anywhere.

"I've only been here three months. I was lucky to get it," she went on as she continued arranging items that didn't need arranging.

Looking out the patio window gave a view of the river and the city a few miles upstream. I could enjoy this view for a while, but I'd miss the activity of the city looking out my office-apartment window. Then again maybe not.

She lit the fireplace and curled her feet under her as she sat in front of it. The flames highlighted her hair and gave a luster to her face. She looked at me with those eyes, and I wanted to join her and forget everything else. It would be nice to be able to spend a normal evening with this women and let nature have its way.

The mood was broken as the phone rang. She got up to answer it, and I started thinking of the disks.

It was Shannan's mother. Nothing much was said—normal sympathetic female chatter. Both were in tears by the time the conversation ended.

I gave her a few minutes to get control and then reminded her that we had some work to do and that it was getting late. She calmed down, and we started reviewing the disks.

It was about 1a.m.. There wasn't much in the journals: usual stuff, met boy, liked boy, lost boy, problems with classes, some professor trying to put the make on her—he was old enough to be her father. There was a mention of some oversexed football player that was going to be interviewing for the position of eunuch if he didn't leave her alone. I couldn't wait to see how this one ended.

She dwelled on a weekend trip with her roommates, Betty Jean Brewster and Katherine Kaye Kantrel. I called out to Sam, "Do you know a Betty Jean and Katherine Kaye from your school days?"

"Yes, they were the girls from the Chowan County area I was telling you about," she answered as she approached me, looking over my shoulder.

"How do I print this?" I asked, not seeing a printer handy.

"Just push print. Augh!" inferring my caveman upbringing.

"Betty Jean was the daughter of a Baptist minister, Katherine Kaye was from an influential peanut-farming family. The girls were childhood friends. I thought they were sisters the first time I met them.

"They really liked Shannan, and she would go with them to their homes on weekends. Shannan was taken with the beauty of the area. There were plantations and historic sites going back before the Revolutionary War. Her descriptions were more than one of observation. They were more like a living entity. In fact she commented that she felt she lived there at one time. She was able to get around without anyone giving her directions other than to a specific restaurant or person's house. The area mansions, plantations, historic sites—they were all known by her. It was very strange. This was the introduction to her belief in reincarnation.

"Betty Jean and Katherine were into reincarnation more as a fad than a real belief, but they managed to talk Shannan into believing and seeing their spiritual leader, Conrad Johnston." Sam stopped for a moment as she looked at the screen.

On the computer were comments about this guru. Shannan dwelled on him, outlining how he wanted to raise her level of consciousness of her past life. This would bring into focus her "life force eternal."

"Now where did I hear that before," I thought out loud, only to receive a slap on the back of my head. "Ouch," I cried in mock pain.

The journal continued describing Johnston's group of five that met every Saturday promptly at 3:00 p.m. and how she was invited to join them.

Shannan went on explaining how she kept trying to convince Samantha to come with them, and if not interested in the group, at least enjoy the beauty of the Chowan County area.

In the notes Shannan went on to say, "Samantha was so taken by Conrad's explanation of the life force and past lives that she let him hypnotize her in front of the group."

Shannan described the event. "Samantha rolled back her eyes and started answering questions in a foreign language. No one was able to pick out the language, but it was thought to be a form of Arabic. Conrad managed to get her to speak English. It was exciting, the things I heard that Samantha said. She was back in time in ancient Egypt at her temple. She said she was IN RA TU, the high priestess of the Temple of Isis.

"I am so happy for her. I just knew she was someone of great dignity and importance. She is so warm, friendly, and helping."

Shannan went on to describe how the other members were hypnotized but never mentioned it happening to her.

I was brought out of deep concentration by Sam calling out, "Earth to Falco, Earth to Falco—anyone home?"

I turned to answer her. She had a concerned looked on her face as she said, "Are you all right? I've been calling you for some time."

"Yes, just a bit wrapped in this journal, that's all."

"It's getting late. The birds are starting to stir. Want to stay here for the rest of the night?" she asked in a way as to say "don't go."

I'm far from old-fashioned, but I didn't think this was the time to get involved, but I sure entertained the thought.

“I didn’t realize how late it was. I better be going.” I got up, put the disks in the box, turned to leave, and there standing inches from me was Sam. She had a determined look on her face that I was staying.

I started going around her, but I could only grab her and pull her close to me. She gave no resistance and melted in my arms. I pressed my lips to hers, and the passion welled up in both of us as we were lost in the magic of the moment.

“I don’t think we should let this happen while we’re involved with this case,” I said as I searched the depths of her eyes for signs of agreement.

“You’re right,” she said, pulling me back to her as we fell to the bed.

CHAPTER 10

It was still morning as we were driving to my place when the phone rang. "Hello."

"Vince." I knew the voice. It was Mike, and it didn't sound like a wake-up call. "Where are you?" he asked in his police voice.

"Why, couldn't your tail find me after the slip?" I asked, just to rub it in.

"Okay, Vince, I shouldn't have had you watched, but I need to see you now at the McCready place. So how long before you can be here?" he said, more as a command than a request.

"I was just getting a coffee want me to pick one up for you and the twin?" I asked, to delay my arrival.

"Sure, but make it quick." He hung up.

I looked at Sam and said, "We can have lunch. I think it will be too late for breakfast after I see Mike. Look, no matter what, don't mention the journals to anyone. Mike isn't back at Shannan's for lack of something to do. Whatever it is, he thinks I'm involved. I think it would be best if you didn't come along."

Sam protested, "I think I should. We were together at Shannan's, and we didn't do anything wrong. I had a right to be there, and I'll tell him so."

"Look, Mike doesn't know that we are together. He's used to me working alone. I think it would be best if he continues thinking that way. This gives us the advantage," I assured her.

As I parked in front of Lilly's Cafe, I looked over to Sam and said, "I'll leave you here. If I need you, I'll call you here, all right?" I said, watching her shake her head in agreement.

Lilly was glad to see us, made the normal greeting, and put two cups on the counter for us, then he asked, "Vince, you got anything yet?"

"Nothing yet," I acknowledged then continued. "I need you to take care of Sam for a little while. I have to see Mike and I don't want her getting on his hit list yet. I'll call as soon as I get out of there."

"Sure, Vince. Sam can stay as long as she likes."

I took three coffees, two black and one with a nipple on it for Pete. He likes a little coffee with his milk and sugar.

I pulled up to the house; there were five squad cars plus Cavanaugh's car. It looked like the circus was back in town.

I was set back on my heels as I walked into the room. It was trashed from one end to the other. Mike met me as I entered the room.

"The look on your face says you didn't do it. Callahan thinks you did," Mike said, watching my reaction.

I handed him the bag with the coffee in it. I looked at Callahan and said, "Callahan's an ass. You know I was here last night. You also know that two uniforms responded and checked out the place. You told me that. So when did this happen anyway?"

Mike started to tell me when Callahan broke in, "We got a call from burglary about 7 a.m. They said the McCready place was broken into around midnight. The neighbors called, complaining of loud noises coming from the townhouse—"

I interrupted, "Don't tell me, they dispatched the closest to the scene and they came with sirens wailing. By the time they entered, no one was to be found."

"That's about it," Callahan said almost apologetically.

Mike asked, his voice more sincere and friendly than last night, "What were you looking for, Vince? Maybe it can shed some light on what this is all about."

"I was hoping to find something that could give me a reason for her murder. Nothing in particular, just reaching for a brass ring.

"This whole thing doesn't make any sense. The kid wanted to know about a person long dead because she thought she was that person. I know it sounds crazy, but there is a lot of people out there that believe the same thing. Some profess it, others just keep it to themselves, but they are still out there. Shannan had the resources to have someone research it for her.

"That's all I've got, but in it is the answer to this whole sorted affair and I will find it," I said assuredly.

Callahan looked at me as if to say he understood but could only get out, "Okay, Vince, but stay in touch. We may have more questions before the day is over."

Mike looked at him and then back at me, shook his head, and put on a grin just like a father when his children are trying to settle their differences but can't find the right words.

I raised my arm in a gesture of good-bye and left.

Outside the clouds were gathering. It was difficult to tell if it was going to snow or rain, but something was coming, I could feel it.

CHAPTER 11

On the way back to Lilly's, I started thinking of the events since this all started. There was a fictitious note. The killers tried to make it look like suicide, but they failed to leave the object that would have caused the cuts. Then there was that person hanging out in the cab. He showed up on two occasions. And now someone trashes the place and leaves empty-handed, or did they.

There are a lot of bits, but pieces are missing that could put them together.

Speaking of the devil, I noticed a black Mercedes in the rearview mirror. I slowed down gradually. I wanted to get him in a position he couldn't turn and run from.

I turned onto a one-way street I knew had parking on both sides. Now all I needed was someone to pull up behind him and then he would be mine.

He must be a mind reader because he just kept going straight. I floored the Bird, squealing my tires as I turned left and squealed them a second time as I turned left again. Turning right against the light as I came back to main street caused some minor swerving by drivers approaching me, but I kept going. I could see the Mercedes up ahead about five cars in front. I started to accelerate when lights started flashing and sirens began warbling. Whoever this person is, he sure is lucky.

I made a quick call to Mike. I figured I would need a little help to get out of this one. The police frown a little on reckless driving. Mike answered as I pulled over to the curb. I gave him a brief rundown on my predicament. I could hear him holding back his chuckles.

"Let me talk to the officer but remember, buddy, you owe me," he said.

As the officer approached the car, I held the phone out the window and with my best boyish smile I said, "It's for you."

She reached out with her left hand, a quizzical look on her face and her right hand on her gun.

"Hello," she said then went quiet for a few seconds before continuing, "This is Officer Davies, traffic."

I don't know what Mike was telling her, but she had a smile on her face that wouldn't quit. She looked at me like I was crazy or something.

Then she spoke, "Yes, sir, I'll do that . . . Good-bye." She handed me the phone, looked at me, and said, "Please get out of the car, sir."

She stepped back, her hand on her gun. I asked her what Mike had said. All she did was repeat, "Please get out of the car, sir."

"What if I refuse?" I asked.

"I'll have to shoot you. Now please get out of the car," she repeated.

I got out.

"Give me your license and registration, sir."

"My registration is in the car, and I'm out so as not to be shot," I said whimsically.

"Then I guess you'll have to bend over and get it, won't you?" This was said with some humor in her voice.

She took my license and registration, looked at them then at me, and said, "Okay, assume the position. I'm sure you know what that is."

I just turned and spread eagle, wondering what in the hell Mike had said to her.

She began a slow involved personal search. I didn't know if I should be mad at Mike or have his children. Officer Davies was a doll that could handcuff me to her bed any day of the week.

She spoke, "Okay, there isn't much here."

I broke in, "Wait a minute!"

She put her hands on her hips, only emphasizing her shapely figure, laughed, and said, "Don't let me catch you driving like that again. You're lucky nothing happened and no one got hurt or your friend, cop or not, wouldn't be able to help you."

I was ready to break out in a chorus from one of those musicals from the fifties where the gang members are being chastised by the infamous officer "Krumky" and sing, "Yes, Officer Davies. Thank you, Officer Davies," but I forced myself to be polite and said instead, "Thank you, I'm terribly sorry and I won't let it happen again."

Then I winked at her as she smiled, turned and walked away, shaking her head.

My chances of finding the black Mercedes now were slim to none. I headed back to Lilly's to pick up Sam.

When I arrived at Lilly's, Sam was sitting at the counter and Lilly was leaning against it as they were talking about everything and nothing.

Lilly looked up as I entered and said, "Falco, what've you got? You've been gone a long time."

I sat down. He poured me a coffee, and I told them what happened. I didn't go into detail about the search, but the look from Sam told me I better make up my mind about women. It would be her only, no sharing and all this after one brief encounter. I wondered what two days of knowing her was going to bring. Wedlock! These thoughts were getting scary.

On a serious note, I turned to Sam and asked, "Are you going to the funeral home this evening?"

She had a sorrowful look on her face and said in an almost inaudible tone, "Yes."

She continued, "I called Shannan's mother. She would like Lilly and me to be with the family at 4:00 p.m. Viewing is at six for everyone else, so we will see you then."

"I'm not going." My words seemed to catch them a little off guard. They gave me a look that, metaphorically speaking, made me lower than whale shit.

"I'm going, but I'm not going inside. I want to see everyone that shows up, but I don't want them to see me. If I go inside, I'll have to meet the family and friends, maybe even tell them some things they don't need to know. It's better if I stay out of the way. You do understand, don't you?" I asked, hoping for a quick yes.

Lilly answered first, "Sure, Vince, at least you'll be in the area."

"What if the family asks for you? They know what you're trying to do. I told them about you," she asked.

"I'll be right outside if you need me," I assured her.

It was going on 1:00 p.m. I wanted to talk with the funeral director before anyone showed up, so I bid my farewells and took Sam home, telling her of my intentions on the way. She seemed to feel better knowing that I was going to see Shannan anyway, even if it wasn't with her.

"If you really need me inside, just come out and wave or let Lilly come out and get me." The look on her face showed her relief.

CHAPTER 12

I arrived at the funeral home shortly after dropping Sam off and was greeted as I entered. She was an attractive elderly woman possibly in her mid to late sixties looking like a Bee Archer wannabe.

"May I help you, sir?"

"I would like to see the director."

"That would be Mr. Rogers. I'll check to see if he is in his office; and your name, sir?"

"Falco," I answered, having a sudden urge to remove my shoes and put on a sweater.

"One moment, please," she said as she walked to his neighborhood.

It couldn't have been two minutes when a man came walking out of a wall. At least that's what it looked like.

"Mr. Falco, how may I help you? I'm Bob Rogers, the director," he said as he held out his hand to me.

"I'm looking into the murder of Shannan McCready and would like to know if anything strange has happened since she's been here?"

He looked at me strangely then answered, "Nothing that I would consider strange, just the usual calls, friends and family of the deceased wanting to know the schedule.

Nothing out of the ordinary . . . well . . . maybe just one thing, now that you ask." "Please, anything might help. What were you going to say?" I asked.

"This morning, rather early, there was a gentleman who came and asked if he could view the body. I told him she wasn't ready and to come back at six this evening, but he was persistent, said he was going out of town and couldn't make the viewing schedule and assured me it would be all right for him to view her while she was being prepared because he was a doctor. Well, naturally, I asked for credentials, but he didn't have any with him, he said, so I couldn't allow it. He seemed very agitated and insisted on viewing her. He gave me his driver's license to verify who he said he was. I immediately picked up the phone to call for verification when all of a sudden he pulled it out of my hand and said he had to leave and then left rather abruptly."

And this didn't seem strange, I said to myself.

"Do you remember his name and could you describe him to me?" I asked hopefully.

"Yes, of course, I do," he said in a manner that asked if I doubted his mental capacities.

"His name was Lawrence Rutledge. He was a tall, thin—not frail, mind you, just thin—man. He was in his late forties at the most. His eyes were very penetrating. His stare—it would be almost frightening anywhere but here," he answered with a chuckle. "I see that stare a lot in my business, maybe that's why I took notice to it. He was still breathing." A faint smile crossed his lips as he continued, "He had a noticeable scar on his left cheek that reminded one of the late-night horror shows. I do hope I've been of some help, Mr. Falco."

"Yes, you have. If he shows up again, please call me," I said as I handed him my card. "Also, if he comes this evening, please point him out to Miss Samantha Richards.

She will be with the family and knows where to get in touch with me."

"Miss McCready is ready for viewing in Parlor A if you would like to pay your respects now since you won't be available later," he said in a sincere tone.

"Sure, now would be fine," I lied. I'm not one for these events, but I followed him to his neighborhood with a song in my head.

Shannan looked, to use a cliché, like she was asleep. Her hair sparkled from the lights shining over her. Her lips were red and appeared moist with color in her skin that made her seem alive. They did an exceptional job on her to present her in this fashion.

It made my blood boil to see this young woman lying here, cheated out of life because of some crazy. I knew how Lilly felt. I could still hear him in that voice of terror,

"I want him, Falco. I want the killer. You gotta get him." Yeah, I knew that feeling. I've had it before. It kept me alive in some tough places.

Looking down at her, I said silently, "I'll find him," as I reached out and touched her hands clasped over her heart. I only knew her for a short time, but it seemed like forever.

I left, assuring myself that I wouldn't kill the son of a bitch that had done this. There were worse things than death, and I would make him feel the pain before I gave him up.

In some organizations, you could say I was going to "terminate with extreme, and I mean extreme, prejudice."

The funeral home was situated on the corner across from a small shopping plaza that was always full. It provided a good cover. From this vantage point, I could easily see the side and front entrances of the funeral home. I situated myself, parking close to a public phone at the end of the parking lot facing the home.

It was close to 4:00 p.m. The sky was filled with dark clouds, the air was cold and damp, it had rained earlier and promised to have snow showers by evening. It was getting dark earlier now that fall had arrived, and the evenings were getting colder than usual.

People were beginning to show up. An older couple got out of a Lincoln Town car with Florida plates as Sam and Lilly arrived in a cab. Sam rushed over to the couple and embraced them. Lilly approached, hand extended and shaking his head sorrowfully.

The men clasped hands and embraced, while the women came closer to do the same.

From the exchange, I knew the couple was Shannan's parents.

The older woman from the distance looked like Shannan. Her hair was the same red color, sparkling from the parking lot lights. Her walk was graceful and sophisticated. Her color had the same ivory tone. The only differences I could make out was the age, and this woman had about twenty pounds on Shannan; still she was a very attractive lady.

Shannan's father was close to Lilly's size with a full crop of gray hair. He stood solid, not hunched over like some men in their seventies, and had the look of a prize fighter. They made an interesting couple.

It was a sad portrait, the four of them standing in the wet, dismally lit parking lot.

As they walked to the main entrance, Sam gave a quick glance around to see if she could find me. She appeared satisfied when she saw me at the phone. She turned and they all went inside.

I paced back and forth, pretending to use the phone, checked my oil a dozen times, and just sat and watched the activity across the street. It's times like this that I wished I'd never given up smoking.

I was cold and wet, standing at the phone and tired of walking in circles, so I decided to sit in the car to warm up. There wasn't anything out of the ordinary happening across the street—people going in, people coming out, some laughing, some crying, and a few not showing any emotion at all. It must have been the same inside.

Sam didn't come out. Everything was quiet. I looked at my watch to see how much longer until they close. It was eight thirty. Viewing was over at nine. I didn't think anything was going to happen tonight. Tomorrow would be another day.

As I started to turn toward the car, I felt a sharp pain in the back of my head, and I could feel myself falling. I was quickly supported on both sides and directed to the back seat of my Bird. As I fell to the seat, I heard a voice say, "Don't kill him yet, mister . . .," then I felt another blow to my head and darkness set in.

CHAPTER 13

My head was throbbing. I couldn't get my hand to move to rub it. My eyes opened slowly. As I started to focus, the only light was coming from overhead and what appeared to be pin points of light from the distance. The place was dark. I could barely make out my surroundings. It appeared to be a big empty garage or warehouse.

I found myself hanging with my hands tied, extended over my head and attached to a hook extended from the ceiling, my feet barely touching the floor, with my arms extended, supporting the weight of my body. I felt as if they were going to pull out of my shoulders.

My eyes now focusing, I could see the light was from an opening in the roof and some cracks along the walls. In the distance I could make out two shadowy figures.

I called out, "Who are you? What do you want? Why am I here?" These were questions I knew weren't going to be answered. Still I had to ask. The exertion caused my vision to blur again, and I felt lightheaded.

I must have blacked out because now I was rudely brought around by what seemed to be an ocean rolling over my face. My head still throbbing as I tried to catch my breath, I was gasping and choking from the inhalation of water.

As I regained my senses, I found myself to be shivering from the cold, realizing that my jacket and shirt had been removed. The water over my body only increased the chill I felt.

All of a sudden a bright light appeared in front of my eyes, causing me to blink rapidly as if a flash went off from a camera when it wasn't expected. I squinted, trying to see who was out there. If I was prone to flashbacks, I was hoping this was one of them so I could wake up and walk out.

It didn't happen. I was still dangling like a side of beef when a voice, deep and menacing, called out.

"Mr. Falco, you are here simply to answer some questions. You have some information I need, and if you cooperate, you may be released."

He hesitated for a moment, probably to watch my reaction to his comments. I didn't give him any satisfaction as I hung there waiting for him to continue.

"Tell me what you know of Elizabeth Anne Barrette."

The words barely out of his mouth as I, in a surprised tone, asked, "What?"

"Tell me what you know of Elizabeth Anne Barrette."

I was dumbfounded at the question. I didn't know who this was, I couldn't see him, and I didn't see any purpose to the question.

I spoke out to the light, "She's dead, a hundred odd years or so. You didn't have to put yourself to so much trouble to find that out. A phone call could have gotten you the same answer. So what do you really want?" I asked flippantly.

"Mr. Falco, please don't insult my intelligence. I will give you another chance to tell me what I want to hear."

"I told you what I know."

My body swayed outward as a blow was delivered from behind to my right kidney, the ropes keeping me from doubling up or falling down. The pain rolled across my body as I tried to catch my breath.

I attempted to display my best macho impression, but I'm sure it didn't fool anyone as I said, "I don't know what you want. I told you what I know."

Two more blows were administered, one to the lower back and the second to the left kidney. I expected more to come and had tensed enough not to have the same severe pain of the first blow. I was certain that whoever was doing the hitting was no slouch.

I think I was about to receive another blow when I heard the voice, "Hold it, Mr. Smith. Now, Mr. Falco, I'm a busy man and I have things to do besides standing here and watching you get beat. This can all be avoided by telling me what I want to hear and that includes where it is. Do you understand, Mr. Falco?" His voice was slow and commanding as he spoke. I didn't have a clue of what he was talking about.

"Mr. Smith is an expert in administering pain. He would like nothing better than to extract each and every letter of every word slowly and painfully. I hope you understand me, Mr. Falco?" His voice, more menacing than before, made my skin crawl. If I were loose, I'd rip out his throat so he wouldn't be heard again.

"I've told you everything I know. It looks like we're in for a long night."

"Mr. Smith, I believe you were right. Our Mr. Falco wishes to prove his manliness.

Please see to this matter. Maybe our Mr. Falco will be ready to talk to me when I get back."

I heard his footsteps diminish, and seconds later, Mr. Smith delivered his next blow.

It landed solidly to my left lower ribcage. I could feel the bone break and the air rush from my lungs. He followed with a series of jabs to my stomach. He was using me like a workout bag in a gym. The rapid succession of blows weakened my ability to tense myself enough to lessen the sting of the assault.

I must have passed out because the next thing I knew, water was rolling off my face as I hung limp from the hook.

I was no stranger to pain. There was a time when I had to live with it or die, but that was a long time ago. Now I had to pull from the depths of my soul that which was taught to me . . . to withstand pain.

I couldn't see Smitty with the lights shining in my eyes, but I could smell him. He started toward me. I pulled with strength I didn't know existed and lifted my legs a perfect ninety degrees. My stomach, aching from the bruises, and the rib cage, feeling like a million splinters, were piercing me. As Smitty advanced toward me, I could make out his image as he stepped into the light, and I managed to push down with my legs catching the back of his head with my heels sending him to the floor.

I hung there for a few moments, regaining some strength. Smitty was either dead or out cold, and if he wasn't dead, I had better move fast to get out of here. I tried to take a deep breath and felt the pain race through my body. I held what breath I took and managed to pull myself up on the ropes, holding my hands together just enough to release me. I fell to the floor and lay there for a moment, mentally arranging myself to continue.

I untied my hands and feet and turned the light on Mr. Smith. He was out cold. I could see a sign of blood on his forehead where he had hit the floor. Mr. Smith was a big man.

Had we met on the field of honor, it would have been a David-and-Goliath grudge match.

I quickly bound him with the ropes he tied me with. All of a sudden I heard a car outside. It had to be the mystery voice. I could hear him talking, faintly, then two doors slammed shut. I ran in the opposite direction. I would settle this later. Smitty and I would have our match and Mr. "In the Shadows" would get a piece of the action too.

I reached the back of the warehouse and jumped off the dock, my ribs absorbing the Shock, creating a nauseating pain. I struggled to my feet and ran for the light in the distance.

Somewhere between the warehouse and the light I lost consciousness. I awoke lying in a field curled up like a baby. The ground was cold but not as cold as the air. My body felt like it was run over by a truck.

I tried getting up, but the pain in my side caused me to nearly lose it as I fell back to the ground. I was cold and hurt too much to remain here. I held my arm tightly to my side, putting most of my weight against my right side, and managed to lift myself to my knees. I staggered to my feet, the pain making me stop and catch my breath as I headed to the gas station I saw in the distance.

Outside the station by the curb was a phone. I called Sam. The phone rang for what seemed forever. Finally she picked it up. "Hello." The voice from the other end sounded distant and seductive. "Sam, I need you to pick me up. I'm at . . . wait, hold on." I put the phone down to see where I was. I walked toward a lady pumping gas. I must have looked a sight because she dropped the nozzle and ran inside.

A young athletic type came running out toward me. I wasn't in any condition to run so I just stood there.

"What do you want here?" he shouted.

"Just wanted to know what street this was." The pain in my side flared, causing me to lose my balance and fall.

"Shit, he's drunk, lady. I'll call the cops." He turned and headed back to the station.

"Lady," I strained, calling to her.

She looked at me with a squint and came closer. She half bent down, looked close at me, and said, "You're not drunk. You're hurt. I've got to tell that boy."

She started to run. I called out to her, "Wait, please, there is someone on the phone. Just tell her where I am and ask her to come and get me."

She looked at the phone hanging and walked to it, picked it up, and hesitantly spoke into the speaker. "Hello? Yes, he is here, but he can't come to the phone. He's hurt."

There was a pause then she continued, "I don't know. He fell down and asked me to have you come and get him . . . Miss, please calm down. He's at the corner of Decker and Main . . . yes, the police have been called . . . hello . . . hello?" She turned to me with a look of surprise and said, "She hung up."

"Help me up," I said as I reached out to her. She was hesitant but started toward me. "I'm Falco," my introduction causing a look of trust on her face. She helped me to my feet and into the station.

Inside the warmth embraced my shivering body as I leaned against the counter watching the look of concern on this woman's face.

I wasn't in the store long when the police arrived.

"This the drunk?" they asked as they approached me.

"He isn't drunk. He's been injured," she said in my defense.

They walked over to me and could see she was right. One officer spoke up, "We better get an ambulance here. Joe, get a blanket out of the car. He could use it."

"There's no need for that. Someone is coming to get me. I'll be okay."

"I don't think you're in any condition to walk away, and we will need a statement of what happened. We can start now while we're waiting. What's your name and what happened to you?"

"Falco, and I really don't need an ambulance." I kept going before we got into the game of twenty questions.

"The last thing I remember, I was standing at a phone across from the Rogers Funeral Home. I was going to see someone there, and then the lights went out. I awoke half dressed, with a splitting headache, ribs that wanted out of my body, and cold."

I didn't tell them exactly what happened so I gave them the Readers Digest condensed version. I knew this was all going to get back to Mike, and I didn't want to have to explain any more.

The athlete handed me a cup of coffee. It was hot, it was good, and it hurt like hell when I tried to swallow, but I managed.

The ambulance was turning in the drive, followed by two cars. It looked like a parade. I didn't say any more as we all watched the new arrivals.

Mike got out of his car. Sam got out of hers, and the boys in white got out of the meat wagon. I was impressed that all of the performers weren't tripping over each other.

Don't let me forget Callahan. He wouldn't miss this opportunity to save his life just to watch me squirm my way out of this one. It could be worse. Mike could have stayed home.

Although Sam arrived behind the ambulance and Mike, she was the first to enter the building. I was sure Mike made the connection between Sam and me as she ran to me, arms outstretched and calling my name with some real emotion. She wrapped her arms around me, nearly causing me to lose my balance. Her embrace felt like I was being squeezed by a bear. Although it hurt, it still felt good all at the same time.

"Vince, what happened? I didn't see you last night. I was worried sick." I let out a slight groan, indicating that I was in a little pain. She let me go to quick. It felt like everything inside wanted to be outside. I grabbed my side and braced myself against the counter.

"I'm sorry," she said sympathetically as she reached out to help me.

I could hear Mike speaking to the officers. "I'll take care of him. He's part of my investigation in a homicide. I'll see that he gets to the hospital. Thanks for the help."

Then he turned to me and smiled. "Vince, as far back as we go, it's always the same. You keep making friends," he said sarcastically as he looked me over bruise for bruise, "and I keep collecting the remains."

"You know you love me and we don't want to forget you owe me," I said in my most endearing manner.

He smiled, shook his head, and said, "You're right, pal. Now let's get you patched up."

Sam looked at us in wonderment but didn't say anything.

The med techs had me cleaned up and ready to go. I looked at the driver and couldn't resist saying, "I know how you boys like to wake the dead, so what say you blare the sirens and lead the parade."

He just smiled and away we went, wailing like a banshee.

CHAPTER 14

In the hospital the doctor did his thing, told me two ribs were broken, that I was lucky they didn't separate, and that the cold helped tremendously to keep the swelling and bleeding at bay. He emphasized not doing anything strenuous. He insisted that I should remain in the hospital for observation, but I convinced him, with Sam's assurance, that I would be a good boy and stay home, eat my soup, and get plenty of rest.

Mike just smiled and said, "And elephants fly." He continued as they wheeled me to the door. "We have to talk, Vince. Your place or mine?"

"I need a coffee. Let's meet at Lilly's."

"We'll see you there," he assured me.

I got in the car with Sam groaning for sympathy as I sat back in the seat. She turned, gave me a worried look, and said, "Maybe you should just leave this investigation to the police . . . before you end up dead." This wasn't the kind of sympathy I was looking for. This is why I stayed single all these years and pretty much unattached.

No one to worry, no one to really care. Just do the job and live or die. Just a day's work.

But now I think I cared just a little. I'll see what tomorrow brings.

"I definitely have someone worried, but I haven't a clue of what it is he wants and I'm not going to let the bastard win, not after last night."

"I want them. I'm going to have them. They're mine!" I said in my best impression of Lilly's wrestling voice. Sam laughed, but I could see the worry in her eyes.

Nothing more was said for a few miles, then Sam looked over to me and asked,

"You said Mike owes you. What does that mean?"

"Nothing, really. Mike knows it's just a joke." She could read more in my tone than I was telling her, and she wasn't going to settle for this answer.

"Vince, I would like to know what this bond is that you and Mike have. I can see it in both your faces when things get serious, so tell me!"

I had mixed feelings about this subject. I never told the story to anyone, and I wasn't sure if I should start now. After all it was just another day in the life of Vincent Falco.

Sam looked and waited for my response. I figured, what the hell. She wasn't going to tell anyone. It wasn't like it was "News at Eleven." I looked over to her and then just stared out the window as I started the story.

"Mike and I were in the same unit in the army. We were in a few firefights in places left unsaid and managed to come out without a scratch. The heroes, bless them all, are on the Wall in Washington and on war memorials in cities throughout the US.

"It remained quiet for a year or so, then we were assigned to Central America as advisers, did some TDY . . . oh, I mean temporary duty, in a few other places, and then word came down that a Middle East country had acquired some nuclear weapons from a US military base. Our team was assigned to retrieve or destroy them. Emphasis was on the retrieval.

"The general location was known, but not the specific storage area. The intelligence group had managed to get someone into the camp, so all we had to do was get in, get the missiles, and get out. Sounds easy . . . right?

"It takes a little planning to get it right. The target area was ideal for a halo assault—that is, a high altitude jump, opening the chute at low altitude. Usually the jump is made at about twenty-five thousand feet, free fall to around two thousand feet, then pop the canopy and float in. What a way to crash a party." I was remembering how cold that altitude was and the rush of jumping into what could have been oblivion.

"Vince, you make it sound better than sex."

I just smiled, thinking that maybe it was. Then I continued, "We landed undetected and headed to the target area. Our teams' objective was to blow the ammo dump, radar unit, and get the weapons out. Three groups were assigned for this endeavor, a security, surveillance, and an assault team. The surveillance team took up position over the rise of a hill looking down on the camp. They had a good vantage point. Not too far, not too close from the objective site.

"My team secured a truck and car so we could blend in as locals. We approached the compound entrance. Two men came to the truck to check for authorization passes. We had two Sons of the Desert with us—Rashid and Ramah. They engaged the guards in conversation until our men took them out. Ramah and Rashid took the post. We went into the compound.

"Two attacks were launched simultaneously. The assaults were directed at the observation towers and barracks areas. Gas and smoke grenades were used to establish cover and immobilize any would-be attacker.

"That's when we went in. It was our job to secure the missiles, rig the dump to blow, and get out. We had fifteen minutes from the time we hit the gate.

"Everything was going according to plan. We got in and started looking for the missiles while the rest of the team took up their positions of defense and setting the charges. We located the crates. There were three of them. We grabbed the boxes and headed out. The fighting had settled down to a few shots. Smoke still lingered in the area, allowing some cover for us to get a good distance from the munitions dump, then from overhead there was a burst of machine-gun fire. I took two hits, one to the shoulder throwing me to the ground; the other just missing the kidney. Both were clean shots. They went all the way through. I rolled and saw Mike hit the ground; he was lifted and thrown by the next burst of fire. I thought for sure he had bought the farm.

"From the distance the security team knocked the bird from the sky. The remaining members of the team picked up the boxes and headed to the truck. I got up and ran to Mike. I wasn't going to leave him there to rot. He wasn't going to own any real estate in some foreign country while I was still breathing. When I got to him, he was still breathing and still trying to give me orders. He didn't look good, and I had my doubts about him making it alive.

"I put his gu . . . I put the pieces back in place the best I could, wrapped him, picked him up, hoping not to make the damage any worse, and headed to the LZ. All the way I figured we were goners no matter if we made it or not. You see, our protective gear had been compromised, but fate was smiling on us and we went unscathed. The rest is history. We survived after some hospital and rehab time. Mike stayed a little longer than I did. He had more to fix."

I didn't notice we had stopped until I turned and looked at Sam sitting behind the wheel, face white, tears in her eyes, but thank god there was no sobbing or water running down the face. After all it was a long time ago. Too late for tears now.

Sam reached over, put her arms around me, lay her head on my shoulders, and said, "Not all the heroes are on the Wall."

Nothing more was said, but I knew she was wrong.

CHAPTER 15

When we walked into Lilly's, there were a couple of truckers sitting at the counter.

Lilly was reading the paper by the register, and a young couple was sitting in a booth doing things that they should have gotten a room for, and Callahan and Mike were sitting close to the counter waiting to hear the latest exploits of The Amazing Falco or Captain America, as Callahan would say

Lilly looked up and almost flew around the counter. "Vince, you look like shit." He was all heart. How couldn't you love this guy.

"Come over here," he said as he was pushing me toward the booth at the far end of the room, "and I'll get you some coffee. You want something to eat, anything? Come sit down."

"Just coffee, Mom," my words bringing a wry smile to his face.

"You sure had Sam mad as hell last night when you disappeared, right, Sam?" He didn't wait for an answer. "If she would have found you last night, there is no way you would be walking straight up today, but then maybe she did because you sure aren't walking right," he said with a smile. "But I'm glad you guys made up. Anyway, what happened to you?"

Sam just looked at him with her eyes wide, her mouth held open, wanting to speak, scream, or yell a few profanities at him, not believing that he told me all of this, but it just wouldn't come out. She saw me looking at her with a grin from ear to ear as I said, "And you were just worried sick about me?"

She went to hit me. I moved quickly to dodge the blow, maybe too fast as she saw the pain roll over my laughing face and said, "Serves you right."

Lilly spoke up, "Something I shouldn't have said, Sam? I'm sorry."

"It's all right," she said, almost laughing.

Callahan was choking on his coffee as this comedy went on. Mike had enough.

The look on his face said it all. I was beginning to wonder if he and Callahan had switched roles. Callahan seemed to have hints of humor while Mike was getting to serious.

"All right, Vince, what happened last night and how is it you end up half naked and beat up . . . again? Please don't leave out any of the details. I would like to sort them out myself for a change."

I told him everything that happened. The look on his face said he believed me. Even Callahan nodded, with his furrowed brow giving a sign of belief.

"I think you have someone worried, Vince. The question is who?"

"I did find something at the apartment." The words barely out of my mouth when Callahan bolted upright. I continued before he started. "It didn't strike me as being anything. She had a name written down. It was Dr. Jonah Hyde. It could be her gynecologist, for all I know."

I saw Sam's eyes flare. "It isn't," she said, obviously annoyed at my suggestion.

"When I left the apartment, there was a man in a cab watching the happenings. Didn't think much of it the first day since the world was outside watching the circus."

Callahan interrupted, "The first day—how many times were there?"

"Three, to answer your question. Now let me finish. This guy looked at me and then had the driver take off. I took the cab's number. It was the Area Cab Co. number five forty-seven. The next day when I left, he was outside again, this time in a black Mercedes, latest model. I got the plate number. It was one of those designer plates. It read, '4 A Good time call.'" Callahan's brow furrowed even deeper. Mike just rolled his eyes, put on a sly grin, and shook his head. "Pete, I'm just joking. It read '2 C L O S E.'

Then yesterday when I left you, I was followed by this same car. That's when—and thank you, Mike—I was stopped by the police." Mike gave me a smile that said, "You're welcome, buddy."

Sam watched us and knew we were communicating but couldn't figure it out.

"Didn't you think maybe I'd be interested just a little about this kind of detail? Or maybe after the chase?"

"Like I said, I didn't give it much thought. The circus was in town. The second time, well . . . I figured if he showed up twice, there would be a third time, and I was right, only I didn't get to nab him. Yeah, I should have shared it with you, but . . ."

Mike jumped in, "You wanted to get him all to yourself. The hell with the investigation. Falco would solve the case."

Mike was obviously annoyed at me again, but what's new. I looked at Mike and in answer to his gaze, I said, "Yes, I got a good look at him. His face was narrow with a prominent nose, dark Freudian beard, round wire-rim glasses, and a black hat."

"Are you sure you're telling me everything this time?"

"Would I hold information from you of all people?"

"Yes!" he said boldly.

"Mike, you wound me."

He just looked then turned to Sam. "Miss Richards, do you know or have you seen Shannan with this person?"

"No, she never told me about seeing anyone remotely fitting this description. I don't know what to think, and Mike, you can call me Sam. I feel like we are old friends."

Mike looked over to me with a questioning glance, didn't say anymore, and he and Callahan got up, bid us farewell, and left. He knew he didn't have to say anything. He had said it to me to many times in the past, and he knew I would give him what I had when I felt it was the right time.

Lilly looked at us. "What're you gonna do now, Vince? It seems to be getting a little Sticky, wouldn't you say?"

I just stared at him, wasn't anything to say, so I just picked up my coffee and figured I'd get my chance at Hyde or whoever this person was.

I could feel the pain start again. I knew I had to get some rest. Sam was watching me and noticed it also. "Let's get you to bed. You need some rest. Mike will take care of your Mr. Hyde," her voice commanding me as she was forcing me to my feet and out the door. Lilly's voice trailing behind us, "You kids take it easy."

CHAPTER 16

We got back to my place; the door was open, and sitting on the leather sofa in all his glory was our Mr. Hyde. I started toward him when he began to speak.

"Mr. Falco, I presume. After yesterday's chase, I felt we should meet in order to avoid such dangerous happenings. I came here yesterday, but you were out. Today I felt it necessary that I wait." He spoke with a European accent, maybe German, more likely Austrian.

I interrupted him as I took a seat behind my desk, Sam taking a position on the arm of the chair near Hyde. I have to admit the only good thing that came with this office was the furniture, rich, soft, and attractive leather chairs and couch. The desk was dark cherrywood with matching credenza and book shelves. It gave the place a little professionalism.

Looking at Sam over my shoulder, I said, "This place is worse than Grand Central Station. Remind me to get the lock changed." I turned back to Hyde, "If you thought it important that we meet, why didn't you just stop yesterday when you saw I was trying to catch up to you?"

He didn't answer the question and obviously took offense to the tone in my voice.

He sat farther back in the chair, letting the leather engulf him as he crossed his legs, and with his arms resting across his chest, he put his hands together as if in prayer, fingertips touching, and every once in a while pivoting on his thumbs as he would open and close the fingertips. His stare was one of a person in thought as he continued bouncing his fingertips off of one another. I just stared back, wondering whether or not he was going to continue talking or get up and leave.

"Mr. Falco, please, I'm here to offer assistance. I believe you are involved with finding the killers of Miss McCready. She was a patient of mine." His tone quite conservative as he sat there continuing to exercise his fingertips, similar to the exercises the girls use to do to build up their breasts when I was in school. I still wonder if that really worked.

"What do you mean she was a patient?"

"Miss McCready came to my office three months ago telling me she was having some disturbing dreams. She went on to tell me about her belief in reincarnation and believed these dreams had their base in her past lives. I have experience with past life therapy and agreed to help her understand her beliefs.

"I felt, much as she, that if we brought it to the surface, she would be able to understand the meanings of the dreams and possibly end them. Past life therapy isn't new, and there are a lot of non-professionals out there who prey on those that believe in reincarnation. You have to understand that Miss McCready was a very astute young lady and had her mind set on finding out who she may have been in another life.

"Being a doctor of psychiatry specializing in this behavior pattern, I took her on as my patient. She told me of her dreams, and I directed her thoughts to look deeper into her immediate past. Usually that is where problems arise. However, she insisted that it was further back than this lifetime and wanted to be regressed. I found her to be quite headstrong as most of my patients do as I suggest, gradually building to hypnotism if warranted. She wanted to be hypnotized then. I explained to her that I felt preparation was a necessary part of the process, but she was most insistent. I consented only after she agreed that it be gradual. She agreed to fifteen-minute intervals in the hypnotic state."

"Well, Hyde," I started to say when he broke in. "Who is this Hyde? How do you know him?" His tone set me back as Sam and I glanced at each other and back to him. I thought I had him figured out. "Shannan had the name written down in her phone book, and if you're not Hyde, then who are you?"

"Oh . . . please forgive me," he said sincerely, "I'm Dr. Wilhelm Reinhardt. I question the name Hyde because during one of my sessions with Miss McCready, there were very short mentions of this Hyde. Please, allow me to continue from the beginning.

"When Ms. McCready walked into my office, the look on her face told me that she approved of the surroundings. My office overlooks the river and one can see for miles on any given day. It has a very soothing effect on my patients as they relate their problems. In the winter the ice sheet that forms on the river brings a different calm, one of solitude as you stare out to the serenity of this once-energetic entity. It's overpowering to most ills, puts one's mind at peace as it searches the void looking for its past. And I find it relaxing as I contemplate the day's events and write them in my journal."

The doctor went on, and from his description it was like being there. I could see and hear them in my mind as Shannan opened the door into the spacious office, chairs of deep, rich, dark brown leather shining from more than occasional use, was set off by shelves that lined the walls that were full of books of all sizes, being held by crystal formations of all colors and shapes, adding a mystical charm to the surroundings. The view out the window of the river lazily flowing by. The last remnants of sails skirting the waves and swells before the last days of Indian summer became autumn's chill and turns into the winter ice. Behind the desk standing to greet her was the doctor, bearded and wearing round wire-rim glasses.

I could hear her as she asked, "Dr. Reinhardt?" and extending her hand in greeting.

"Miss McCready, please, sit down. How may I help you?"

As she sat down, slowly crossing her legs and adjusting her skirt, then looking up she said, "I've . . . I've been having dreams that seem to reflect events of the past. I don't mean the immediate past, but a past life experience. I believe in reincarnation and from my study of this subject, I believe that what happened to me before this life is creating the problems I am now experiencing."

"This doesn't sound too crazy, does it, doctor?"

"Not at all. I have been involved with past life regression for many years. I'm sure we can work through this without a problem, Miss McCready. The first step has already been taken. You recognize the reality of your belief."

"Doctor, I would like to be regressed as soon as possible, perhaps today."

"Miss McCready, I would like to approach this slowly. First, we should find out as much as possible that your conscious mind knows of this past, then see how that relates with the dreams you have been having. Understanding is the key to retaining these memories. Only after we find the obstacles that lie in our path can we remove them."

Shannan, getting up from the chair and walking to the window, stares out into the vastness of the clear sky, slowly turning looking at the doctor with those pleading eyes. "I don't know how to explain my feelings, but I have to be taken back now, not weeks from now. It is most urgent that we do it . . . today."

"Please, Miss McCready, you have to understand the necessity of gathering all the known information first . . ."

Shannan interrupted, "I haven't got that much time. Please, can we forego your usual approach and see what is in my past that has me staying up at night and occupying my days?"

"As I stated, Mr. Falco . . . Mr. Falco . . ."

I was brought back to the moment, turned and looked at my caller. "She wanted to be hypnotized, so I consented. When she was in the trance state, the strangest thing occurred. I didn't have to talk her back, she was already there. This was very unusual," his voice in wonderment as he began stroking his beard.

"Miss McCready was a very strong-willed individual, and I could see from her appearance that no matter what I said or did, she would not settle for anything other than hypnosis as the first treatment.

"I began the hypnosis as always by taking the subject back gradually, first asking them to see their surroundings and look for anything that would be recognizable. Then we progress to people and faces, and finally we explore the known places, people, and events."

I could visualize Shannan sitting back in the chair, being cradled by the soft leather as the doctor worked his spell.

"You are going back, back to your past, the past before you were Shannan McCready . . ."

"Who are you?" Shannan interrupting, her voice nearly English in accent, "and what do you want of me, sir?"

The doctor, taken aback, asked, "I'm Dr. Reinhardt, and what is your name?"

"I'm Elizabeth Anne Barrette. Do I know you, sir?"

"No, but I am here to help someone, and your help is needed also."

"How may I help?"

"If you would be so kind as to answer some questions, I'm sure it would be of the greatest help to me."

"What do you want to know?"

"Elizabeth, what is the year?"

"Eighteen twenty-six."

"Where are you now?"

"I'm sitting in my carriage watching the water roll ashore from the Sound, and seeing the children run in and out of the sea."

"Where is this . . . Sound?"

"Why, it's in North Carolina. It's quite lovely here this time of year. I often come here and think of my love," her voice trailing.

"Where is he?"

"He died, sir. He had the fever and passed on. All I have left is remembrance of his smile and how he would hold me close when the cool breeze would blow from the sea, and how he would shelter me from the salt spray as the waves broke against the rocks as the wind carried the spray to where we stood. He was a good man."

"Can you tell me of your family?"

"My father is a businessman and has a very influential standing in the community.

Some say he is intemperate in his business dealings and fear him when they must barter their wants or goods. It's true, he is a stern businessman, but not as voracious as some say. He is a very loving father and would do anything I ask.

"They say his blood can boil like that of his forefathers, having the heart of the pirate, more than the privateer. I vision him at sea as I watch the Sloops gather in the harbor, and hear the jargon of the lads from their long days at sea. He would make a handsome captain commanding his vessel to bring a volley alongside the Ketch of the brigand captain. Guns ablazing, smoke filling the air, and the screams of the crew as they board the frigate, with sounds of steel against steel as the swords meet to ward off harm as they battle for their lives. Then the anxious calm as the fallen leader surrenders handing his cutlass to my father, who, in his mercy, offers him a pardon as opposed to dancing the hempen jig. Although the end of a hemp rope would be more deserving."

"And your mother?"

"My mother is a generous soul, God fearing, and loving. She would not harm a beetle as it chewed through the plants. You would never find a more caring individual as long as you live."

"What can you tell me of your day, besides watching the sea?"

"I have come here to forget my doings of this day; I have not had peace for some time. The doctor has stayed on to help, but it was a ruse. He had only his intentions at heart and that was to sway me to him. He would try to force his affections on me, but I would counter with the threat of my father. I tried to stay with Rainy, more and more, for with her I felt safe.

"I have the rush in my blood from the happenings with that Hyde. I had him driven from the house. He is one who should do the hempen jig, and all should watch and shout in joy of his dance of death, for he did not stay away as he should."

Elizabeth was now showing signs of agitation and starting to convulse as her voice becomes muffled. The doctor trying desperately to bring her back.

"Shannan . . . Shannan, you will be awake when I say three, listen to me, one . . . two . . . three . . ." She still was gagging, as he continued, "Shannan, can you hear me? Shannan, you must come back, now!" his voice raised to get her attention.

Slowly she started to react, still convulsing, unable to move her arms, but her hands moving frantically as if bound at the wrist. "Shannan, where are you? Look at the surroundings and tell me where you are."

"I'm . . . I'm in an office . . .," she said as she turned and looked at Reinhardt, "I'm here, yes, I'm here."

"Mr. Falco, I can say without doubt that this had never happened to me. She was acting as if being strangled, and for whatever reason, she did not want to return at that moment. She was extremely exhausted, and being my last client for the day, I encouraged her to remain and rest for a while. She did just that.

"We met on several occasions without hypnotism and discussed what had happened, trying to bring forward any memory or event that may have had any bearing on her behavior while in the regressive state. We seemed to be making progress, as the dreams were becoming less frequent; however, this ended when she attended a gathering of her friends to discuss their beliefs in reincarnation. This started the dreams again. This was about four weeks ago.

"One morning shortly after her meeting with her friends, she came to my office and told me of the event and the aftermath of the gathering, that being the dreams. She insisted that I once again hypnotize her. I agreed reluctantly.

"This time it went even worse than the first time. She was Elizabeth again, screaming obscenities at this Hyde fellow, insisting that he was the devil himself. It was almost as if she was trying to fight off this Hyde but couldn't move. Then the choking came and the convulsions. I finally brought her back; she said she felt very strange as though she was freed from this plane, just as she put it, 'floating over her own body,' but couldn't remember anything of the events that had transpired.

"That ended the session. She got up, although I tried to get her to stay at least for a little while to calm down. She insisted that she was all right and needed to be alone for a while.

"She called me a week later and told me it was becoming worse. She went on to tell me of an incident that had occurred in her place of business." I stopped him and told him that's where I came in.

"Then you should understand my concern. I immediately began to research her reactions to therapy in hopes of extinguishing this behavior while treatment continued."

I was listening, but it was hard to believe that people really talked like this. I just continued listening as he went on.

"You understand that a person can't be made to accept any suggestion while under hypnosis that the subject does not believe in. At least that has been my experience contrary to some writings. But a person can be coerced in accepting the possibility of events, happenings, beliefs, if properly tutored. That is to say, open their minds to all possibilities. When this is achieved, they have belief in that subject matter.

Then and only then can the subject be implanted with desired thought patterns."

"That, Mr. Falco, is what I believe happened to Miss McCready. Someone had prepared her for this belief in reincarnation, hypnotized her, and planted this Elizabeth person in her mind."

I wanted to take my final examination in this Psych 101 class I've been attending but didn't think this was the time to ask for it, I thought as I kept listening to Reinhardt.

"I thought this Mr. Hyde would be a good place to start. However, I was unable to locate anyone named Hyde in this state."

We sat quietly for a few minutes before Sam broke the silence, "Shannan never mentioned you to me or this Mr. Hyde, but one thing is certain, up until she got involved with some college classmates that were into reincarnation, she didn't even think of it as a word so that must have been when she was being prepared."

"Sam, you may have something there. I think I should take another trip to Chowan County. It seems that it all started there, and maybe I can come up with something that will help end it."

"Hold on, mister, you're in no condition to be traveling."

"I've been in worse shape. Believe me, I can travel and I promise to write every day, Mom." I gave her a smile and a wink to help her accept the idea that I was going.

"You won't have to. I'll be with you."

Then the doc broke in, "Would you mind terribly if I were to join you? I find this rather intriguing." His query more as a way of telling us that it didn't matter what we said.

He was going anyway.

"Well then, let's par-tay, gang," I said in somewhat of a sarcastic tone.

CHAPTER 17

On the way to the airport, I called Mike. "Hey, big fellah, I thought you might want to know that I ran into that person again, his name is—"

Mike interrupted, "Dr. Wilhelm Reinhardt. I got it from DMV. I've tried contacting him. He seems to be gone a lot. I left five messages on his answering machine and had Pete pay him a visit; still haven't heard from him."

"I think he said he was going on vacation, wasn't planning on being around for a while. He doesn't have much to contribute. Just concerned about his client . . . Shannan."

"Vince, why do I have this feeling that you're not telling me everything, again?"

"Mike, I love you. How can you think a thing like that? Look, I'm going on vacation for a week or so. See you when I get back, okay?" I hung up before he had a chance to say anything. Sam was looking at me, smiling and shaking her head.

"I keep wondering how he can control himself around you. I'd lock you away if I were him just so I could keep an eye on you."

I just let it slide as I made a second call, this one to Louis Cohan; that was the name he was using this week. When we first met, he was Justine Armstrong. Since then, he's used a dozen or so aliases so as not to make it too easy to be found.

Lou looks and acts the part of the absentminded professor when he is around people he doesn't know or trust. He is the archangel of hackers. He broke into the Feds' files in the early eighties and didn't make any friends in Washington doing it. He had strong notions of getting into the war room and settling all wars. At least that's what he told me. One thing for sure, if you needed something on someone, he could get it.

I had stopped at his place on the way back after my brief encounter with the Amazon police officer and asked him to look into the list of names in Shannan's book under "Club Members" and to also get a handle on this Jonah Hyde.

When I walked in, Lou was sitting at his favorite spot in front of five monitors. He had them set up like a musician sets up his synthesizers. Lou never pays for the use of the net, Web, whatever it is called these days. He just links through everyone else and lets the corporations pay for his time.

We exchanged greetings. "Falco, my friend, it's been a while. What can I do for you?"

"I need a favor."

"Of course you do. Why else would you be here? By chance to visit a comrade before the reaper arrives or just to watch a master at his task? No . . . none of the above, only to ask a favor." His wit was armed in sarcasm.

"Lou, how can you say these things? I stop by every time I'm in the neighborhood."

"Okay, Falco, let me have it before the pile gets deeper."

"I need all the info you can get on the names in this book, listed here." I pointed to the list. He took the book and thumbed through it. "I don't see anyone here I know." He then scanned the page of the club members and handed the book back to me. "Give me a couple of days. No one can hide in the system. Hell, it's getting so that before the sperm hits the egg, the file is started. You have heard of 'Big Brother,' haven't you, Falco?" His tone most assuring of times yet to come.

That visit is what prompted this call.

Finally Lou answered, "It's your time, so don't waste mine."

"Lou, Falco here. Any word?"

"Cohan, this is Cohan, your brother. So soon you forget." Humor, that's what I liked most about Lou.

"You struck out if you're looking for crooks. Ornsworth is a housewife, has three kids and one in the oven, likes to spend money, has her cards up to the hilt. I cleared a few for her." He chuckled and then continued, "Besides spending her old man's cash, she belongs to a ton of organizations—PTA, Girl Scouts, Brownies—not the ones you can eat . . . yet," then another chuckle. Sam was just rolling her eyes as Lou continued, "The only interesting thing she has going is this thing about coming back from the dead. You know, reincarnation. Neat. If it happens, I wouldn't need this Web to get around. I'd know everything.

"Pat Smith is an executive assistant, and from her rap sheet, she has executive-bed privileges with some of our leading citizens. I found her style unique in the system. I'm sure she thinks putting this info into the computer's locked files can't be accessed. Real naive, aye?

"Foxmore, the first three letters of her name describe her well. She is known under the pseudonym of Erica Jason, a well-known local model aspiring fast to reach the top. She's getting help from her friend, Patty. If you know what I mean.

"Morely and Washington work for Paragon. They're researchers, single, looking, nothing worth getting excited about. And finally, Jonah Hyde. I couldn't locate anyone in the tristate area, but I pulled up two Jonah Hydes in North Carolina. One deceased about one hundred and fifty years, and the other, just hanging by a thread. He's in his nineties. Anything else you need?"

"I'm on my way to the airport. I'll check with you later, pal. I owe you."

"Do you owe me? Oh, do you owe me! I should live long enough that you could pay me back."

As I hung up, Sam just stared at me and asked, "Where did you get those names?

I know these women and would never have thought anything like that about Pat or Anne. Wow, what a surprise. Falco, you don't cease to amaze me."

I leaned back in the seat and just smiled.

When we arrived at the airport, I placed a call to Lou and had him fax the information he had on Hyde to me. The girl at the counter was looking me over like a panther on the prowl. Sam stepped up to the counter, put her arm in mine, and asked in a voice that warned of possession, "Is it soup yet?" Her eyes let this airport vixen know not to mess with her prey. This wasn't going to scare the young lioness. As she approached, her claws extended, her eyes hypnotizing, and lips inviting as she reached across the counter to me. Sam stepped up, reaching out and pulling the pages from her hands saying, "Thanks for all your help . . . kid."

As we walked away, Sam had that look on her face of victory. She clipped the ears of her aggressor, she would retain the title, and she would be queen. I wasn't sure how I felt about this possessive nature she had, especially since we only knew each other for a couple of days.

As we approached the gate, we could see the doctor sitting, patiently waiting for us.

"Doc, been here long?"

"I arrived about thirty minutes ago. I have the tickets. As soon as they announce boarding, we can get on the plane."

The doctor sat down, opened his magazine, and was lost to us. Sam stared out the window. Her mind was a thousand miles away, and I was adrift in thought going over everything that had happened to date, hoping to find some connection between Barrette, myself, and Hyde.

Finally, the announcement came for boarding. I looked up for Sam, but she was gone. I turned to the doc, ready to ask if he had seen her leave, when he said, "I believe she went to the ladies' room. Perhaps you should get her."

I went in the direction of the restrooms and saw Sam hurriedly approaching me. She put her arm in mine when she finally reached me and in a nonchalant manner said,

"Vince, with all the things that had happened, I forgot to tell you about the night at the funeral parlor. There was a visitor there that looked exactly like Conrad Johnston, only he had a scar running down the right side of his face. I approached him, but he denied being Conrad. Said he was Lawrence Ramsey, a friend of Shannan's. I got Lilly. We went outside looking for you, but you were gone. Anyway, I just saw the same man standing by the convenience counter. He looked right at me. And by the time I got there, he was gone."

"Are you sure it was the same man?"

"Yes, I wouldn't make that mistake, and I'm sure his name isn't Ramsey. I never forget a face."

The mention of the scar brought to mind what Rogers had told me at the funeral home, and then there was the similarity of the names.

"Well, he's gone now and we have a plane to board." I guided her through the rush of the crowd and headed to the plane.

The doctor had gotten us first-class tickets. Bless him, he knows how to fly. We all settled in to our seats and didn't have much to say on the way. I was able to get some necessary rest for my aching bones.

CHAPTER 18

It was 4:00 p.m. when the plane landed down. Outside the airport, it was a picturesque setting, blue sky, dotted lightly with billowing white clouds lazily floating by, and temperature in the seventies. You couldn't ask for a nicer day.

We picked up the rental and headed for US Seventeen. According to the map, we had about an hour or so drive. We took in the sights as we headed south. The doc was amazed at how open it was, having spent most of his time in and around the city since coming to this country.

"It is very lovely around here, would you say, Miss Richards? It reminds me of my home. Of course the Alps are a little higher, but nonetheless, it is similar. I could consider relocating to this area just for the serenity."

"Yes, it is a beautiful area. I enjoyed driving along the rural roads while I was going to school. Shannan and I would drive to Virginia Beach on the weekends or sometimes head south to Myrtle Beach, wherever the notion took us. Even in the winter, it was nice. Sometimes it would snow, but never like home. I remember one time when we woke in the morning to what looked like a light dusting of snow, you know, just enough to make it white. Well, everyone was outside scraping the walkways clean to make snowballs. I thought it was funny, but later found out that a lot of the snow scrapers never played in the snow or had to shovel it or get stuck in it. To them, it was amazing. But of course, you know that the child in us never really goes away, don't you?"

"Miss Richards," he said with a smile and distant gleam in his eyes, "I hope we always keep that part of us to help us remember what life really is about."

When we arrived to our destination, we looked for one of the better motels and settled for three rooms. I would have liked a bed partner, but the doc wasn't my type.

So since Sam was new to me, although you couldn't tell it by her mannerism, I thought separate rooms were best. Besides, my ribs weren't going to let me do much anyway.

We met for dinner and at the table I laid out the plan for the morning.

"I'll look up this Hyde fellow in the morning, and then I'll head to the county clerk's office and see if the info package is ready yet. I might even be able to pick up something on this Conrad character since he keeps popping up."

Sam looked at me and said, "You concentrate on Hyde. Dr. Reinhardt and I will go to the clerk's office. What did you say her name was? You remember the strawberry blonde with the Southern belle accent, don't you, Vince?"

I just smiled. "Betty Lou Barker. Tell her Falco sent you."

"Do you think we might have time to tour the area? I would like to see some of these historical sites that are on the signs we passed, and of course we will go to the county offices," the doctor said without really directing it to anyone.

I wanted to tell them we weren't on vacation, but then I thought this would keep them out of my way and still let them think how much they were helping. Life was good.

It was settled. My newly acquired staff would rent a car in the morning, and I would go in search of Hyde. I felt a little disappointed not going to see the voluptuous Miss Barker, but I guess it was for the best.

After dinner, we headed to our rooms. We all were a little tired from the day's activities and the flight.

The room had a queen-sized bed with a Jacuzzi in the corner next to the patio door that opened overlooking the pool. The adjoining room was a kitchenette with a coffeepot and coffee packets supplied. We chose well. This was better than my place. I could get used to this, I thought.

I lay down on the bed to see how it felt. The next thing I knew, there's a knock on the door. I must have fallen asleep. I was still in my clothes from the evening before. I struggled to my feet, feeling the rush of pain from my side, having forgotten all about it, and opened the door. Standing in front of me all wide-eyed and bushy-tailed was Samantha.

She looked me over like a potential buyer of livestock then said, "Good morning, Falco. Having a late night?"

"I forgot my PJs. Isn't it a little early?"

"Vince, its gorgeous outside," she said as she closed the door behind her. "It's 7 AM. We can have a leisurely breakfast and still have the rest of the day for whatever you want. I've already called Dr. Reinhardt, and he will be joining us. So let's get the show on the road, big fella."

She reached over and wrapped her arms around me. "We do have time on our hands while the doctor showers and dresses." She had that naughty twinkle in her eye. I winced from the ache in my side. "Oh, Vince, I'm sorry, I forgot about your side."

"To hell with my side," I said as I pulled her close, falling into the bed.

CHAPTER 19

As I stepped outside the room, I looked at Sam and said, with a smile on my face,

"It is a nice day, isn't it?"

When we reached the restaurant, the doc was reading the local paper and drinking coffee. He looked up as we approached the table. "You two have finally made it. I had thought perhaps you left without me. I have already ordered."

"That's okay, Doc. I just want some coffee, maybe a Danish." His eyebrow rose as I called him Doc, obviously not an endearing term to him.

"Make that two; I have to powder my nose." Sam got up and headed to the ladies room.

It was 9 AM when we left the restaurant. Sam and the doctor decided to walk to the county office. It was only three blocks away, according to the waitress, and most of the tours leave from there or just a few blocks farther south at the visitor's center

I headed to the Balmorial Home for the Aged. That's where Mr. Jonah Hyde has taken up residence.

The home was an old plantation manor built in the Victorian style. The grounds were well-kept, with flowers planted along the drive. The lawn areas were shaped to test the groundskeeper when he mows the lawn.

There were mixed groups sitting on the porch talking, reading, and some just napping, I thought. They all stopped doing whatever they were doing and took notice of me as I walked inside the leaded glass doors.

Inside, about fifteen feet and attached to a long staircase was a reception area with a young man in attendance. As I approached, he asked, "May I help you?"

"Yes, I'm looking for Mr. Jonah Hyde."

"I haven't seen you before. Are you a relative of Jonah?"

"No, I'm Vince Falco and I'm looking into some of the history around this area. I was told he would be a good source, that he knew everything there was to know about Chowan County."

"Then, you're with the press?"

I was getting tired of playing twenty questions, but I continued, "No, I'm a freelance writer. Is he in?"

"No, sir, he left yesterday and isn't expected back until later today. I'll be glad to tell him you called."

"When he gets back, please call me at the Olde Towne Inn."

"Yes, I can do that. However, since you are here, Charlie, I mean Mr. Charles, Hands is also quite the historian of these parts. He and Jonah talk for hours on end bout the way it used to be." He let out a small laugh then continued. "They sit and argue something fierce about the past even before they were born, and mister, I do declare that's a long time ago.

"Jonah and Charlie are the resident historians in these parts. Charlie is the better storyteller. We sit with him for hours, sometimes just to hear the stories. I declare he has some good ones, and it's hard not to believe that it was really the way he tells it. "Charlie is here if you would like to talk to him."

I wanted to see this Hyde person, but figured since Hands is a close friend, I might be able to get a feel for Hyde before I met him. "Sure, that would be fine. Where would I find this Charlie Hands?"

He walked to the front door, stepped outside, and pointed to the end of the porch. See the gentleman standing with those two ladies knitting by the end column? That's Charlie. He's hot with the ladies, blows the myth about no sex after sixty. Hell, he's ninety-two."

"The man wearing the black-and-white striped pullover?"

I attracted a lot of attention as I walked the length of the veranda. As I approached Charlie, I could see he was a well-weathered man, had the appearance of spending most of his life outside. Besides natural aging lines, he had skin of leather. He looked to be in his late seventies at the most. He still had a full crop of hair, more white than gray, with some brown strands still surviving the ravages of time. His eyes were blue and actually twinkled in the sunlight. He was unshaven, maybe three days, stood like an old sailor keeping his balance in rough seas, hands on his hips, and elbows pointing out. He was a fine figure for a man his age or any age for that matter. No wonder he was a hit with the chicks, or maybe I should say hens.

I reached the end of the line and by now I was the center of attention, the new kid on the block, and I mean kid. "Mr. Hands, I'm Falco. I was told at the desk that you could possible help me."

He had a grip of steel as we shook hands. He must have been a formidable foe in his day and probably still was. He looked me over as he kept the vise closed on my hand. He wasn't going to let go until he felt it was all right.

"Falco, is that your full name?"

"Vince Falco."

"Vince, is it? Well Vince, it depends on who you want eliminated." He grinned ear to ear as the ladies joined in.

I smiled at his remark and continued, "I'm doing some research on Elizabeth Anne Barrette . . ." Before I could finish, Charlie's expression changed. His eyes became narrow and piercing, his jaw firm, and his brow furrowed.

"Why would you be looking for information on the Barrettes? Hasn't been a Barrette living in these parts for a hundred and fifty years or so." He waited for an answer as he stared at me, stroking his unshaven chin.

I figured if I told some of the truth, he would be more likely to cooperate. "This may sound crazy, but about a month ago, this young attractive woman came to me with a story that she was Elizabeth Anne Barrette in her past life and wanted to know more about that person and her life. Well, I'm not normally drawn to this kind of story, but something about her made me want to look into it. I finally found two Elizabeth Anne Barrettes, both in North Carolina and both dead. One died in 1972, the other in 1826." The look on his face changed. He seemed willing to talk as he guided me to a seat in the midst of the ladies, who by now had put down their knitting and were all ears to the tale about to be told.

"It all started a long time ago. You see, Elizabeth was the daughter of Edward Hardie Barrette II. His father was the grandson of Edward Teach. You do know who Teach was, don't you?"

"No. Should I?"

"Edward Teach was the infamous Blackbeard. You do know of Blackbeard, don't you?" I just shook my head as he continued. "That's where I'll start."

He began rubbing his chin as if stroking a beard and looked out to the horizon as though he could see what he was about to describe.

"You have to understand this man, Teach. In eighteenth-century England, reading and writing wasn't known to many, but young Mr. Teach came from an educated family and learned to read and write. It was said that he read everything he got his hands on. He had a sharp mind and a heart set for adventure that he had read about. He put to sea with the one man that was to change his life to one of piracy, and that man was Captain Benjamin Horngold.

"He was the most feared pirate of his time throughout the West Indies. Young Edward learned well." Charlie stopped for a second, looked up to the sky as if to pray, put on a little smile, and the twinkle returned to his eyes.

"Aye, piracy. It's still happening, you know! Adventure on the high sea. You have to be careful if you go sailing in the Caribbean and other seas as well.

"Well, that's where it all started. My grandfather, four times removed, was Israel Hands, the first mate to Edward Teach. He escaped on that fateful day in 1718 when the British Navy killed Teach at Ocracoke Inlet. There were rumors that he was killed or captured, but he weren't. He lived on to make his fortune.

"Teach had a boy on board, said it was his son. He was fourteen years, a scrapper like his dad, it was said. The navy took the lad and put him in servitude on their vessel. At fifteen, he jumped ship in South Carolina and took up Articles with Sir Marion Fairweather, a pirate of the Caribbean." He stopped and looked at me. "What's the problem, lad?"

My expression gave insight to my ignorance. "What exactly are Articles?"

He gave a hardy laugh, "Articles, mate, were the rules while on board the ship. Pirates were the true democratic government. The capt'n was elected by the crew, and all decisions were the result of a vote by the crew. Sure, the capt'n had his command, but the majority could change his orders.

"Young Edward, who had assumed the name of Edward Thatch Barrette so as not to infer his father's lust, was taken on as the son Sir Marion never had. But young Edward had the blood of his father coursing through his veins and wanted more than Sir Marion could give. Young Edward tried to convince Marion to take bigger ships, change his route, and head to the Red Sea, but he wouldn't hear of it and ordered the lad to be still. Well, the lad knew where his father had buried his treasures on the Ocracoke, Albemarle, and Pamlico Sounds, and knew he could do well by himself, didn't need Sir Marion. So he picked ten members of the crew he felt would follow him. One of these trusted men was Israel Hands. The lad and Hands agreed to say nothing of their acquaintance while on board. The ten drew up Articles among themselves and waited for the right time to seize the ship. When it came, the devil himself winced at the bloodletting that took place.

"It was a dark night, not a star to be seen, and on occasion the devil moon would be seen coming through the clouds. It was an evil omen to the men on board. Even the ten felt it wasn't the right time, but young Edward would defy Neptune if it was in his best interest to do it.

"Sir Marion ran with a light crew on board his ship, the Reginagaye. The crew numbered twenty-five, and ten were signed with young Edward. That left fifteen to be taken."

"Young Edward set to the task. He entered Sir Marion's cabin. While he lay asleep, Edward placed his hand under his chin. And as

Sir Marion opened his eyes, Edward pulled back his head and ran his razor-sharp blade across the throat of Marion, feeling him struggle and listening to him gag as the blood flowed. Then Marion lay still. The mutinous ten locked the hold to the crew's cabins and seized the ship.

"Edward had the capt'n's body brought on deck and strung up by the legs hanging from the yard arm over the rail of the ship. He had the crew brought up from the hold, and in front of them all he began to dismember Sir Marion's mortal remains. This ran shivers through their very souls, not knowing if their fate was to be the same.

"Soon, gale-sized winds began to blow and Edward ordered the ship to sea. The crew said the night was full of evil omens and they had to stay close to shore, but young Edward wouldn't hear of it. He laughed and shook his fists to the sky as he shouted that he was the master of his destiny and to hell with the devil, Neptune, and any other deity that would try to stop him. When he turned to his men, the look on his face commanded strict obedience. They set to sea, unnoticed by the remaining three ships of Sir Marion's fleet.

"Edward wouldn't hear the pleas of the crew willing to join him and had them fed to the sharks one by one as he headed to Ocracoke Island.

"By twenty, Edward was a more seasoned seafarer than most of the capt'ns afloat.

"The times were getting hard with privateers and the navy out for hides of pirates.

He decided to give up the sea and head for shore. Only five of his men wanted to join him, so the six took up Articles, a pact. A blood oath would be better said that they were bound to. You could say that they started the society of 'the Brethren of the Coast.'

Although the Brethren originally was formed in the seventeenth century, still it was said that this crew started it. Not too smart in those days. Aye, it were a loose collection of pirates and privateers known as buccaneers in those days.

"He knew he couldn't let the four remaining crew live. They would surely give him up to save their hides, so he and his mates killed them as they slept."

I was listening to the story like a kid. I didn't see what all this had to do with Elizabeth, but I didn't want to miss a word. Even the ladies stayed awake to hear the tale and Charlie was in his glory having an audience to tell it to.

He continued, "On land, Edward conducted himself like a real gentleman. With his learn'n and all, he became a pillar of the community or at least it seemed, for he had a heart as black as coal. He bought land, built his plantation, bought and sold slaves, grew tobacco, and bought and sold anything or anybody. It was said he would deal with the devil and win.

"That's where my grandfather, four times removed, had dealing with him. He knew Edward better than Edward knew himself. He ran the company and Edward handled the politics. This pact ran the coast buying and selling and stealing whatever they could.

They were the best liars, cheats, and thieves. They were the original Murder Incorporated.

"Edward married to give the illusion of a settled gentleman, and at twenty-four, his wife gave birth to Edward Hardie Barrette. He was a frail lad and was left with his mother to care for. The lad didn't know why his father wouldn't have anything to do with him, and as he grew, so did his resentment for his father. Although he would remain weak of body, his cunning was better than the best.

"Whilst the lad resented his father, he still looked to him for approval, but none came. The lad watched everything his father did, the way he talked to people, the things he said, and on many occasions followed his father and watched his transactions, be it murder, slaving, or whatever ill-begotten deed he was doing. The boy took it all in; he learned well. He liked what he saw and felt the power of being feared.

"He hired some unsavory types that hung out at the local tavern, and they began to intrude on his father's business. The lad learned well indeed.

"The father was infuriated with the loss due to this ghost dealer he believed to be one of his own and had Hands set up the trap to catch the ill-doer. This wasn't difficult to do since Edward was connected as far north as New York and south to the West Indies.

But the surprise came when he had his men in waiting all around the Edenton Bay where the transaction was to take place. He would have these natives drawn and quartered.

"Now, if the elder Edward had a heart, black as it was, it was said that tears came to his eyes when he saw that it was his son cut'n him short. The scuffle didn't last a minute as the elder embraced his son. There and then, they agreed to be one. You could say the Barrettes merged to form a giant cartel. By now, Edward was twenty and the elder was forty-four. Together, they ruled the coast.

"The young Edward married Penelope Bennett and had a son in 1750.

He was christened Edward Hardie Barrette II. He was all a grandfather wanted in a son; he was strong, smart, and cunning. It seemed this lad had all the finer traits of the family.

"As he grew, he leaned more toward running the plantation than taking up the family enterprise. He had his eye on politics; he wanted to be governor. This infuriated the grandfather, and the elder Edward had many an argument about the younger Barrette's ambitions and how it would be taken by the other members of the pact.

Edward didn't care what his son did as long as he did well.

"One night, the elder Edward was drunk and kept going on about it until the son knocked him down. The elder hit the hearth with his head and was dead on the spot.

Edward took his father to the road and reported to the local authorities that they were assaulted by highwaymen and in the struggle, he was knocked unconscious. When he came to, his father lay dead beside him. All the highwaymen in the area worked for the Barrettes, but nobody could prove it so it was an acceptable story.

"Edward the second never took over all of the family business, just the more prosperous end bordering on the illegal. But as he became older, he had more of his grandfather's temper and was known to be cruel when he didn't quite have his way.

"He married late in life to the widow Emily Maye Barker. She was thirty and he was forty. Her first husband was thrown from his horse and found on the road with the horse standing over him. He was kicked in the head by that horse. She had it shot.

"Edward and Emily wanted children, but it seemed that Emily was barren. Edward took it in stride and went about his business. Emily was a little forlorn, but managed not to show it. Nine years went by when the miracle happened or so it was called. You see,

Emily was found to be with child.

"Elizabeth Anne Barrette was born in the year 1800. Her father had a party the town still talks about. Everyone was invited who was considered to be anyone. You know, the uppity-ups and the wannabes.

"Edward couldn't do enough for that child. He taught her how to handle herself,.

There wasn't a lad in the parts that could hold a sword to her, outride her, or throw her.

Her mother saw to it that she also knew the refined ways of a lady. Elizabeth did them both proud. After all, they sent her to the best schools, gave her the best clothes, and everything and anything her heart desired.

"Elizabeth never married. She had many proposals. Some she turned down, but two she accepted." He chuckled a little before he continued. "Of course, they were on separate occasions.

"First, there was young Thomas Maynard. It was said that he was a descendant of Lieutenant Maynard who killed Blackbeard at Ocracoke in 1718. This could have been his undoing if the family held a hundred-year grudge. But after all,

Elizabeth loved him and if that was what she wanted, then she was to have him. The family accepted him as the son they never had.

"Elizabeth was eighteen when the wedding was set. All the arrangements where made, people invited, you name it, and it was done. The father of the bride was as happy as a lark. He was having a house built on the plantation for their wedding present.

"It was never finished. Three days before the wedding, Thomas took ill. The doctor stayed with him night and day, but on the day of the planned wedding, young Thomas expired. The townsfolk sympathized with both families, but none took it as hard as Elizabeth and her father. He more for his daughter's grief than his own.

"It was a few years before Elizabeth went out with another man, though many tried to court her. Her grieving was long, but finally she came around to the fancy of Charles Geoffrey Eden, said to be of the bloodline of the first governor. He had uppity airs, but Elizabeth controlled his mannerisms.

"It must have been fate 'cause if it weren't for bad luck, poor Elizabeth wouldn't have had any luck at all. Charles came down with tick fever, same as young Thomas, and passed on days before the wedding was to be. Seemed strange that the same doctor took care of this lad as well.

"Elizabeth withdrew from society, stayed in the house, and was said to be a recluse for some time. Her father's heart was broken seeing her like this. He had the best doctors look at her, and all said the same thing, that he should have her put in a place where she would be watched day in and day out. He was about ready to follow their suggestion when Dr. Jonah Hyde said it would kill the girl if she was taken from her home. It would be best if she was kept at home and let him take care of her.

"Elizabeth threatened to kill herself if her father made her leave; that's what made Edward do what Hyde suggested. He consented to keeping her at the plantation and gave Hyde permanent residence so he would be able to watch over Elizabeth.

"Hyde stayed with the Barrettes four years. It was said that he made advances toward Elizabeth one evening while the family was retired. Elizabeth fought him off, and her scream brought her father and the house servants to her room. Hyde was said to be on the floor bleeding from the head with Elizabeth standing over him brandishing a poker. Needless to say, the father was enraged enough to kill him on the spot, but Elizabeth stopped him and instead had him thrown off the property. The servants were said to have beat him all the way to the road's end.

"That's the part where Hyde and I argue." Charlie got that sly laugh of his in again then continued, "He says the girl caused the ruckus, but everyone knows better. Too many stories telling it different, yet they all say the doctor started it and should have been put to the stock or worse.

"It was said that Elizabeth reported seeing the doctor on the grounds by the graveyard. No one ever caught him there. He was like the wind in the night, there but not to be seen. Edward caught up with him in town and confronted him with the accusations, but the doctor denied it. Edward didn't let it be. He started spreading rumors of Hyde's drunkenness and forceful affections to women in the surrounding areas. This eventually drove him away, what with business declining and the townsfolk treating him like the plague.

"Now, 'our' Jonah is a squirrelly old coot. One minute he's nice as can be and the next thing you know, well . . . all hell breaks out. His faces change with the wind." The women sitting and listening to the saga just shook their heads in agreement. "If he had been on m ship, we'd keelhauled him. I'd say, he had the temperament of his grandfather four times removed.

Charlie had a sly smile on his face as he rubbed his unshaven chin. "He has a grandson, claims he hasn't seen or heard from him for years. He used to live around here, and like many others he was determined to find the Barrette treasure."

"What treasure? I haven't heard about any treasure."

"The story around these parts is that Teach's son brought back most if not all of his father's bounty and buried it on the plantation. The location was given to each of the sons, and it was thought that Edward the last gave it to Elizabeth. But if he did, she took it to the grave. To this day, it hasn't been found and that property has been plowed, shoveled, and God knows what else, but it still ain't been found. I could lay claim to part of it because my grandfather and his grandfather before him were in the pact."

Charlie continued, "As I was saying, the boy would go to the old mansion and tear up the place. He took apart walls and floors, but ain't no one found nothin' yet.

"Now, I ain't saying this as fact, but my grandfather four times removed would have made a map of where he hid the treasure and on the map he would have put a big 'X' to mark the spot. Well, there ain't no 'Xs' on the floors or walls, trees or noth'n, so why even try?

"If it weren't for the hens in the Historical Society, that place would have been torn down years ago. And then if there was any treasure, it would have been found."

"Where is Hyde's grandson?" I asked.

"He vanished some time ago. Took off and ain't been heard from since, so Hyde says. I know better, but ain't get'n into it. You see, he was involved with this group of women. Some said it was a cult of some kind, worshiped the devil or something like that. Anyway, two of the ladies seemed to have committed suicide and slit their wrists at the old Barrette plantation. They were found on the floor five days after they were reported missing."

"How were they found? Kids or cops?"

"Weren't neither. Local gal found them when she went up to tend the graves. No one knows why she does it, but she's been doing it all her life."

"How does Hyde's grandson fit in to it?"

"They belonged to the cult. He was the leader or priest. When the rest of the women were questioned, it all come back to him. He was last seen with both of them heading in that direction and weren't seen since the first day they came up missing.

"He always hung around with this big fellow, had to be heavier than a prized hog at the fair." Charlie got another chuckle out of this. "He even snorted when he walked and had a peculiar odor about him too. Anyway, like I said, it all comes back to him. The authorities watched Hyde for some time, but never found nothing that gave the whereabouts of his grandson."

"Has this younger Hyde got in touch with him recently?"

"First of all, his name ain't Hyde. His mother was a Hyde. Hard to believe it when you met her; she wasn't like the rest of them. She was a real nice woman, rest her soul.

No, he wasn't a Hyde by name, but he had the Hyde temper. His name is Conrad Johnston."

I almost fell off the chair. I knew the name. I heard it more than once in the last three days. Now, I wondered why he was at the funeral home and the airport. But would he risk coming back here? The Barrette place has to be the connection, and I was determined to find out how.

"What you thinking about, young fella? You seem to be out to sea or something."

"That name, I've heard it before. Seems he was seen not too long ago by a friend of mine."

"I ain't surprised none, not after the way Hyde's been acting."

It was 4:00 p.m. Time really went by listening to the history lesson from Charlie.

The old goat sure could tell a story. I wondered how much was truth and how much was fairy-tale.

"Charlie, thanks for the information, and would you give me a call when Hyde shows up? I'd like to talk to him also."

"Ain't no need, lad. He'll only get it all twisted 'round, but if you like I'll give you a call. Be sure to come back now, ya hear?"

After spending all day with him, I had this uncontrollable urge to sing "sixteen men on a dead man's chest, yo ho ho and a bottle of rum" and maybe even stagger a bit like the sailors do. I got to the car after all the goodbyes and headed back.

I arrived back at the motel about five. Sam must have been looking for me because the moment the door on the car opened, she was at my side.

"Well, what kind of day did you have?" she asked.

"Very interesting if you're into history."

"What?" she said as her brow wrinkled in a quizzical fashion. I didn't answer, only started to my room with Sam following.

"Are you going to tell me what you found out or am I to guess?" she asked.

"Right now, all I want is a hot shower and a nice cold drink, and we can talk over dinner. How does that sound?"

She put both hands on her hips, eyes opened wide, and her mouth slightly opened as if she wanted to say something, only it wouldn't come out. She was still standing there when I closed the door to my room.

CHAPTER 20

The water ran down my face as the shower thundered in my ears. The warmth of the steam rising from the water embraced my body, giving me a feeling of magic fingers massaging away the cares of the day. I started to stretch in rhythm with the water as it rolled down my body. Pain quickly took control of the moment. My arms dropped, embracing my side to subdue the feeling of my ribs coming through my side. The doctor said it would take a good six weeks to mend, but I felt good all day. It must have been the wonder drugs. I would have one or two as soon as I got out of the shower.

Standing there letting the water run cold, I thought about everything Charlie had said, then all of a sudden the lights went on in my head. I guess someone was home up there but left the lights out. It was something Charlie had said that finally got through.

He said that Johnston was involved with two women that committed suicide. That in itself didn't mean a whole lot, but then I remembered what Lilly had told me about two women that had done the same thing, not to mention Sam's two friends that lived in the area. It had to be more than coincidence.

I got out of the shower and made a quick call.

"Balmorial, Bob speaking. How may I help you?"

"Charlie Hands, please."

"I'll connect you."

"Your nickel, mate," came the voice from the briny.

"Charlie, it's Falco, and I think its thirty-five cents now. I need a little more information. Something you told me may be of help, but I need to know the names of the two girls that died at the plantation if you remember."

"What! Do you think I'm senile or something?"

"I didn't mean that, Charlie. Just a figure of speech."

"Let me see if I can remember back to yesterday."

"Charlie, give me a break here, okay?"

"Yeah, I know them like the back of my hand. Fine girls, they were. Good families.

It was a rotten shame what happened." There was a pause. I wondered if he fell asleep.

"Yes, they were Katherine Kaye Kantrel, always a kidder, her being the only real KKK person I knew, and Betty Jean Brewster, a sweet kid, use to sit for hours and listen to me talk. Yeah, they were two very fine young ladies. It sure was a shame." His voice remorseful.

"I appreciate the help, Charlie. Take care."

I had to make one more call. The phone rang maybe eight, nine times. I was just about to hang up when a voice sounded on the other end.

"Hello."

"Lilly, Falco here."

"Vince, where are you? Find out anything?"

"I'm in North Carolina. I need some information."

"Sure, Vince. What can I do to help?"

"You told me you had some friends here. I need to know where they live and the names of the two girls you said committed suicide."

"I don't remember their names . . . wait, I think one of them was a Betty Joe, Betty Sue, or something like that. I don't really remember. My friends lived between Edenton and Valhalla. Closer to Valhalla. They moved to Florida since then."

"Wouldn't Odin keep them?"

"Who?"

"Forget it. Thanks for the help, Lilly." I hung up before he started. He could talk forever if you let him. Maybe he should get with Charlie, and they could go on for hours.

Things were beginning to fit. Conrad Johnston definitely had a place in this affair.

The question was, where?

Sam knew the two women and this Conrad. Maybe she could shed some light on this relationship and why they would have killed themselves. I figured I'd approach it at dinner.

I just finished wrapping my ribs when the phone rang. "Falco here."

"Are you going to join us for dinner?" Sam asked.

I looked at my watch; it was 6:00 p.m. Time has a way of flying. "I'm on my way."

My room was on the second floor, giving me a great view as I stepped out onto the veranda. The doc was standing beside the car, arms crossed, looking into the sky.

Sam was leaning against the hood, with her arms behind her and hands resting on the hood. Her one leg extended stiff and the other bent with her foot resting on the bumper, and her dress clung to her body as the wind blew her hair gently across her face. It was a seductive picture, making dinner the last thing on my mind.

The doctor turned. "Ah, Vince, you have decided to join us. How nice." His voice displayed his acrid side.

Ignoring the doctor's remark, I asked, "Where do you want to go?"

"There is a nice 'atmospherey' place just the other side of town. The doctor and I went there for lunch."

"Oh 'atmospherey.' By all means, we have to go there," I responded in an uplifted tone.

Sam looked at me and smiled. The doc just grunted something in his own language and got in the car.

On the way to the restaurant, the doctor started the conversation. "I like this area.

It's full of historical culture. Even the younger people seem to have pride in the events that have made it what it is. What do you think, Mr. Falco?"

"Well, Doc . . ." He grimaced, obviously disliking to be called "Doc." "I haven't had much time for sightseeing, but I'll take your word on it."

"I always found it to be quite beautiful around here. You have four seasons, none of them in extreme, and the people are so warm and friendly accepting you for what you are. I could easily live here, but I don't know what I could do for work. Although Norfolk isn't that far to travel if one wants the serenity of the country." Sam's voice trailed in sighs.

"Turn here, Vince." Sam directed me into the parking lot of the restaurant. As we walked inside, I had to agree with Sam: it was nice, it had atmosphere, and it smelled of old wood. That must have been the "atmospherey" part Sam spoke of.

We were seated by the fireplace in the middle of the room. Not my favorite place to be, but the two with me seemed to like it.

"This place reminds me of a place in Austria, not that it has American revolutionary artifacts on the walls as there is here, but it has a similar decor with a cozy fireplace in the center of the room and the old world woodwork that highlights the craftsmanship of the era," the doctor said in a respectful tone.

Sam spoke up, "It has romance, intrigue, and adventure reaching out to touch you, and yet it gives off a warm and friendly feeling. Don't you think so, Vince?"

I just listened to them going on about all the feelings this old world atmosphere gave them. Me, well, all I saw was old wood, rusted swords, flintlock relics, and farm tools that made my back ache just looking at them. I couldn't say that to Sam, so I went on with the poetry. "Yes, it sets my heart fluttering as my mind wanders through the past. I can see the smoke rise as the fire flashes, launching the cannon balls to their destiny and hearing the screams of men as they do their dastardly deed. Yet through the smoke and screams rise the spirit of freedom, as men and boys rush to fight the British, some falling to meet their maker as others march forward to battle, perhaps to die, but certainly to claim this land as their own."

My speech ended. I looked to Sam and the doc, both just staring at me as if I knew what I was saying.

"God, that was beautiful. You should write it down. I'm sure the owner would have it hung for all to read," Sam said in sincerity.

I just looked at her like she was tripping and let it go. Just then, I had a reprieve.

"Can I help y'all?" came a voice out of nowhere.

I looked over to the doc on the way to the voice. He had an expression on his face that you find in grade school when watching the girls in the locker room. The one where excitement glares from your eyes and your body tenses with desire. This person arriving at our table was able to remove his somber look and make him human with just a few short words. I looked up to the good witch of the south that had produced this transformation of would-be prince from the frog that he was. It was easy to see why.

She was in her early to midforties, auburn hair, green eyes, had a soft come-hither look, and skin tone that glowed in the light of the fire. She was wearing a smile that held you to her face.

I looked over to Sam; she was smiling and showed approval of the would-be match as she nodded her head and raised an eyebrow at the doctor.

"Yes, we would like some drinks to get started." I could that see my eagerness to get things going had changed the mood, causing the starry-eyed doctor to return to his bland-looking self.

She was looking at the doc the whole time I was talking and had a twinkle in her eye. Maybe she has a thing for the Freudian type.

As we waited for dinner to arrive, Sam started the conversation, bringing us back to why we were here.

"Wilhelm and I went to the county courthouse and met Betty Lou. She remembered you very well." Sam's expression matched her slow musical tone, hesitating to give me a chance to put my foot in my mouth, but I wasn't going to do it. I just sat and waited. Sam finally continued, "She apologized for not having the information she had promised. She said the printer was slow in getting it out. She gave us a copy of the proof and asked us not to show it around. There's about a hundred pages. It's a fascinating read, but doesn't really say much to help us.

"After we left the courthouse, we went on some tours. It was very interesting. This place is alive with history. Did you know that the first

Capitol during the revolutionary war was here. Not to mention that Blackbeard and other famous pirates walked these streets and that they even buried treasure in this region. Most of it still is unfound."

"I agree with Samantha. It is a stimulating experience talking to these people. It is history that builds the character of a town and its people. I'm sure Samantha agrees that when the people we talked to gave us information on events that have taken place here or in the immediate area, it was told with pride and reverence," said the doctor.

Sam looked at him thoughtfully and shook her head in agreement. Then took it farther.

"The history just keeps going on and on. Chowan County, some say, was named after a tribe of Indians who lived here around the mid-1600s. They were known as the Chowanokes, and Edenton was believed to be the first settlement in North Carolina. Some call it the 'mother town' of the state. It was the capital of the colony, and in 1715, it was named 'the Towne on Queen Anne's Creek.' It had a run of names, but in 1722, it was named Edenton and then became the county seat for Chowan County.

"Edenton was named to honor the first governor, Charles Eden, who died in 1722 and is buried in the St. Paul Episcopal churchyard. There seems to be a history to the burial as well. He was initially buried near the Salmon River, but in 1889 due to erosion on the banks of the Salmon River, he was moved to St. Paul Cemetery here inEdenton.

"Edenton residents, from what we learned, were what could be called 'rebels' in their time. It seems they didn't all agree with the Crown. In fact, Governor Eden was accused of excusing pirates' behaviors and was said to be especially easy on Edward Teach, 'Blackbeard,' and may have enjoyed some of his bounty.

"In 1786, the first US Post Office in North Carolina was here.

"There is so much history here that I never it knew when I was here with Shannon." Her voice trailed, thinking of her lost friend,

"All right with the history lesson. I'm more interested in having dinner, So what say we eat?" I said, thinking how much they found out in just one afternoon. Too bad they didn't find the alleged treasure.

The expression on the doctor's face told me that dinner was about to be served.

This woman sure had an effect on him. He acted like he just went into puberty.

Sam looked to me and asked, "What did you find out?"

As the waitress set the plates in front of us, I gave the condensed version of the story from Charlie. Sam sat attentively with the doc coming in and out of the story as the waitress moved about the room. She had a hold on him, and he didn't even ask her name.

At the conclusion of the report, Sam looked at me with her head half-cocked and said, "That's fascinating. I would like to meet this Charlie and I'll bet he has a hundred stories to tell. Just think, personal ties with pirates, buried treasure, and highwaymen, it's so intriguingly romantic. I would certainly like to see that plantation. Who knows what we could find."

The doctor didn't say much, having spent most of the time watching every move the waitress made, but finally interjected, "It is curious, even for that time, that a doctor would give up his practice so readily for one individual. I would have to think that he had an ulterior motive. Yes, there must have been something there that he wanted. Four years is a long time to limit a practice to one person or family."

I caught myself shaking my head and rolling my eyes in agreement with the doc.

This reaction must be contagious. The doc sure had a way to make you think. Things were beginning to churn in my head. I needed a few more pieces of the puzzle to make it work, but I had a good idea of who may have caused this mayhem. The question is, where do I get the pieces?

I didn't mention the double suicide or the connection of Conrad Johnston with it, but knew I was going to have to. I looked at Sam for a moment, not saying anything, but the look on my face told her I had something to say because she put on the California Valley girl look and said, "What?"

"Betty Jean Brewster and Katherine Kaye Kantrel, what can you tell me about them?"

"Not much. They were really friends of Shannan. I knew them through her. They were her roommates at college. I went with Shannan to Katherine's home a couple of times, but we never really talked much, mostly about school, and there were the occasions when I went to the meetings with them since I was IN RA TU."

Sam had a quizzical look on her face as she was answering me as did the doctor, with one eyebrow a little higher than the other.

"Forgive me, but I do not know what IN RA TU means, so I cannot see the connection between you and these women," asked the doctor.

Sam controlled herself from laughing, knowing that the doctor was sincere in his question. She looked at me to answer him while she composed herself.

"IN RA TU was the alleged high priestess of the temple of Isis a few lifetimes ago. Sam thinks she was IN RA TU." My voice showed signs of amusement as I answered the query.

Suddenly, I let out a breath and groaned as Sam, not caring that my ribs were still unprepared, let her elbow slam into my side looking at me with a devilish smile in her eyes.

"I was only joking, take it easy." I held my side looking for sympathy, but none came.

"I didn't know you believed in reincarnation, Samantha. I find the subject rather fascinating. We do have to take time and discuss this IN RA TU," said the doctor.

Sam was still glaring at me when she continued.

"As I said, we only met a few times. I didn't have much time on my hands, with me going to school full-time and working. Anyway, what does this have to do with anything?"

"Did the girls live near here?" Sam still looked at me with that wondering look as I avoided answering her question.

"Katherine lived near Valhalla. I don't know where Betty Jean lived, but it had to be close to Katherine's place because they talked about how they were inseparable as children," she answered with questions in her eyes.

I continued with Charlie's story as a way to answer Sam's question. "It seems that this Conrad Johnston is the grandson of Mr. Jonah Hyde and he mysteriously disappeared a few years ago after a bizarre double suicide. The two involved in the suicide were Betty Jean and Katherine."

Sam froze, tears welling in her eyes. She gestured to say something, but the words didn't come out. The doc handed her a napkin to wipe the tears as he put a comforting arm on her shoulder.

After a few moments, she spoke, "I didn't know them all that well, but to think of them as dead, it's just awful."

The waitress, seeing there was a problem, came over to the table. "Can I help, honey?" she said as she put an arm around Sam.

Sam looked up, her eyes thanking her for the offer. "Yes, would you please get me a double brandy?"

"Sure, honey, I'll get it," she said, looking at the doc asking, "What was the matter?"

"She just found out that two women she knew had died," he said quietly as he lost himself in her hypnotic gaze.

We all sat quietly waiting for the waitress to return. When she arrived, she put a hand on Sam's shoulder and said, "Just take it slow, honey. Things have a way of get'n better."

We sat for a little while longer. Sam seemed to have pulled herself together, and the doc, well, the doc was in love. He hadn't taken his eyes off the waitress since she made her presence known.

I started to pick up the check when all of a sudden it was scooped up by the doc.

"I'll take care of this, Mr. Falco, while you and Samantha get the car. That is, if you don't mind?"

"No, not at all. Please be my guest." I smiled and winked at Sam as I helped her up.

We waited about ten minutes for the doc to pay the bill. I guess they didn't want his money and he was forcing it on them, or maybe he got lucky and was visiting the back room with the belle.

Sam was up close and starting to get personal when he finally came floating out of the place. After quick adjustments, which weren't noticed by the doc, we drove away.

Sam was staring out the window, the doc was lost in his own world, and me, well,I was just there.

"Vince, where is the Barrette plantation?" Sam asked.

It was a clear night and I was curious about the place anyway, so I suggested we drive there and have a look around.

"I would like to see it. Wilhelm, is it okay with you?" Sam asked.

There wasn't any response. Sam turned to see if he really got in the car.

"Wilhelm!"

She was a little louder this time, and it brought him back to reality.

"Oh my, I'm sorry, I wasn't paying any attention. Just . . . just thinking. What can I do for you, my dear?"

"We were going to go to the plantation and wondered if you would like to come along or be dropped off at the motel."

"I would love to see the place. It seems to be important to this case. Perhaps we may find something of interest there," he replied.

It was an eerie setting in the moonlight, with the house sitting high on a hill and the moon near full and bright hanging over the mansion. As we drove up the winding road, I couldn't help thinking that I've seen this picture before, probably on some paperback novel with a gothic setting in the background and some fair damsel running down the hill for whatever reason.

Sam let out a shutter, "This doesn't look like a nice place. I feel cold and depressed just looking at it. Maybe this wasn't such a good idea. Let's go and come back in daylight. Maybe it'll look better then."

"What do you think, Doc?" I asked just to be polite as I started to turn around.

"Did you see that?" he blurted out, nearly causing Sam to have an accident in her seat.

"See what?" I asked.

"There was a light flashing through one of those windows."

I turned the car around again and stopped as we faced the house. We waited a good ten minutes, but nothing happened. I looked over to Sam and then back to the doc. "Do you want to go up to the house and look around? Maybe there's something there."

"No, it must have been a reflection when you were turning around. Perhaps it would be better if we come back in the daylight. We will be able to see a lot more then.

Is it all right with you, Samantha?" he asked.

"Yes, that's fine with me. Tomorrow, in the daylight, early, so we can be out of here before dark. That will be fine with me," she said hurriedly.

"Okay, Sam, I got the idea, you can stop. We're going back," I said.

"I'm sorry, Vince. I don't know what came over me. I just don't feel good about this place, this evening anyway."

She had a shy little smile on her face highlighted by a glimmer of blush in her cheeks visible from the light of the moon.

It was 11:00 p.m. when we returned to the motel. We bid our goodnights at the car and went our separate ways. I had hoped Sam would have liked a little company, but didn't think I should say anything in front of the doc. Sam didn't give any indication that company was wanted anyway.

CHAPTER 21

I woke up at 5 AM and just tossed and turned. Finally, I gave in to the fact that I wasn't going back to sleep, so I got dressed and headed to the cafe for coffee and a place to think.

I ordered a coffee and just looked out the window not really seeing anything as I started going over the events that had me here. I knew that Shannan thought she was this Barrette person and Sam was the lost Egyptian priestess. Hell, maybe I was King Tut, who knows. But how did Betty Jean and Katherine Kaye fit into the picture?

Suicide or murder by three girls that were close at one time, and several hundred miles apart at the end. This Conrad definitely was a connection, but how? Yeah, I was full of questions and no answers. I needed to find out more about these two girls. It could push me in the right direction or drop me for a loop, but I had to find out.

I called Sam's room and a sleepy voice answered, "Yes."

"Good morning, bright eyes, this is your wake-up call. Is there something madame wants?" I said playfully.

"Yes, madame wants to sleep. Falco, it's 6 AM. What do you want?"

"Let's get some breakfast, talk a little, and get an early start. I'm in the café. I'll have coffee ready for you. See you in fifteen minutes, all right?" I hung up before she could say no.

As she stumbled to the table, she looked at me and flopped down. She put both hands around her cup as I poured coffee into it from the pot on the table. Slowly, she raised her eyes to mine as she sipped from the cup, then slowly locked her gaze on me and said, "It's almost six thirty, so what's so important that I had to get up this early?

Nothing is open, no one is going to want to talk to us this early, and I'm tired." She lay her head down on the table in a fray attempt for sympathy, hoping I would tell her to go back to bed.

"It won't work. I need you," I said without sympathy.

"Not now, I have a headache." She looked up smiling. "So why didn't you call the doctor and let me sleep?"

"I didn't want to bother him. I thought you could do it and take him with you." I hesitated, waiting for her reaction. She just looked at me waiting for more, so I continued, "I figure you and the doc could talk to the families of Betty Jean and Katherine since you knew them, and I would visit the local authorities and see what they remember. After that, I'm going back to the Barrette place."

"Okay, but I'm going to take a warm bath to get this body going before I call Wilhelm."

CHAPTER 22

We finished our coffees and went on our separate ways. It wasn't far to the police station, but then it wasn't far to anything in this town, that is, until you get to the outskirts, then it feels like forever to anywhere.

I was greeted by a burly sergeant walking past the door with a coffee in one hand and the proverbial donut in the other. "Morning. You must be new in town, haven't seen you before. Can I help you?"

"I'm Falco."

He interrupted, "You definitely aren't from around here."

"You don't sound like a nativc cither," I said in response.

He grinned. "You're right, I'm from New York. Came here a few years ago on assignment and stayed. Life is sure easier here than up north. Not many people shooting at you around here. I actually stand a chance of retiring in one piece. So what can I do for you, Falco? You look like a cop, you got cop eyes."

"I used to be. I'm private now. I'm working on a homicide and everything leads back to here. I'm hoping you can shed some light on the matter and I can settle it."

"Who you working for, private or you hooked up with the police?" He watched my face as he asked to see if there was any sign to dispute my claim.

"Private, but I do have connections on the force working the same case. You can call Detective Lieutenant Mike Cavenaugh. He'll vouch for me."

"Maybe I will, but first let's hear what you want." His manner was pleasant. I felt we hit it off okay.

I explained the events leading to my being here, leaving out certain details. He must have liked what I had to say because he started talking almost before I stopped.

"It was my first case here. I had the most experience with homicide and vice. For openers, it was thought to be a cult thing, but lacked any real evidence of that.

Secondly, these girls had plans of going to Atlanta and opening a small advertisement business, made inquiries for business loans, property, the whole nine yards. And the clincher, we couldn't find the object that made the cuts."

"Then it was murder . . ."

He stopped me as he took a drink of his coffee. "Now, I didn't say that." He stopped and looked around the room. Some officers were coming in the room. He got up, held up his finger in a gesture meaning "just a minute," and walked into an adjoining office. He was back in a flash.

"Let's take a ride, Falco. You may find it interesting." He directed me out the door while looking around the room as if he was doing something wrong.

In the car, he took the last bite of his donut, gulped the last of the coffee, and turned to me. "I told the chief that you were an old friend from my precinct and I was going to show you around town. We're pretty loose here. Nothing much ever happens.

O'Leary's cat gets in the face of the neighbor's dog, Foreman boys stir things up a little when they come into town, and once in a while, someone tries shoplifting just to keep us on our toes. Now, don't go thinking we don't get our share of action around here. We do get an occasional homicide, three since those girls."

"It sounds too exciting for me," I said jokingly.

"I had twelve years in Brooklyn and saw things that would make an M.E. puke.

When I was sent here to follow up on a tip that would blow open a case I was working on, I made a few friends here. Oh, I went back to New York, resigned, and took the job here. That brings me to your problem."

He paused, so I took advantage and asked him some questions. "You said it wasn't suicide, but everyone I've talked to still say it was. Didn't anyone here pursue it?

Didn't you tell them what you thought?"

"Whoa, hold on, you're gettin' the cart before the horse. I was enthusiastic when I first started here and given this assignment because of my background only made me want to solve it quickly. I brought up the facts that there was no instrument found at or around the scene that could have made the wounds, and the wounds looked more like surgical incisions than slashes. The chief, he's retired now, brought up the fact that there wasn't any motive either.

"I was determined to prove that it was homicide. I called for the medical examiner, the only one being fifty miles away, and to make things worse, he was on vacation.

Well, they sent his assistant. He was new to the position and quite inexperienced, but sure thought he knew it all. He looked at the surface: wrist slit, blood lying in a central area indicating that the victims hadn't been moved. Hell, he just made a judgment call on the spot, signed the papers, and took off."

"How could you just let it go like that?"

"Hold on just a minute. You may think this is Mayberry, but I'm not Barney Fife.

Let me put it this way. Like I said, we're a little loose here on procedure and we don't readily air our dirty laundry for the world to see. After all, these girls were part of an alleged cult because of their belief in the mysticism of the afterlife. Even one of the girls' father, who is a Baptist minister, condemned his daughter being a member of this group. Anyway, I didn't just blow it off as a suicide. I continued questioning the group, and during the interviewing process, I got a call from James Robertson. He was apprenticing as an undertaker so he could take over the family business, Robertson Funeral Home. He said he had to see me right away.

"When I got there, he was waiting in the front parlor just pacing up and down.

When I walked in, he didn't say a word, just grabbed me and headed to the basement. I still remember his words to this day as we walked. Hell, as we ran down those stairs.

He started talking the minute we hit the first step. He kept repeating himself all the way down the stairs.

"He said, 'Bill you ain't gonna believe this, you ain't gonna believe this, believe me, you ain't gonna believe this. Boy, did that coroner mess up this time. I'm no medical examiner, but I did go to medical school for a while, and boy did he mess up.'

"He just kept on going, then at the bottom of the stairs you could see the two girls lying on the tables. He directed me to Betty Jean first, then we went over to Katherine.

On both girls, there was a bruise just inside the hairline at the base of the skull, and a few inches away was a definite puncture wound about the size of a fine needle. There was a faint scab on the wounds indicating that the girls were still alive when they were cut. As you know, there wouldn't have been a bruise if they were already dead when they were hit in the back of the head.

"I figured they were knocked unconscious, then slipped the hypo to make sure they would stay out, then the sick son of a bitch slit their wrists.

"I called the chief, had pictures taken, and about to call the M.E. to get back and do it right, when the chief stepped in and said there wasn't need to make the families go through any more hardship than they already were. He said we could just put it down as a possible homicide and continue the investigation on the QT, and let the girls rest in peace.

"You went along with him?"

"I didn't know what to do. My instincts told me to push it to the hilt, but then looking at the community, I figured it was their way of handling things. So, yes, I guess you can say I went along with him but I didn't drop the investigation, only the fact about pushing for an autopsy.

"I talked with everyone and anyone hoping to find a motive or anything remotely involved with these two girls, but there wasn't anything except that damn cult thing.

"It's recorded as a probable homicide. The file is still open. We, the police, don't talk about it. If the people knew we suspect murder, they would be clambering at the door, so the chief just kept the investigation to a couple of officers. I'm the only one left."

"What happened to this chief? Is he still around?"

"Not long after this all happened, he retired. Came down with some kind of thyroid problem, really put on some weight. He had twenty years in when he left these parts and no one has heard from him since. His checks are deposited electronically."

"Where did you find the girls?" I asked.

"There was a call from Bob Hansen. He was out at the Barrette place surveying for the Historical Society when he heard a scream up at the house. It seems that one of the local ladies keeps up the Barrette graveyard and was walking through the house when she found them.

"As I got more into the investigation, it made sense, in a sick sort of way, that they would meet their end at the Barrette house. You see, these girls believed they were ladies of the manor in their past lives. I don't remember who was who, but one claimed to be Penelope Barker-Barrette and the other was Mary Elizabeth Hardie-Barrette. They were from the 1700s or something like that.

"They were both reported as being last seen with Conrad Johnston. He was never found. There is a warrant out on him. His grandfather still lives around here and every once in a while, I'll go over and talk with him just to see if he heard from Conrad."

"So, has he?" I asked.

"He keeps saying no, but my gut feeling is that he's lying. With his age and all, it wouldn't do much good to pressure him. He might die. Not that it would bother the townsfolk; he isn't particularly liked as much as tolerated. He's a real cantankerous old coot. One thing's for certain, if you want a history lesson of this burgh, he could tell the story from the time of Adam and Eve. I think he knew them personally," he said smiling.

I knew the country side we were driving in. Up ahead just around the curve was the Barrette place. I was planning on coming here, so this may save me a trip. But I had to ask anyway. "What are we doing here, Bill?"

"I thought you'd like to see the place. They say that the original Barrette buried treasure here. Stories say he was the son of Blackbeard. There's a lot of pirate history around these parts, and almost everyone you meet claims ancestry to one or the other of these pirates we read about in history.

"Most of the place is stripped from treasure hunters. Once there was even a group out here with sounding equipment. They went through every room reading the walls, floors, and ceilings. Seemed they found some hidden passages, but that was all. Most of the grounds have been dug up, but still no sign of treasure. I think it's just another folklore to keep tourists coming."

We drove up the drive and stopped in front of the house.

"Come on, Falco, I'll show you where they were found."

Bill led the way. At the top of the stairs, there was a hole in the porch. Bill almost missed stepping over it as he kept looking back to see if I was following like a good little puppy.

On entering, you could smell the mildew, urine, and other foul odors. It reminded me of some condemned buildings I had to go in back home. As you stepped past the vestibule, the smell diminished. The broken windows served a purpose, giving the place flow through ventilation.

The house was mammoth. There were three floors, plus an attic, and I got the grand tour. We entered into a long hall with doors or remnants of doors on either side.

The staircase was set to the right heading to the second floor. It was a grand stairway in its day. There were rosettes carved the length of the stairway on the stair brackets, and as the stairway ended at the second floor gallery, there were remnants of spool-turned balusters supporting the railings. The stairway was replicated on the second floor going to the third, with rooms being on either side of both floors. The only indication of the attic from where we stood was the hole in the ceiling.

I must have looked like a New York tourist to Bill, head turned up, looking at the sights. When I turned, he was standing there, hands on his hips looking all around like me.

"You can see the craftsmanship that went into these old houses. It isn't like the assembly-line woodwork of today. My father was a cabinetmaker and he did this kind of work. Real quality." There was reverence in his voice as he talked. "People still want this kind of workmanship, but you have to pay through the nose for it, and then you have to watch them to make sure they don't take shortcuts. Hell, some of the homes around here that have been restored cost what I make a year for the next twenty years, and that's just the restoration price, not the price of the home. Most of the pieces put into the restoration are made on machines, lacking that handmade quality, but then most of the so-called craftsmen don't have the patience to labor by hand to achieve the original look, so they sacrifice and accept a copy, that's progress for you."

He took me through door number one. It was an opening sized for double doors that led into a room that most homes I've been in would fit in. It had a hand-carved mantle overhanging the fireplace on the outside wall of the room, with traces of murals painted on the ceiling and along the walls and sections missing where the vultures tore the walls apart for hopes of finding their pieces of eight. For some reason, I thought of the Egyptian tombs and how they were spoiled by the robbers of their day. This could have been a grand ballroom, but instead it was now a ruin of a once grand house.

"Falco", I could hear a voice bringing me back to the living, "you coming or looking for termites?"

I walked over to the far end of the room thinking I should have packed a lunch for the trip across the room. When I arrived, Bill was pointing to the floor. "This is the spot where both girls were found. You can still see the bloodstains. They never cared about cleaning the place after the incident. It was supposed to be torn down.

"We searched the area as far back as we could, never found anything. Tire marks are always present, so we couldn't rely on them. I've gone over the place more times than I can count, still haven't found anything. I didn't always get my man, but this time it hurt because I know in my gut that Conrad did it, but I can't prove it.

"The warrant out for him is for questioning, so you know how much attention anyone is paying.

"I was out here last night, and it might not be anything, but for a moment I thought I saw a light coming from the house. I waited for a few minutes, but never saw it again.

Maybe we can look around a little."

"Sure, but with the kids always coming up here, it could have been anyone. The kids use this place for fun, you know, initiations, sex, or just to play, not forgetting the treasure hunters. We get calls all the time from the Historical Society reminding us that this is an historical site and that we are charged with preserving its integrity." His voice was almost laughing.

We walked throughout the house. Most of the rooms have similar features, trim, fireplaces, murals, and the like. The second floor gave me an eerie feeling like it wanted to open under the weight of my body. The floor creaked as I stepped from room to room, sometimes giving in slightly under my feet. This floor contained some bedrooms and what appeared to be a reading and writing room. From this room, there were doors that opened to the outside gallery overlooking what appeared to be a pond, but now it's just a sunken hole overgrown with weeds. But in its day, this view could have taken your breath away. In the distance, you could see the centuries-old sycamore, magnolia, pecan, and willow trees placed as though by hand just for the view.

The third floor creaked even more than the second. It was mostly bedrooms with what had to be the indoor toilet. It was a room that resembled an outhouse, having a seat with a hole in it that seemed to drop to an area under the house. It must have been a first. The attic was as big as the other two floors; however, it's now just one big open space. The roof was a good eight feet above the floor. There were broken chairs, tables, and other things scattered about. I was surprised that the antique hunters hadn't grabbed these things and sold them.

You could see through the roof in a few places. The watermarks doted the floor and walls. On all sides, there were windows, some still containing the original glass.

Looking out the window, the graveyard was visible. Somewhat reverent in its day, but now it's overgrown and unkempt except for what appeared to a small area. I got Bill's attention, and we started down to the graveyard.

When we reached the graveyard, we heard a car in the distance kicking up rocks and speeding away. I took a close look at the graves that had been attended to. At my last visit, the area was overgrown completely. Now, this spot was manicured and most of the headstones where straightened. The area that was now cleared was the grave of Elizabeth Anne Barrette and the cross monument to the rear and right of her grave. All the names were here that I have heard in the last two days: Elizabeth, Penelope, Mary Elizabeth, Edward Thatch, Edward Hardie Barrette, l and ll, all the names of the family. I felt like I knew them after listening to Charlie.

"Falco, we've got to go. I got a call."

We left, but I had a feeling that we were being watched the whole time we were on the plantation. More questions: who could it be and why? I should write a book of questions. Maybe the readers could send in the answers.

CHAPTER 23

It was still early, a little after 1:00 p.m., when we got back to the police station. I wanted to have a look around the Barrette place without having to answer to anyone, soI headed back.

As I drove up to the house, I could see a car in front of it and two people walking around on the porch. As I got closer, I could make out the doctor and Sam.

I pulled alongside the car. Sam came over to greet me. "Where have you been, big boy?" she said in her best May West impression. "You wanna come up and see me?"

I just smiled as I got out of the car. "How long have you been here? I just left not more than twenty minutes ago with the local gendarme."

"We just pulled up. I thought maybe you would be here. You know, it doesn't seem so bad in the daylight. Actually, it's quite charming.

"We didn't find much more than you already know about the girls. Betty Jean's father still mourns her death and insists it was his fault for being so strict with her. Her mother just shakes her head as he goes on. They have two other daughters and a son.

He's also a minister. The daughters are married and live in Raleigh.

"Mrs. Brewster can't understand why Betty Jean committed suicide. She had so much going for her. Betty Jean and Katherine were going to start their own advertising agency. Everything was ready: building, stationary, the works. They were all set to leave for Atlanta and start their new career when they came up missing.

"The Kantrels have accepted it and blamed Conrad for their daughter's death.

Mrs. Kantrel couldn't understand how Katherine believed she was Penelope Barker-Barrette. She said she used to tease Katherine about how nice it would be if she could remember where the treasure was. There wasn't much after that, just girl talk."

We both looked up on the porch and watched the doc look into each window and door. He was a curious individual. He stopped at the window that still had some glass in it, leaned forward, then suddenly whirled around. "There was someone here last night! This is where I saw the lights last night."

Sam and I walked over to him and looked inside. "Doctor Watson, what makes you so certain this is the spot and that someone was here last night? After all, people come here all the time. So I'm told," I said in my best British accent.

"Reinhardt, not Watson." Then he got it. "Oh, of course, Sherlock Holmes and all.

Yes, I see". He gave a little chuckle at the humor and continued, "Here, look at the boards. See how the edges have fresh marks. Look how the dirt is disturbed near the far end of the boards." He pointed to the perimeter of a section of the floor.

We climbed in the window and walked over to the spot, trying not to disturb anything on the way. I slipped the blade of my pocketknife into the separation between the boards near the area that looked as if it was intentionally covered with dirt, dust, and debris. The board started to lift up, and with it came more. It was a trap door. Inside was a narrow stairway leading down to what appeared to be a room. I looked up at Sam and the doctor, and both of them had the same surprised yet quizzical look on their faces.

"Well, do we stand here and gawk or do we explore? I say we get down there and have a look-see."

As we started down the stairs, the doc said, "I think we may need a light. It appears to be getting darker."

"Don't worry, Doc, I've got a small flashlight." No sooner had I said that that another light joined mine. I turned to find Sam holding the cousin of mine in her hand.

"Mine's bigger than yours," Sam said with that devilish smile of hers.

The ceiling was about six feet from the floor. The room was close to ten foot square, give or take a couple of inches. There was a table with two chairs to match; they were twentieth-century landfill salvage, or to please the environmentalists, recycled discards. Sitting on the table was a lamp; it was one of those neon camping types and not very old.

The doc seized the lamp and turned it on. At the other end of the room was a passageway leading away from the house. It was three feet wide, but not more than five and a half feet high. We all had to bend to get through. It brought back some memories of the past when searches in tunnels in foreign lands were a necessity. It wasn't the happiest of times, I thought.

We walked a short distance in this cramped passage before it opened up. The structure had changed to a more defined passage. It opened up to about five feet with a ceiling height of about seven feet. There was a pungent odor that reminded me of some place else I had been, but I couldn't remember what it was but I knew where it was.

We were not far into this section of the passage when Sam let out a scream that could have waked the dead. We were lucky that it didn't because on either side of us were the mortal remains of two unknown souls. They were laid in ledges that had been cut into the walls. Again, I flashed back to the days when such things were common to me. Some people used to bury their dead in tunnel walls back when. Sam grabbed my arm with one hand and covered her mouth with the other. The doctor approached the remains and did a quick examination on the exposed skulls, careful not to disturb their rest.

"I think, by the structure of the frontal area, that these are the remains of the Negro species. I would venture to guess that they were the servants."

"You mean slaves, don't you, doctor?" Sam asked.

"Considering the times, I would say you were right, Samantha. But they must have been treated fairly well to be allowed burial rights this close to the main house. Wouldn't you think? This is reminiscent of the catacombs in Rome and some other areas of the world," the doctor related.

We walked further along the passageway with more remains showing on all sides.

Soon, the ceiling started sloping down or we were going up. We hunched over and continued to follow the path. Sam started singing, "we're off to see the wizard," then she stopped abruptly and stared straight ahead.

"My god, it's a coffin."

Directly in front of us, jutting out of the wall was a wooden coffin with the end torn open. It was empty and didn't look as though it had ever been used.

The passage made a sharp turn in both directions. The passage to the left ended after a few feet. Its appearance indicated a cave-in, but how long ago? The grounds didn't show any signs of it when I had walked around. I didn't dwell on it. I figured I could look a little closer when we got out.

We turned and headed in the other direction. Up ahead, we could make out another stairway leading up about three steps. Sam was still hanging onto my arm, nearly stopping the circulation, as the doctor followed nonchalantly as if on a tour. Soon, we came to a room that had slabs in it, like the ones found in crypts, but I didn't remember seeing a crypt in the graveyard.

As the doc shined the lantern around the room, we could see oil lamps hanging on the walls. I lit one on each wall. The mirrored reflectors behind the globe on the lamps highlighted the illumination. The room definitely had the look of a crypt. The slabs attached to the walls were unmarked. The floor was tiled with two-foot squares of black marble trimmed with a silver inlay sitting on what appeared to be concrete. At the corners, etched in the marble, was the Jolly Roger. In the center of the floor was a coat of arms with four distinct etching, one in each section. One at the twelve o'clock, three o'clock, six o'clock, and nine o'clock position. The etchings left no doubt that the Barrettes were descendants of pirates. At the top was a frigate with full sails. To the left, pointing in, was a cannon with a pyramid of cannon balls of silver. On the right was an angel holding a sword, and on the bottom was a cutlass with indentations that could have held jewels of some type. Under the blade was inscribed the word "Teach".

The doc was feeling and pounding the walls, obviously looking for a way out.

"I can't find an exit, but there has to be one," he said.

Sam had a worried look on her face." I can't take closed spaces for long, and it has been too long already, so you better get us out soon."

"There has to be a way out of here. No one digs a tunnel to a dead end." I took one of the lanterns off of the wall and held it to the perimeter of the large stone slabs. At the third slab, the flame from the lamp was drawn toward the wall. I quickly extinguished the flame and watched as the smoke was drawn behind the block. This stone was etched with the same two angels found in the graveyard by the big cross.

I took hold of the edge of the slab and tried pulling it out, but it didn't move. The doc came over and took hold with me. As we strained, we could feel some movement.

We pulled harder and nearly fell as the stone gave way and swung toward us. As it opened, rats came running out and Sam didn't know which way to turn to avoid the rush. They weren't interested in us as they scurried out of the room.

On the other side of the opening was another stone stairway leading up. This passage wasn't like the others. It obviously hadn't been used for years as the cobwebs covered the opening and the steps had layers of dirt and debris on them. At the top of the stairs was a faint light.

"Where do you think this one goes?" Sam asked.

She didn't wait for an answer as she pushed past me and started the ascent.

"It goes up, and please don't let me stop you," I answered in a whimsical manner.

At the top of the stairs was another stone slab. There was a visible strand of light showing from the crack. Sam tried pushing it open, but to no avail. The doc and I tried also, but it didn't give way.

"Let's give it one more shot. If it doesn't open, then we head back the way we came."

As the doc and I started to push, Sam leaned against the wall to give us more room to push. All of a sudden she started falling back and the block we were pushing sprang outward, causing us to tumble out, nearly falling from the stone platform we had exited to.

As I looked back inside, I could see another block etched with that same angel pointing to the opening while holding a shield that was extruding from the tile.

"We're in a graveyard!" Sam said.

"Yes, isn't it amazing? From the grave to the graveyard, strange turn of events."

"You're not funny, Falco," Sam said.

"I thought it was. I'm going to close up the place like we found it if I can get the other stone to close." Back in the crypt, I took one last look around before putting out the lamps. I didn't see anything out of the ordinary for a crypt. As I stepped inside the passage, I looked to see if there was anything on the walls that would close the door.

Sure enough, there on either side of the opening was that angel. To the right was an indentation and on the left was an extrusion, just like the one at the top of the stairs. I pushed it and the door slowly started to close.

Outside, I found the handle to close the opening. It was a cross sitting to the side of the opening attached to a rod sticking out about six inches. I pushed it in and the stone slab sealed itself, not showing any signs of intrusion.

"I thought this looked like a mausoleum when I first saw it, but then I waived it off because of the external size. I never figured it to be an entrance to an underground burial chamber," I said.

"If you look at it carefully, it is very remarkable. From the surface, it appears that each of the deceased are buried beneath their headstones, when in actuality they are each in a separate vault. It would be quite deceiving for a grave robber. All that would be found would be an empty coffin like the one we encountered. I do find this ingenuous, don't you?" the doc said as he looked at me and then Sam for signs agreement.

"It certainly was exciting, don't you think?" Sam said enthusiastically.

The doc looked at Sam like she should make an appointment to visit his couch.

"If you're into gothic romance, you know, wearing black makeup, dressing funny, and making love on graves, then it may be exciting."

They both looked at me like I needed to be committed.

"The person who was here last night certainly went to some extreme to hide the passage. The dirt and debris was arranged carefully so as not to call attention to the opening. I wonder why. There wasn't anything down there I thought was of any importance. The remains showed no signs of disturbance, so why the tunnel?"

The doc asked more for himself than an answer from us, but I thought I'd give him a little more to dwell on. "You're right about nothing being disturbed. Did you notice that the exit, which is also the entrance, wasn't disturbed either? And don't forget the passage that was filled in; it looked like it was done a long time ago. If you look around out here, there isn't any evidence of where the cave-in occurred. Whoever dug that passageway obviously doesn't know about this entrance under the cross."

Sam walked around looking at the tombstones, stopping where the name matched those she had heard. She got to the cross as I was coming around from behind. She looked up at it. "It doesn't look as large from a distance, and even up close, I find it hard to believe that there is a vault under it."

"Vince, over here, look over here."

I turned to see what the doc was whispering about.

"Look over there, by the tree line, see the reflection of the light? Someone is watching us. Can you make it out?" he asked.

I caught a faint glimmer of a reflection, then it was gone. As I moved toward it, I could hear a car starting and then gravel being thrown as it raced away.

"Did you see that? Someone is definitely watching us," he said.

"Yeah, Doc, I saw it. I think we should keep alert from now on. Make sure we aren't being followed and be cautious about what we say to anyone. Also, make sure you check who's at the door before you open it." I was hoping my words of caution didn't fall on deaf ears as Sam looked over to me with a concerned look.

"I think we should leave. I've had enough fun for one day. I don't know if I can sleep without a light on tonight," Sam said softly.

Back at the house, we covered the hole pretty much as we found it. If we were watched long enough, then it's very possible that the entrance at the cross was spotted and this hole wouldn't be used again.

As we walked back to the cars, the doc looked like he wanted to say something but didn't know how.

"I . . . I was wondering if you two would mind riding together. I would like to go into town and, well . . . just look around for a while."

"That's fine, Wilhelm. I don't mind riding with Vince. You go and have fun, and we'll see you back at the motel." She looked over to me with her devilish grin and that twinkle in her eye. "Will we see you for dinner?"

"I'll get something while I'm in town, but thank you for asking," the doc replied.

CHAPTER 24

It was a long night as I tossed and turned thinking about the past day's events. I couldn't stay in bed any longer, so I got up, went to the window, and looked out the curtain to get a feel for the new day.

It was a picture setting of the sunrise in a red sky. I thought about what my grandmother always told me, "Red sky in the morning, sailor take warning." I wondered what this day was going to bring since the omens weren't on my side to begin with.

I looked over to the phone and saw the red light blinking. I called the desk to see what the message was.

"This is Falco. You have a message for me?"

"Mr. Falco, let me check . . . Yes, you have a package that arrived yesterday, and Mr. Reinhardt would like you to call him."

"Thanks." I looked at my watch as I hung up; it was 6:30 AM. I figured, what the hell, I might as well call the doc. After all, the clerk did say when I got up, and I was up.

The phone rang about eight times before I heard a groggy voice fumble for words.

"Hello, who is this?" the doc asked.

"Falco here. You wanted me to call when I was up?" I said cheerfully.

"Mr. Falco, do you know what time it is?" he asked more as a statement than a question.

"Why, yes, I do, and I thought it was strange that you would want me to call you so early, but after all any request from you is a request to fulfill," I said jokingly.

"We will talk at breakfast. Say about 10 AM?"

"Doc, let's make it 7:30. That gives you plenty of time to get up. I'll see you then," I hung up quickly so I didn't have to hear him mumble in his native tongue.

I was waiting at the table when Willie walked in. He had his usual pair on, an outdated three-piece suit, black pinstripe, with a white shirt and matching tie. He approached the table and drew looks from the locals.

"Have a seat, Doc. I have your coffee coming. By the way, are you going to a wedding or a funeral?"

"I beg your pardon?" he said quizzically.

"The suit, Doc, the suit."

He just looked at me and didn't answer.

"Now, what was so important that you left me a message?"

"I had dinner with Ms. Wesslow last night. Oh . . . Ms. Wesslow is the waitress we had met at the Broad Street Pub the other night. Jennifer Leslie Wesslow is her full name."

"Mr. Reinhardt, you sly devil you. You came all this way just to pick up a honey," I remarked with a smile and a wink.

Willie raised one eyebrow and just looked at me. He didn't say anything; his face said it all. He had that expression seen on one of those alien heroes with pointed ears that dare go where no man has gone before. After all, he was an alien.

"I was telling Ms. Wesslow what we were doing here. Nothing specific, but I did mention that the Barrette place was of some interest to you. I was surprised at how fast Ms. Wesslow joined in the conversation. She began telling me of this family she knows that had ancestors who worked for the Barrette family as far back as the 1700s."

I interjected, "They were slaves if it was the 1700s."

"Uh . . . yes, slaves." The doctor repeated as he picked up his coffee and took a drink.

"I really am amazed at how many people take such an interest in the Barrette plantation and still let it go to ruin," he said in wonderment.

"Doc, it's like this, every newborn is told of the jewels, gold, silver, or whatever this treasure is supposed to be. And as they grow, it festers inside them that they will be the one that finds it and becomes the hero envied by the town. I'm surprised we haven't seen it on one of those prime-time news shows.

"What are the chances of meeting with Ms. Wesslow? I'd like to talk to her. Would you mind arranging it?" I asked.

"I thought you would and I have taken the liberty of making arrangements for dinner this evening at the Lands Cove Tavern. It was recommended as being one of the three dining establishments four-star-rated in this area. Our reservation is for 8:00 p.m.

Ms. Wesslow and I will meet you and Samantha there," he said rather proud of himself for anticipating my request.

I asked the doc to let Sam know that I was heading out to Balmorial and that I would call her later.

CHAPTER 25

When I arrived at Balmorial, Charlie was outside entertaining the ladies, three of them to be precise. So who said you couldn't fool around after sixty?

"Falco, you got my message already? I just called half hour ago or so," Charlie said as he offered his hand in greeting.

"No, I thought I'd check and see if Hyde was back yet. What did you call about?"

"Hyde, he came back last night. Didn't say much, seemed a little more grumpy than usual. I asked if he heard from his grandson; he just closed the door in my face.

Now, he's an ornery old coot, but he never closed the door in my face without say'n something."

"Where can I find him, Charlie?"

"He ain't come out yet. Strange, now that I think of it. He's usually the first one out." Charlie had a look of concern on his face as he spoke. "Tell ya, it ain't like him. Better get over to his room. He ain't no spring chicken," he said as he started toward the building.

I did all I could to keep up with him and him being ninety-three. On the way to Hyde's room, Charlie got one of the orderlies to come along. The look on his face was one of worry now.

When we reached the room, the orderly knocked and called out his name. There was no response. He knocked again before using his key. When we got inside, we found Hyde on the floor. He looked like he had been lying there for a while. The orderly pushed a button, setting off an alarm at the front desk as he bent down to check Hyde for vital signs. He looked up and said, "He's still alive, but we better get him over toMercy before he's too far gone. Lord knows how long he's been like this."

The orderlies arrived and picked Hyde up, placed him on the gurney, and wheeled him to the ambulance area. The residents were gathering to see who was being taken out. Charlie was walking around assuring them that Hyde was still alive and joking that "he wasn't one to give up the ghost just yet." "It looked like a heart attack to me. What do you think, Falco?" Charlie asked, trying to hide any emotion and not expecting an answer.

Charlie and Hyde were the oldest residents at Balmorial by at least fifteen years.

He would probably feel alone without Hyde regardless of his cantankerous ways.

"How many heart attacks has he had, Charlie?"

"First that I know of, if it is one," Charlie replied.

"What kind of work did Hyde do?" I asked out of curiosity.

"Jonah was a teacher. Kids had a saying 'bout his classes. It went like this: 'Jekyll or Hyde, Jekyll or Hyde, which will it be when we get inside.' Sure does explain his moods."

"Never really saw the man sick. Had the flu once or twice, some aches and pains, but hell, at our age you expect one or two." Charlie just smiled.

"You know me and Hyde were born the same day. Maybe that's why I put up with him."

I just smiled and thanked him for his time. "Let me know what you find out about Hyde. If he's okay, I'd still like to talk to him before I have to go home."

"Sure thing, Falco. You take care now," he said as he turned and headed down the hall.

"Falco," Charlie called, "I can't say for certain, but when Jonah came back last night, I was sitting on the porch and it sure looked like Conrad helping him out of the car.

"I wouldn't doubt if these two had an argument or something getting him all riled up. There wasn't many meetings with them two that didn't end up in one"

"Charlie, did you happen to see anyone else with them? Maybe a big, heavyset man, late forties, smells?"

"Nooo, can't say that I did. Why ya ask'n?"

"Just curious that's all. And by the way, what time did you say he came in?"

"I didn't say, but it was about ten. You know, young fella, I ain't lost my marbles yet. I remember you say'n how you were writ'n a piece 'bout the Barrettes. You sure do ask funny questions, if that's what you're doing. You act like a cop. So what is it you're looking for?"

"You're right, Charlie, I'm a P.I. and I'm here to find out as much as I can about the Barrette plantation and anyone having anything to do with it. Some investors have hired me so they can decide if it's worth their time and money to make it one of those Jamestown attractions or not."

"Look, I'd appreciate it if you kept it under your hat. If it got around, it could ruin the deal. You know what I mean?"

"Sure, why didn't you say so in the first place? I know when to keep my mouth shut. Don't you worry none."

As I reached my car, I turned and saw Charlie in the middle of the three ladies pointing his finger at me and I knew how well he would keep the "secret." I chuckled to myself as I drove down the drive.

I knew Charlie would let it all out, so I didn't feel bad about planting a seed of deception. Besides, it would give them something to talk about for a long time.

While driving back to town, I wondered who could play the parts of the Barrette clan if it were converted. It was still early, so I headed to the historical museum to see if they had anything on the Barrettes or the plantation yet.

CHAPTER 26

The historical preserve was a mid-seventeenth-century Georgian-style manor house overlooking the Sound. It was said that the ships would pull into this bay and their captains were obliged to fill a bottle with rum that was set in the mangrove tree in the harbor for the outgoing vessels. It was supposed to bring them good fortune on their venture to sea. Here, also, they would barter for the best price for their goods, and I wondered how many of the acclaimed pirates took of rum and women while exchanging stories of the briny. This town was rich with folklore of an era rich with daring adventure, mystery, and romance of these pirates, highwaymen, and privateers. Their stories filled books for the world to read, but here you walked the same streets and touched the same things that they touched; you were part of the past.

As I walked inside, I heard my name being called. "Mr. Falco, I do declare . . . what a surprise see'n y'all here. Did you have a chance to read the report I sent over to you with that nice Ms. Richards?"

"Sho' nuff did, honey chile," I said smiling. She just looked at me and batted those deep rich blue pools. She was a siren that escaped from the sea to taunt man. She could have any man do her bidding if she wanted.

Grabbing my arm, nearly cutting off the circulation, she headed me down the hall.

"Oh, Mr. Falco, you sure are a card. What brings you here anyway? Is there something I can do for you?"

The sound of her voice was an invitation to explore the Southern architecture of this coquette.

"I was wondering if the Historical Society had any pictures, I mean portraits of the Barrette clan. I would like to see what they looked like."

"Why lan's sake, yes, we do. We had most of the portraits restored for when we finally get the plantation. They're upstairs in the bedrooms."

After all, I thought, I had to do my duty. I followed her to the second floor bedrooms. As I started to step over the cord that acted as a barrier, Betty Lou pulled up on it as if to unfasten the catch. Instead, all she caught was a very personal part of my anatomy. She looked at me with those wanting eyes and smiled. "Are you all right, Mr.Falco? I am terribly sorry." Her voice told more than her words as her eyes roamed my body as if I were the prized bull at the auction.

"Here . . . let me get this rope out of the way." She reached between my legs, slowly gathering the rope and watching my reaction all the time. "There now, Mr. Falco, everything's all right," she said with that Southern drawl, bedroom eyes, and devilish smile.

I didn't give in to this seductress, but God knows how difficult it was.

"Here is the first lord of the manor. He liked to call himself Sir Edward, but he was no knight. Next to him and so on is the family. Sir Edwards's wife was Mary Elizabeth Lloyd, plain woman. Next to her is their son, Edward Hardie Barrette and his wife, Penelope Bennett. Then, we have Edward II. Makes you think of royalty, doesn't it?

Now, we come to Emily Maye Lynn-Barker; she was a widow. She was an attractive woman for her day and it was said that she was a devoted wife and mother."

I was left standing there with my mouth open as I looked at the next portrait. It was Shannan. Those eyes piercing my body, her lips slightly held open, red hair glistening from the overhead lights, and that ivory skin not darkened by the years. Whoever repaired these portraits must have had a vision to make this one so lifelike.

"Mr. Falco, are you all right?"

"Yes . . . fine, just fine. This must be Elizabeth Anne Barrette."

"Yes, it is. You look as though y'all seen a ghost or something."

"Almost. I've met a woman that could pass for her double."

"That's about it, Mr. Falco. Is there anything else you would like? Anything at all".

If this was another time, I wouldn't have hesitated to accept the charms of this vixen, but this wasn't the right time. Sam, what have you done to me? I asked myself as I slowly examined this mortal monument to the goddess Venus from her shapely legs up through that hourglass figure with her breasts exposed enough to make a blind man see and an old man dream, and finally reaching her face that said I'm yours, just take me.

As our eyes met, I said, "I have to go, but thanks for your help." As I started to leave, I could see the sadness in her eyes and the victory of knowing that I wanted her.

"Mr. Falco," she called as I reached the bottom of the stairs, "if you change your mind, I'm in the book."

CHAPTER 27

When I got back to the motel, I checked to see if there were any messages. The clerk handed me an envelope; it was from Sam. Seems she decided to take a tour of the local mansions and said to pick her up at her room for dinner.

It was only 4:00 p.m., so I lay on the bed figuring I'd rest for an hour and then get ready for the gathering.

I was shocked to awareness when the phone rang. It was 6:00 p.m. and I had fallen asleep. I answered the phone and it was Sam.

"Vince, I'm running a little late, but I'll be ready by 7, okay?"

"Sure," I said half asleep.

"Are you all right? You sound strange," she said.

"Yeah, I'm fine. I'll be there at 7."

I hung up, tried to stretch, but I still wasn't heeled enough to pull on my one side.

I did a quick shower and shaved, wondering how Hyde was doing and thinking about what Charlie said about Conrad being in town. It seemed he would be taking a big chance. If what Charlie said was true about Conrad and Hyde always arguing, it wouldn't make any sense coming back just to fight. There had to be something, but what? All I had were questions and a big headache trying not to think of them.

I stopped at Sam's room to escort her to the car. I started to knock on the door when it flung open, and standing there with the light behind her emphasizing her curves and highlighting the color of her hair was Sam. The smile on her face said it all. I must have looked like a dumbstruck kid going on his first date.

She was wearing a navy blue tank dress with a heart-dipped neckline exposing just enough of her to make a statue sit up and take notice. The hemline was well above the knee revealing the graceful curves of her thighs down to her ankles. The dress had a way of clinging to let the less imaginative be able to dream about the unseen portions of this enchantress.

I started to speak when she reached out, embraced, and kissed me. Her warm moist lips and the softness of her body against mine only emphasized how much of a woman she was. I didn't want to go and meet the kids; I wanted to stay home and play with mama. When she let me go, I asked in my best macho voice, "What's that for?"

"I'll show you later . . . if you're a good boy, Falco," she said in a seductive tone as she walked past me in an alluring motion with her hand rubbing across my cheek. I was hoping for a quick dinner and prayed that I could be a very good boy.

I was wearing a double-breasted taupe-colored suit with a light beige banded collar shirt and no tie. I felt a little out of place next to this goddess, but she was going to have to live with it.

In the car, Sam started telling me how to behave, not to call the doc Willy and to be hospitable, as though I was anything other than a perfect gentleman. All I could say was "yes, Mom" as I waited for her to wet her fingers, rub the dirt from my cheeks, and push the hair out of my eyes. She just smiled.

We arrived at the tavern, where a big, big boy grabbed the door on Sam's side of the car and couldn't take his young eyes off of her chest. She could have been the headless horseman for all he knew. She was halfway around the car before he realized that she was gone. I brought him back to earth.

"You going to stand there with the door open all night or would you like to park it?"

His wide eyes blinked a couple of times as he was making his way back to earth.

"She's my mother. What do you think?" I said jokingly as I watched his face turn three shades of red. Sam looked at me with a look of disdain for taunting this young admirer of hers. I could tell she was eating every bit of it up.

Inside, we were greeted by the hostess. "We're here with the Reinhardt party," Sam said.

She looked at her seating chart and said, "This way please. He and Jenny Lee are next to the hearth."

When we arrived at the table, the doc was seated to the right of Jenny Lee, his hand on hers as they stared into each other's eyes, or so it appeared.

She was wearing a little black slip dress with white straps and bodice trim. Her skin was lightly tanned, emitting a golden glow from the light of the fire place. The doc, dressed in the latest stuff shirt attire, nearly jumped out of his skin as we stood there waiting for a greeting. He jumped up looking like he was caught with his hand in the cookie jar. Stammering, he said, "Miss . . . uh . . . Ms. Richards, Mr. Falco, this is Ms. Jennifer Wesslow." Sam offered her hand as both women had that smile on their face of sheer conquest of the male species. "I'm Samantha, thanks for your support the other night."

"Just call me Falco," I said as I reached out to shake hands.

"And you can call me Jenny Lee or just Jenny, if you like," she said with a smile.

The doc, still stumbling, finally suggested that we sit down.

"Will . . . Wilhelm said you knew a family that had close ties to the Barrettes. I would like to hear more about them if you don't mind." I asked to get things going.

"That would be the Weavers. Ashta and I worked together for years before her mother took sick and she had to take care of her. We still visit from time to time. She lives just past the Barrette place."

"What could you tell me about the Barrette plantation?"

"Nothing anyone else couldn't. It is the dream of every child to find the treasure hidden on that property. As a kid, I used to go up there after school, on weekends, and any old time with friends in hopes of finding it."

"People would dig, pull the walls apart, and dig in the cellar. That cellar must have a hole clear through to China by now." She was smiling as she mentioned the cellar.

"We were out there and didn't see a cellar. There were no doors leading to the basement," I said.

Jenny interrupted, "I said the cellar, not a basement. To get to the cellar, you have to go around back of the house, although there may be a cover over the stairway now.

Seems young Jimmy Booth fell down those stairs a couple of years ago and broke both his legs. He wasn't found for two days. I haven't been there for years."

"Have you ever found anything different about the place as time went on? You know, anything that you would consider unusual?" I queried.

"No, not really. Everybody at one time or the other has been there. Ashta might be able to tell y'all something more. She takes care of the graveyard up there."

"Why does she do it?" I asked.

"Don't really know. I never did ask her why. I thought it was a kind thing to do. Lord knows I never would have done it," she said.

"Why not?" I wondered out loud.

"The Barrettes weren't what you would call the best of people, except for the last generation according to the stories. I would get an eerie feeling every time I was up there." She had a very sincere look on her face as she talked about this.

"Why did you keep going then?" I asked.

"I was a child. I didn't want my friends calling me a chicken and such. But as I got Older, I went less and less. You know, I get goose bumps just thinking about that graveyard." She leaned over and showed us her arm with small bumps.

The doctor took advantage of this moment and put his hands on her arm and started rubbing them. This man was obviously lovesick, or horny as hell. I'm not sure there is a distinction between the two anyway.

"Could you arrange a time when we could meet with your friend Ashta?" Sam asked.

"Sure, we can go over there anytime. She would like the company. She doesn't get out much anymore, with her mother getting worse and all. Her mother has that Alzheimer's thing. Keeps forget'n things. Only now there isn't anything to forget; it's all gone. They won't put her in a home, said they didn't want their mama mistreated."

We covered everything we could about the Barrette place. Sam carried the conversation with Jenny, while I just ate and listened. The good doctor was in dream land and I'm sure he didn't have visions of sugar plums in his head. It would be more like Georgia burning and Southern belles ringing in the new year.

We said our goodbyes and left around 11:00 p.m. The boy was waiting earnestly at the door to get the car. When Sam walked up to him, he couldn't raise his eyes to her face. She just smiled and asked for the car. This boy had to be six foot five, one hundred sixty pounds and built rather well. I would say he was seventeen, eighteen at the most. Sam just sparkled at the way; he behaved.

CHAPTER 28

On the way back to the motel, I began to think out loud about the cellar. Why didn't I see it? I had walked around that house fifty times at least.

"Do you want to ride up there now?" Sam asked.

I was somewhat startled. I didn't realize I was thinking out loud.

"I would, but I don't think you're dressed for a field trip to the local haunted house."

"I would like to see it if it's still there," she replied.

"Let's do it."

We arrived at the plantation and started a slow walk around the house. It was a moonless night, with heavy cloud cover overhead. There was a cold steady wind blowing, causing Sam to stay close to me for warmth. It didn't make things easy with the small flashlights we both had.

At the rear of the house was an angled rock form covered with dirt. I started pushing some of the dirt away with my foot. It was lightly packed as if it was newly placed there. I felt something give under my weight. I bent down and started removing the dirt with my hands. Sure enough, there was a board placed on top of the rock foundation. Sam helped me lift it out of the way, with most of the dirt still on it.

There were five rock-formed steps leading to the bottom. We went down to the cellar. It had a dirt floor, musty old place smell, and a low ceiling. In the far corner was a table, lamp, and two chairs. Leaning against the wall were two shovels and a pick. Sam was walking closer to the stairs when I heard her call in a low muffled voice.

"Vince . . . Vince, come here."

I hurried to her side.

"I saw someone run past here. He looked big from the size of his legs," her voice excited.

"Stay here, I'll take a look," I said as I started up the stairs.

"Be careful," I heard her say as I stepped out on to the ground.

I heard a rustling noise in the hedges in front of me. It was too dark to see anything and the light I had wasn't bright enough to shine that far. I carefully approached the area where the sound came from. There was a quick motion as the hedge parted and this dark figure came bounding out of the foliage. Instantly, I could see light flashing overhead to the rear of the hedges; it was reminiscent of my days at war. I couldn't be having flashbacks. I was too aware of what was going on. The figure reached me. I reacted by turning my body, grabbing his arm with one hand and his chest with my other, flinging him over my shoulder and watching him fly by, landing with a crushing sound. He was quick to his feet, displaying his talents of the martial arts by making his karate sounds to scare me, I would guess. But God knows I've been scared by better men than him.

He came at me with a double punch to the chest. I blocked the blows and countered with one to the sternum, causing him to bow a little, and followed by another to the throat as he began to bend forward. I could hear him strangling from my punch.

He stumbled forward for a second, caught himself, and ran off holding his throat and chest.

I started to chase him when my body remembered the two broken ribs and let me know that what just took place wasn't in the best interest of recovery. I went to my knees clutching my side.

I heard Sam running to me calling my name. I lifted to my knees and waived one hand to let her know I was ok.

"What happened? Are you all right?" she asked as she helped me to my feet.

I thought for a moment about the last encounter of this kind, but it couldn't be. Or could it?

"This guy was big and he smelled just like Mr. Smith from the other day. That smell of an overdose of cologne and cheap cologne at that. But why was he here and where was the voice?" I asked myself out loud.

"Sam, stay here, don't move." I said as I started toward the cemetery still clutching my side.

I reached the cemetery and was standing in front of the big cross. It was raining more as a mist than falling droplets. Lightning could be seen in the distance, followed by the increasing rumbling of thunder.

As I was looking up at the cross, there was a brilliant flash of light. In the center of the light between the two stone angels was Shannan McCready. It looked like her, but there was something about the face that was a little different, yet the same. On either side of her were faces I hadn't seen before. They were staring at me too.

The movements where distinct and slow, almost as described by Shannan in my office. I could see her mouth moving, but words failed to be heard, yet I knew what she was trying to say. "You must free me. Let them know who took my life. Tell them. You must tell them. Look to hallowed ground." Then everything went dark and silent.

I could hear my name being called in a frantic tone. "Vince . . . Vince, are you all right?" It was Sam. My head was in her lap and her hand was on my face. Kneeling next to her was the doc. He was moving my eyelids around while shining a flashlight in my eyes. I wasn't sure what the hell was going on and words weren't coming out of my mouth, though it felt like I was trying to talk.

When the doc was finished, I started to move but my head felt like it was stuck to her lap. My vision was a little blurred and my body ached more than before. I could hear the doctor talking, "Samantha, we should get him to the hospital. He was lucky the branch only hit him and not the lightning."

I could feel them pulling on me and myself pushing to get up. There was ringing in my ears and bright spots in my eyes like the ones you see after your picture is taken with a flash.

Once I was on my feet, I started getting a little more control of myself. I wavered a bit as a drunk might do trying to walk. The ringing in my ears wasn't as noticeable, but my head ached and my eyes burned. I looked over to Sam. She had a worried look on her face, but the doc was one cool character. He still had that "Mr. Spock" look. They where guiding me to the car, telling me to take it slow.

"I'm okay, you can let me go. I've been worse," I said in a rasping voice.

Sam still held on to my arm. The doc let me go, but not all at once.

"You are a very lucky man, Mr. Falco. If you were five feet closer, you wouldn't be alive. I haven't seen lightning strike with such intensity since my days in Salzburg."

"I was coming up the drive and could feel the pressure from the force of it. Yes, my friend, you are a very lucky fellow," he said sincerely.

"We better get you to the hospital, Vince," Sam said earnestly.

"Jenny, would you get the door, please?" I heard Sam ask.

The whole gang was here for this moment. I wondered where they all came from.

"Look, Sam, I'm ok. Doc, did you see any signs of a concussion, bleeding from the ears, eyes, nose, or mouth?"

"No," he uttered.

"Then, let's go to the motel and if anything strange comes up, I'll scurry off to the Hospital. I promise, Mom." I said as I turned to Sam. She put on a little frown, pouted her lips a little, and asked the doc if he thought I was all right.

"If he stays in bed and rests, perhaps it will be all right. I don't think he should be alone tonight," the doc replied.

"I'll stay with him," Sam offered.

So it was settled. I was going to have a babysitter and the doc was going to get laid. Hell of a night, I thought, as I got into the car.

Back at the motel, I lay on the bed and watched the ceiling spin around as Sam curled up next to me. She was soft, warm, and from the points of interest resting against my body, inviting. I couldn't help but think how this night could have been if only I wasn't so damn curious about that cellar. I reserved myself to the fact that I was to be celibate for another evening. I might as well become a monk.

CHAPTER 29

I was aroused by a loud ringing. I opened my eyes and couldn't help blinking a couple dozen times trying to adjust to the light. Then all at once, the light was subdued and there in all her splendor was Sam staring down at me. This was beginning to be a habit with her. She stood there with a tie-front bodysuit with a snap bottom clinging to her shapely torso, ever so inviting. My mind wandered in lust only to be brought back by the throbbing in my head and side.

"Vince, you have a call. It's Charlie," she said as she handed me the phone.

"Charlie, what's up?" I asked, still half asleep.

"Jonah . . . the old coot, didn't have a heart attack or stroke, just had an anxiety Attack, they said. He'll be kept in the hospital for a couple of days. Thought you would want to know. Oh . . . there's been some calls for him this morning. Could be Conrad wanting to know if he was dead yet." Charlie laughed on that note.

"Thanks, Charlie. Let me know if anything else happens."

I figured I should let Bill know what was happening just in case Conrad decided to show at the hospital. If Bill could grab him, I'd have my chance to get some answers.

I felt 100 percent better than when I dragged my body in last night. The boulder that was being balanced on my head was now gone and only the ribs throbbed.

I could live with that. I grabbed my wallet, took out Bill's card, and dialed the local number.

"Hello, Sergeant Lextor. Can I help you?"

"Bill, Falco here."

"Hey, Vince. What's up?" he asked cheerfully like we were old pals.

"Yesterday, Jonah Hyde was taken to Mercy Hospital. He had an anxiety attack.

Anyway, Charlie Hands said he swear he saw Conrad Johnston helping the old man out of the car when he came back to the home the night before.

"Charlie just called me and said Jonah had a call a little while ago and he thinks it might be Johnston. If it is he, he may be going to the hospital. But then again, maybe not. I thought you might be able to get there before I could and grab him if he showed up."

"Thanks, Vince. I'm leaving now. See you when." He hung up.

I turned to Sam and told her what was happening and asked if she wanted to come with me.

I jumped in the shower and rushed to get dress. It must have taken all of thirty minutes. I opened the door to go outside and there stood Sam ready to go. Must be a record, I thought, a woman ready in less than an hour or two. I'd check with Guinness later.

I approached the car when Sam spoke up. "I'll drive. I've been by the hospital Before, so we won't have to guess on how to get there."

"Fine with me. Let's pick up a coffee on the way," I said as I laid my head back against the seat and started recounting the events of last night. There was a bright light; it seems it was lightning. Then what was the image I saw? It looked like Shannan, but who were the other two? She spoke but didn't make any sense. Something about hallowed ground.

Sam touched my arm and asked, "Penny for your thoughts?"

"It's the nineties. Make it a buck," I said jokingly.

"You had that distant look on your face again. Where were you?" Sam asked.

"I was thinking about last night." I told her of the vision to see what she could get out of it. She was quick to guess.

"Shannan is trying to tell us who the killer is, and the other two women could be Betty Jean and Katherine Kaye."

"That's why you were so lucky, that flash of lightning hit the tree seemed to bounce and then hit the cross. You went down when the branch flew off the tree and hit you in the head. That's the spot over your left eye," Sam said as she lightly touched the spot.

"Okay, okay, I know where it is. You don't have to push on it.

"I'm sorry, Vince," she said with a big smile.

We arrived at the hospital and Bill was outside standing by his car. Sam parked the car close to the main entrance and we walked over to Bill.

"Vince, what in hell happened to you?"

"I had a bout with a tree limb and it won."

"Do tell. Must have been a big one."

"I'm Samantha Richards. You must be Bill."

"Pleased to meet you, ma'am." He couldn't take his eyes off of her either. I figured he was related to the young sex fiend we met last night.

"Bill, do you have a son that parks cars at the Land Cove Tavern?" Sam glared at me but didn't say anything.

"No, my boys not old enough to do anything but deliver the local paper. If you were there, then you met one of the Foremen boys. Big, ain't they?"

With all the chitchat out of the way, Bill got down to business.

"Vince, you were right. Conrad was back in town. I pulled up just as he was walking toward the door. He saw me and took off. I chased after him, but he got away.

Some guy was in the car with the engine running."

"I don't think he'll stick around now that everyone knows he's in town. Tell me, did you get a good look at the driver?" I queried.

"No, they took off with the tires spinning. I put the word out on the make of the car.

It was a rental. Had a sticker on the trunk, he got it out of Raleigh. Anyway, I was going to have a word with Hyde. Want to join me?"

"Sure," I answered.

Bill asked at the desk for Hyde's room number.

"I'm sorry, but Mr. Hyde isn't allowed visitors."

"I would like to speak with the doctor, Edna, if you don't mind," Bill requested with authority.

"Okay, Bill, but he's not gonna let you see him in his condition anyway." She turned and paged Dr. Edwards.

Bill turned to me and said, "I have a couple of uniforms coming down to stand guard at his room just in case Conrad decides to come back."

Edna interrupted, "Excuse me, Bill, Dr. Edwards will see y'all in room 414."

We headed to the elevators. When we found 414, there was a young man sitting at the desk. To look at him, you might guess him to be twenty-one or twenty-two. He had light brown hair, military cut, high on the sides, and a boyish smile as he greeted us. He must have read the look on my face because he followed the greeting with a statement.

"I'm older than I look. My family was blessed with youthful appearance. So I'm not out of any TV series, if that's what you were thinking," he said smiling ear to ear.

We all had a little laugh out of it.

Bill spoke up, "Dr. Edwards, I need to speak with Jonah Hyde. I have to know what he knows about the whereabouts of his grandson. I'm also going to place a security team at his door in case his grandson comes back."

"I can appreciate your need, but he's here because of extreme stress. I've given him a light sedative and don't think it would do much good to talk with him anyhow. If you would call me later, I'll have a better idea of when he could see you." The doctor's voice was asking for the reprieve more than demanding it.

"Okay, Dr. Edwards, I'll call you later. However, I'm going to stick around until I get my men set up to watch him." Bill wasn't going to give in completely to the doctor's wishes.

"Let me know if you get anything out of him, ok?" I asked as we turned to leave.

"Yeah, I'll let you know, Vince," Bill said assuredly.

Sam and I started for the elevators when Bill came half running to catch us. "I'm going to get a coffee in the cafeteria. What to join me?"

"We'd like to, but we have to meet some people in a little while and we better get Going," I said as Sam gave me a quizzical look. I could see that Bill picked up on it also.

As we walked away, Sam asked, "What's going on? We don't have to meet anyone until this afternoon."

"I'm going to talk to Hyde," I said flatly.

"But you can't see him yet. You heard the doctor," she whispered.

I didn't answer her. I just continued with my plan.

"This may just work out. Let's take Bill up on the coffee, I'll excuse myself for whatever, and you keep him in the cafeteria until I get back," I said as we turned, heading back to the cafeteria.

We caught up to him as he neared the elevator. "Bill, it seems I was wrong. We aren't meeting our friends until this afternoon, had my times twisted. Let's have that coffee." He smiled and led the way.

It was a self-service cafeteria and all we were here for was coffee and time. Sam picked a table and I got the coffee. Bill obviously needed a fix. He picked up two chocolate donuts and a cheese Danish. I didn't have to say anything. The look in his eye told me he knew what I was thinking.

"I know this looks bad, but I'm on a strict dozen-a-day donut diet. After all, I'm a cop and can't afford to lose weight because I'd have to buy an all-new wardrobe. So you see, it's better that I maintain my waistline so as not to cause any undo financial hardships on my family," Bill said with an enormous grin on his face.

At the table, I took a sip of coffee and then in a sudden motion as if I had forgotten something, I bolted upright and said, "Bill, I'm sorry but I have to make a call to our friend at the motel. He's probably up by now and wondering where we are. I'll be right back. I left the phone in the car." Bill was shoveling a circle of coronary delight into his mouth and only nodded his awareness of my leaving. Sam just looked at me. I wasn't sure if she approved or was disappointed that I would interrupt a sick man.

I stopped at the front desk. “Edna,” I said questioningly. “You remember me? I was with Bill.”

“Yes, I do, but it still stands: Jonah can’t be bothered at this time.”

“I understand, but I was wondering if you could give me his room number so I could avoid any problems with the florist delivering the flowers I’m having sent. Can you help me?”

“Sure I can. He’s in room 234. Where y’all from?”

“Up north,” I said.

“I could tell you were a Yankee,” she said shyly.

CHAPTER 30

I took the stairs to the second floor to avoid running into anyone that may have seen me with the police. As I stepped out of the stairwell, I was next to a door marked "Supply Room." I looked around to see if anyone was watching; I found it clear of prying eyes. I opened the door and stepped inside. There was an assortment of toiletries, gowns, mops, brooms, etc. On a hook just behind the brooms was a smock; I took it and put it on. It was a little tight but who would notice. I grabbed some gowns and headed out the door.

As I approached the nurse's desk the phone rang. No one was there so I started around the desk when I heard a voice call out, "I'm coming, it's okay. I'll get it." The voice put images of female splendor in mind, it having that southern drawl that parallels bedroom eyes. I turned to see where it was coming from, and there rounding the corner was this dishwater blonde maiden dressed in a white extremely short-skirted uniform with white sheer stockings and brandishing a smile that put the sun to shame. She wasn't Miss America nor was her face outstanding, but she had a charm about her that made her average looks wanting.

She rounded the desk, whisked up the phone, and sat down all in one easy motion. As she whirled around in her seat I could hear her say, "Nurses' station, can I help you?"

There was a pause as I watched her face change to one of surprise and concern. She looked down the hallway left and right as if ready to cross a street, cupped the phone to her mouth, and in a semi whisper I could hear her continue, "Conrad, is that you . . . ? My lord, where are you? Yes, your grandfather is here, but you better not come here, the police are waiting for you. They're sending a guard to watch over your grandfather's room."

I looked at the name plate on the desk; it read "Beth Franklin, RN."

She stopped talking as I looked at her, and she gave me a quizzical stare as if to ask "Who are you?"

I nodded my head at her as if I belonged and continued to the far side of the station. "Conraaad . . .," I could hear her stretch out her words as she continued talking to him. "I'm married now. You've been gone for almost three years. You never wrote or nothing in all that time. I declare the whole town thought you vanished from the face of the earth." She giggled and squirmed like a schoolgirl as she continued with Conrad. "'Course I won't tell anyone I was talk'n to you . . . I'd like to see you. Maybe you could call me tomorrow and I could get away for a little while . . . Okay, bye." She just put the phone down and sat there staring into nowhere.

I slipped into room 234 and found Hyde sitting in a chair staring out the window.

He turned as I closed the door behind me.

"Boy, just put that stuff down and get the hell out," he said in a gruff tone.

Mr. Jonah Hyde was a thin man with leathery skin that showed the lines of time, yet didn't give away his age. His hair was reminiscent of Einstein, white and bushy, and his eyes were set in deep sockets. He didn't look like a person I would expect to look who wasn't well. His gaze was piercing as he watched me set the gowns down on the chair next to him.

"You gonna leave that paraphernalia there, boy?" he asked.

"No, sir, I'm not, Mr. Hyde," I continued. "I'm Vince Falco, and I would like to ask you a couple of questions about the Barrette place."

He looked at me with a stern stare and was reaching for his call button when I reached over and grabbed it.

"Mr. Hyde, I'm not with the police. I'm trying to get information about Elizabeth Anne Barrette who died—"

Hyde interrupted, "I know when that wench died. She was the cause of my good family's ruination. She falsely accused my name sake of stalking her. She was the daughter of Satan himself . . . Now get the hell out of here before I call for the nurse!"

I continued, "Mr. Hyde, I was told that you were the foremost authority on the Barrettes by Charlie Hands. He said you could tell me things no one else could." I tried using my best groveling tone.

"Well, what do you want to know, and why?" Hyde said as he studied my face.

"I was told that Dr. Hyde lived with the Barrettes and took care of Elizabeth some four years. Then I'm told that he made advances to her and was removed from the plantation in the middle of the night, and eventually ran out of town. Now that's what I've been told but then that's only one side of the story, and I'm not one to accept a one-sided tale."

"That girl was spoiled rotten. She had everything her way. She flaunted herself at my name sake. In his papers, he tells how she would come to his office from the time she was of age to have him examine her. He told of how she would hold herself in her hands and ask him if any of his other patients had such firm breasts, and as he put it, shapely and wanting womanly attributes." He spoke with that same know-all attitude that Charlie used.

"What happened that made her father throw him out all of a sudden?" I asked.

"In his memoirs, his mention of that night is somewhat guarded. He said that Elizabeth had pursued him all over the plantation that day, from the house to the gardens, approaching him in a 'familiar way' when he was in the barn. He went on to tell how she compelled him to sit in the graveyard while she danced and sang to him. She removed some of her garments revealing herself to him for reason other than professional. He wrote that he held her off from her attempts for an amorous relation until finally he was forced to pursue her desires by her telling him that if he didn't have this affair with her, she would tell her father that he forced himself on her person. After he had satisfied the harlot, she told him that she was with child and wanted him to do something to remove the burden or for sure she would tell her father of their lovemaking." Hyde stopped for a moment as if to turn the page before continuing.

"That night," he continued, "he went to her room to see if she had calmed down from the events of the day, and was going to tell her that what she wanted was wrong by nature and by God. When he arrived at the door, he could hear sounds of moaning and thought Elizabeth was having problems, so he let himself in. What he saw was a disgusting sight, as he put it—there in front of him was Elizabeth in bed with one of the Negro boys. He described the sight a little more vividly than I could, but I'm sure you can envision what he must have seen. Anyway, she sent the boy out the window and put on her nightclothes while he stood there. He told her of his decision, and then she let out a shriek that would wake the dead, then turned and hit him with the oil lamp. You know what happened then. Although they beat him and humiliated him before they ran him out of town, he went on to write that he felt her personality change was caused from the demise of her two would-be husbands, and believed she turned to the coloreds for understanding. In any event, he went on to say she was with child and now believed it to be colored." Hyde was somewhat forlorn after telling the story.

"What about the stories of him being seen in the graveyard at night, trying to see the Barrett girl?" I asked.

"He tells of how he wasn't paid for his services and knew that the Barrettes kept a considerable amount of money at their plantation. I think that's where the treasure story comes from, and if he could get to Elizabeth, he felt she would relent and have her father pay him. Well, as you know, it never happened.

"Elizabeth was found dead not too long after this incident. Her wrists were cut too deeply to be suicide, so the story goes, and no one was the wiser of her condition.

"In the journal he states that the cuts were reminiscent of the slow death given to pirates who stole from their own. He believed that her father found out of her curious circumstance and killed her and the Negro James. For he was dead the same day—found hanging from the willow by the graveyard.

"My kin was chastened by this devil, Edward Hardie Barrette II, and forced through false accusation to leave his home. Banished though he was, he did not take his soul from this county he loved, he returned some ten years later, and at fifty did take a wife. Edward II had died and the widow Barrette was sickly and dying too.

"He wrote that the widow Barrette talked of gold and jewels and would ramble on pointing her fingers as she would relate a sonnet. I have heard it so many times that it still rings in my ears. My grandson would repeat it over and over until the very words cursed his soul and left him burning with desire to find the unblessed mythical treasure of the Barrettes."

It was obvious that Hyde wasn't senile; he was bright, articulate, and angry. His tone was one of reprisal for his family's honor.

"Even today there are some townsfolk that believe the Barrettes were wronged by my ancestor and through the years have shown their disdain on me and my family," he continued.

"When you said your grandson would repeat this sonnet, what do you mean?" I asked expecting to hear the poem.

"As I would repair the journals of my forefather, I would read them to Conrad. He was forever asking me what this meant or that meant as I was reading in the language of the time. Conrad, as he got older, would take notes and delved into the history of that era. He was incensed with finding this treasure that doesn't exist."

"When you say incensed, how was that?" I asked trying not to let out my knowledge of Conrad and his being wanted by the police. Hyde looked up at me questioningly but then continued.

"He was always going to that damn Barrette plantation and doing god-knows-what till the late hours of the evening. Many a time his father would have to go and get him," Hyde said with a little smile of remembrance.

"What was the sonnet anyway?" I asked as-matter-of-factly as possible.

Hyde looked to the sky, closed his eyes for a moment, and then began the sonnet.

"Beneath ye badge of Christian charge

Lies ye consequence of ancestry
Legion will ye Cenotaph be
Whilst Cherub ye isthmus implies."

"It makes little sense as I see it, but Conrad was fascinated with it. He even put music to it and sang it all around the town. People thought he was crazy, and sometimes so did I."

"Where could I find your grandson? I would like to talk to him about the plantation since he appears to be the expert," I asked.

"He moved away a few years ago," Hyde said in a gruff tone.

"Have you heard from him since he's left?" I asked.

"Why do you want to know?" he asked guardedly.

"Like I said, he seems to be an expert on the Barrette pace, so if you have I'll leave my number with you in case he contacts you." I attempted to hand him the paper I wrote my number on, but he wouldn't take it. I laid it down on the table next to him.

"You don't want to meet my grandson. He's in league with the devil." Hyde put his head down as he spoke, his words seeming painful as he continued. "I haven't told anyone before, but my grandson has kept in contact with me since he left here. I'm sure you know why he left if you talked to Charlie Hands. Anyway, he came back a few days ago and picked me up at the home. I was happy to see him and thought perhaps all this nasty business was done since he had come for me. I should tell you that I was fortunate to have made some very wise investments in my early years and it has provided me well since my retirement. When I'm gone, it all goes to Conrad and his sisters.

"Well that's what brought him back. He wanted money and he wanted the journals. He still believes there is treasure on the Barrette plantation, and he will hang before he gives up the search. He went on this time telling me how he was so close by having some women believe they were Barrettes in their past lives and had them doing the search for him." He paused for a moment to collect his thoughts, and then continued.

"I love my grandson but this business has left me a broken-hearted old man. I know now that there isn't anything I can do or say that will change him," he said with remorse then continued. "For two days, he kept at me for the journals more so than the money. I refused hoping he would realize his folly but he never relented. Finally I was too exhausted to continue with him and started to leave. This infuriated him and he pushed me back into the room. I collapsed from the fatigue of his badgering and bullying. He showed a glimmer of remorse and had his friend put me in the car and take me back to the home.

"I was in my room trying to rest when he called, not to apologize, but to continue on about the journals. It infuriated me to no end. I hung up the phone and then my chest started hurting, I couldn't catch my breath. I was sure it was the end just before I passed out."

He was done talking as his shoulders fell and his face showed remorse over this whole sorted affair.

"Are you all right, Mr. Hyde? Should I call the nurse?"

"No, I'm fine, just feel'n a little down."

"Thank you for your help, Mr. Hyde," I said as I started for the door.

"Mr. Falco, please find my grandson before he harms anyone else," Hyde spoke in a tone that said he knew what I really wanted, and it was time to end it.

I looked at my watch; I was with Hyde for almost an hour. I stopped at the nurses' station on the way back to the cafeteria.

"Beth, you don't mind if I call you Beth, do you? I'm Falco, and I heard you talking with Conrad." Her face showed signs of fear, as if I was going to tell on her. "Don't worry, I'm not going to say anything." A look of relief came over her.

"What do you want?"

"You already know that there is a warrant out for Conrad Johnston's arrest. If you meet with him you will be guilty of aiding in his flight from justice and may be looking at time in prison, especially if he is found guilty of murder."

"What can I do? I didn't do anything wrong. I just know him, that's all," she said nervously.

"I can't tell you what to do, but I can tell you what you should do, and that is tell the police of your conversation with Conrad and the fact that he wants to see you. That would get you off the hook and maybe even save your marriage," I said after seeing her ring.

"My husband hates Conrad. If he finds out I've been talk'n to him, Lord knows what he'll do," her voice breaking as tears began to well in her eyes.

"Conrad called you, you told the police. What could he think except that you loved him enough to give up Conrad to the police. Right?"

"Yeah, I guess you're right. Thank you, Mr. Falco."

I passed by two uniformed officers on the way back to the cafeteria. They took no notice of me, and I didn't do anything to give them reason to.

In the cafeteria, Sam and Bill were still sitting where I had left them. As I got close, Sam looked up and if looks could kill I would be dust.

Bill just looked up and said, "Vince, sorry but your coffee is cold. Where'd you park, China?"

"Sorry it took so long but I had a flat on the rental and called to have it fixed. It's okay now," I lied, giving Sam a little smile and a wink hoping to smooth things over.

"It's good your car's okay, but I have to see to my men. I just sent them up to the room to watch Hyde," he said as he started to get up.

From behind me I could hear Bill being summoned by one of the officers. "Bill, this nurse has something to say about Johnston."

I turned to see if my fears were true and sure enough standing next to the officer was Beth. She looked at me as if to ask if I turned her in. I walked over to her quickly and introduced myself. "I'm Vince Falco, you look very familiar. Have we met before?" I asked in a way to let her know I didn't reveal our secret.

"I don't believe we have, Mr. Falco," she replied with relief in her voice.

Sam was watching me, wondering what was going on but not saying anything. Bill got up, elbowed me a little as he walked by, and put his arm around the nurse.

"Beth, what do you know about Conrad?" he said as they started down the hall.

Sam didn't say anything as we left the hospital. She just grabbed my arm as we walked out to the car.

On the way back to the motel, Sam asked, "What was that business with the nurse? And did you see Mr. Hyde?"

"She was talking to Conrad on the phone. I merely suggested that she tell the police before she got into real trouble, that's all."

"She looked familiar but I can't place the name," Sam added.

"Beth Franklin is her married name. She definitely knows Conrad. She was making plans to see him. Perhaps you knew her before she was married," I offered.

"Perhaps, but I need the name. Maybe you could get it from Bill?" she asked. "Now, what did Hyde say?" she continued.

"I recorded our conversation," I said, smiling as I took out the recorder and handed it to her.

She leaned back in the seat, looked over to me as if to ask what else I've recorded without anyone knowing. Finally, she turned on the recorder and sat in amazement as the story was told.

Watching her sit in awe of the tale made me think that this must have been how the days before television were when people sat in front of their radios listening to the stories of the times.

Finally we reached the motel. Sam was still enthralled by the narrative of Jonah Hyde.

"Look, why don't you take it with you and finish listening to it in your room. I've got to make a couple of calls and afterward, we can get together for lunch before we head out to see Jenny's friend." I went back to my room and placed a call to Mike.

"Cavenaugh, can I help you?"

"As a matter of fact, you can," I replied.

"Vince, where are you?" he asked.

"Still in the sunny south. How's the weather your way?" I asked more for conversation than caring.

"I'm sure you didn't call for the weather report, so what's up?"

I gave him a quick rundown of events and brought up Conrad Johnston.

"Why didn't you tell me about him before? Get me a description and I'll run some checks," Mike said half scolding me for withholding information.

"You could probably pull it up from the files. It was put out about two or three years ago by the local police. He's got to be the invisible man. Every time he shows up, I get a headache but never see him. Anyway, I called to see what you had on the case, if anything, it might help me here."

"Nothing out of the ordinary—some hairs, fibers from an expensive suit, and traces of blood from the vestibule," Mike said disappointedly.

"Maybe you can place this Conrad at the scene. I have this gut feeling from everything that has happened to me that he did it or was there when it was done. He has this two-ton friend that seems to do his bidding. All you have to do is prove it." I could see Mike rolling his eyes as I left it in his court.

"Vince, you better be careful. It sounds like you have him nervous and you know what that can get you."

"Yes, Mother, I'll be very careful," I said as I hung up.

There was a knock on the door. I answered it, and standing in front of me was lunch. She stood there poised, wearing a knit tunic with deep V neckline, revealing the natural curvature of her unharnessed breasts and a broomstick skirt that barely made midcalf. Sam just smiled as she watched me follow the curves of her body with my eyes.

"What do you want to do now . . . Falco?" Sam said in a husky voice as she handed me the tape recorder.

I reached out and grabbed her, pulling her inside the room as I closed the door.

CHAPTER 31

The phone rang causing me to stir from a deserved sleep. I reached over the fair maiden lying next to me to answer it.

"Hello," I said with a yawn.

"Mr. Falco, Dr. Reinhardt here. I was wondering when you might be ready to go, and I haven't been able to locate Ms. Richards."

"Yeah, Doc . . . Sorry, I forgot all about it. If it's not too late can we leave about six? And, Doc, don't worry I'll find Sam," I said as my eyes followed the contours of her body barely hidden by the sheet clinging to her.

There was a pause. "Jenny said it would probably be all right but she would like to call to confirm it."

"Okay, let me know, meanwhile I'll get ready as if it were. And, Doc, I think you're ready to call me Falco, the mister is dead many years now," I said jovially as I hung up.

I rolled over, stared at the ceiling for a second then reached back for Sam. She was warm and soft just lying there, wanting to know what was going on.

"What?" I said as she stared at me with a smile in her eye and a whisper on her lip.

"Well . . . are we or aren't we going to get up?" she asked devilishly.

I pondered the thought of staying in bed the rest of the day but knew we had to go. "I think a shower is in order, and then a trip to the country," I said as I showed my true feelings by making a frown and sighing deeply.

"Well, at least we can frolic in the shower, big boy."

After some serious showering, the phone rang again. "Hello, your thirty-five cents."

"Mister . . . ah . . . Vince," the doc said as he caught himself, "six o'clock will be fine. In fact, we have been invited to dinner with Mrs. Weaver and her family. I took the liberty of accepting. I do hope it is all right with you?"

"Fine, Doc, we'll meet you in the lounge in ten minutes."

"We're having dinner at the Weaver place. It will be one of those 'Who Done It' dinners," I thought out loud.

Sam looked at me and said, "I think this whole affair is fascinating. I would never have thought something like this really happens outside of paperback novels."

"Yeah, my life, one big paperback story . . . with an eerie house on the hill, lifeless trees in the background, and shimmering specters reaching out to pull me to them," I said hauntingly with my eyes opened wide and gesturing with my hands, fingers waving as if playing a piano in the air.

Sam rolled her head back, laughed and said, "Let's go, Poe."

In the lounge, wearing his usual three-piece suit was the Doc. Jenny, adorned in a fresh country look of a front button, balmy floral print challis with an exquisite feminine fit as the dress reached her ankles and the buttons undone from the bottom to mid thigh displaying smooth, shapely legs that attract the looks of men and women alike. I couldn't help but wonder if the doc was going to become a country boy, or if he could get Jenny to become city folk.

Sam looked at my admiring eye on Jenny and politely put her arm in mine and said, "Are we all ready?" It was short and sweet, and made the point. Jenny looked over to Sam in that know-all girlish way and smiled. They seem to delight in nonverbal communication.

"Anytime, y'all," Jenny said.

The doc took the lead and we went to the car. I handed the keys to Jenny since she knew the way.

We arrived at the Weavers' place in twenty minutes—back roads all the way. At the door was a slender, well-shaped woman that could have been a model. She stood at least five foot seven, had a very attractive smile that was pleasing to look at, and hair that reached her shoulders, divided midpoint on her head and curly from that point down. She was attired in a similar dress as Jenny but hers was with a more tropical print and color. Behind her was a big man pushing six foot something, wearing a beige double-breasted suit, with a thin double-striped white shirt with banded collar, the jacket straining from the bulk it held confined. It brought vision of that green hulk you see in the comics, only dressed for a date.

He was quick to greet us as he stepped down from the porch and extended his hand. "I'm Sylvester Weaver, this is my wife Ashta, pleased to meet ya," he said with a big grin.

As my hand was going numb from his grip, I thought perhaps he would be a good match for Mike.

Jenny spoke up, "I'm sorry, this is Samantha, Vince, and Dr. Reinhardt. Everybody this is Ashta and Sly. Everyone calls him Sly."

"Y'all come on inside, supper is ready. I'm pleased to meet y'all," Ashta said as we headed inside.

The house was built in the 1800s; it was white with double galleries standing in the shadow of sycamores that had to be older than the "Nina, the Pinta" and the "Santa Maria." The steps led up to the center of the porch to the entrance of the house. The massive door was adorned with a brass door knocker that had to be as old as the house itself. The inside was preserved in near original styling. The entrance hall ran the length of the house with pilaster and pediment doorway casings that reached to the ceiling, giving the doorway a squeezed in look. Heavy walnut trim set around where the walls met at the ceiling and floor. Rosette patterns were in the center of the ceiling where candelabra-type light fixtures hung. The fireplace set into the wall was accentuated by the hand-carved mantle and sideboard trim, inlaid with brass patterned climbing vines. The dining room had a more subdued tone as the trim was lighter in color and simpler in design but showed of elegance for the time.

"You have a very lovely house, Ashta," Sam said as she took in the sights.

"Thank you. Sly and I have tried to restore it to its original appearance. Lord knows I've had the time be'n here all day every day, what with watching mama and all," she said half proud and sad at the same time.

"Now y'all sit down and I'll get to serv'n."

"I'll give you a hand, Ashta," Jenny said as she headed for the kitchen.

"Now, you just sit," Ashta said, only to have it fall on deaf ears as Jenny and Sam both went to help.

Sly looked over to the doctor and me and said, "Would you like a drink? I have just about everything."

"Perhaps a glass of wine," the doctor replied.

"Nothing for me, thanks. You certainly have done a fine job with the house. Was it very difficult to find matching wood patterns?" I asked more to keep the party alive until dinner than to really know.

"I was fortunate enough to have most of the wood in good condition only needing to be stripped and refinished. I did have to have some made but it wasn't as hard as you might think. In this area, we have many restoration businesses because of all the homes that date back to the late 1600s. In fact, my business is in the restoration of fireplaces, chimneys, and such," Sly replied.

The girls were jabbering as they came through the doorway, carrying trays with what appeared to be a feast. There was turkey with the fixings, mashed potatoes, gravy, and salad. I thought maybe we skipped Halloween and went right to Thanksgiving.

"Now everybody find a seat, and Sly will give the blessing and then everybody eat," Ashta announced.

Dinner was great, with light conversation covering the weather, Sly's business, the house restoration, and Ashta's mother. Everyone seemed happy and stuffed.

When coffee was served with a buffet of deserts, and everyone was comfortable at the table, I asked, "Ashta, Jenny said you could tell us about the Barrette place and family. We've heard different stories about the family and have seen some strange sights at the plantation. I was hoping you could shed some light on the truth for us."

"Well, my great-great-great-grandparents were slaves on the Barrette plantation. Their names were Rainy Daye and James." She stopped for a moment, and gave a shy smile as she continued. "She was born at the end of the day, and it had been raining all day long, that's how she got her name.

"Anyway, they were lucky in the sense that the Barrettes didn't want uneducated workers in the house, so they were taught to read, write, and do arithmetic. They learned well and taught many of the others on the plantation to do the same.

"They were dressed properly and treated well for house servants. This tradition of educating the house help went back to the first Barrette. It was said that the Barrettes treated their slaves more like common folks than slaves because of their pirating background, it being known that Caesar, a black man, was a member of Blackbeard's crew and was liked and trusted by Blackbeard. He was hanged shortly after Blackbeard was killed at Ocracoke Inlet.

"But it was expected of them to do as told. It was said that if the selected slave refused to learn, they were killed in front of the other slaves and their peers were made to bury them.

"Now you have to understand that this story has been passed down for generations by mouth. My grandmother said that Grandmother Rainy kept a diary but no one has seen it.

"Grandmother Rainy was born a few days before Elizabeth was. She and Elizabeth where suckled together and grew to be very close. When Elizabeth was sent away to school she would write Grandmother Rainy of her doings and after her return, she taught her the essentials of being a lady.

"It was said that Grandmother Rainy was ready to marry James, but she wanted to wait for Elizabeth to marry before she did. Elizabeth didn't want her to wait, but she wouldn't hear of it any other way.

"Finally, Elizabeth was engaged to be married, and plans were made for a simple ceremony to be done for Rainy and James after Elizabeth's. Everyone was happy. That's when misfortune occurred. The man Elizabeth was to marry took ill and died a few days later. Everything stopped at that point."

She hesitated for a moment and asked, "More coffee? There's plenty of pie, you have to try my pecan pie."

"Yes, Ashta makes the best in the county," Sly blurted out.

Coffee went around and we all had a piece of the pecan pie. Sly was right; it was delicious.

"What happened after the wedding stopped?" I asked to get back to the story.

"Well, Elizabeth withdrew from everything, but kept close to Grandmother Rainy. It was said that her father didn't like her being with the Negroes so much and ordered Grandmother Rainy out of the house and into the fields. Elizabeth wouldn't have it, and she and her mother made him bring her back to the house.

"Elizabeth finally started seeing other folks to keep peace in the house. After all, a woman at eighteen that wasn't married was considered an old maid and must have something wrong with her. Not to mention what the plantation workers were thinking and saying about Grandmother Rainy and Grandfather James.

"Elizabeth knew what she had to do, and soon she had a beau. He was the delight of the family, not to mention James and Rainy, but fate wasn't on Elizabeth's side, and just days before the wedding he died.

"It was said that Elizabeth bore the curse of those done wrong by her forefathers. The poor soul withdrew to her room and wouldn't even let the light shine through the window.

"After a few years, Grandmother Rainy and Grandfather James were married. It was a good thing 'cause Elizabeth started to come out and talk to others on the plantation staying mostly with Grandmother Rainy and her people. Edward didn't seem to mind as long as she was com'n round. He must have felt that once she got over being by herself, she would start seeing others of her own kind.

"Now Grandmother Rainy was pregnant, and Elizabeth's feelings seemed to change toward her. It was thought she was hurt because she was alone and didn't have a man of her own, and at twenty-six it wasn't likely that she would have a husband none too soon. Most eligible men were as old if not older than her father, widowers mostly. But as time went on, Elizabeth was drawn back to Grandmother Rainy, and they remained close right up to the end. Poor Elizabeth was found dead in the graveyard, said to have committed suicide by cutting her wrists, but my grandmother said her grandmother told her that Elizabeth was murdered."

Ashta stopped as if it where one of those late evening radio programs that re-run the old radio mysteries. I just sat there waiting for the sound of a rusty gate to close or a door with bad hinges to squeak. At this point we all got up and headed for the living room.

Sly broke out a bottle of wine and passed glasses around the room. We were all going to drink, like it or not, I thought. I sat back, Sam situated against my side on the sofa; the doctor and Jenny sitting on the love seat by the fireplace; Ashta and Sly occupying the wing chairs, closing the circle in the parlor.

I opened the conversation, "I was told that there was a disturbance in Elizabeth's room and the doctor was thrown off the property. What do you know of that?"

"Oh my, yes . . . it seemed that the doctor came to Elizabeth's room one evening and made advances toward her, but she fended him off, and by knocking him to the floor was able to summon her father, who it was said threw the doctor out of the house and had him whipped all the way down the drive until he was off the property.

"It seems that he kept coming around, he was seen many times in the graveyard. Finally Edward had him run out of town."

As she hesitated, I asked, "Jenny said that you keep up the grave of Elizabeth. Why do you do that?"

"It was passed down that Grandmother Rainy would stay by the grave and pull weeds, plant flowers, and just talk to Elizabeth 'bout anything and everything. She would have her baby by her side, and as the baby grew, she was then the caretaker of the grave site. It has been passed down as tradition. My grandmother thinks it has to do with James being killed not too long after Elizabeth, and his body being buried God only knows where. In fact, Grandmother Rainy is buried somewhere on the plantation, but we haven't been able to find the location. Story has it that all the slaves were buried in the same place, but none of their descendants have been able to locate the site." Her tone was saddened by this fact.

"How did James die?"

"It's not known for sure if he was killed. Some talk was that he ran off, but Grandmother Rainy knew better. She said he was taken from the stables one night by two burly men known to have worked for Hyde, and never returned."

"She had asked Edward if he knew what had happened to her James, but to no avail. Hyde had left the area fearing for his life after Edward threatened him, so she wasn't able to ask him either. Many a night she spent looking over the plantation for signs of a grave, but never found any. So the story goes."

"What can you tell me about the alleged treasure?"

"I doubt that there is any such thing up there. People have been digging ever since the last Barrette was buried there. When I was a child, I used to go up there and look for it myself. I used to dig all over the place hoping to find the graves of the slaves and my ancestors, just to surprise my grandmother. But I never found them or anything that would even resemble treasure," she said with a smile on her face.

"What about Conrad Johnston?"

Her face became stern, her eyes closed for a second before she spoke. "Now that is one man I wouldn't mind whipping the horse out from under myself," she said with emphasis on "whipping the horse" and in a tone used by the best TV preachers you've ever heard.

"He is the meanest man I have ever known. He would pay the other children to beat us black folks for being on the Barrette property, but if he needed something and didn't want to do it himself, he would be as nice as pie, and you would do it for him. Heaven knows what he was always doing at the house. Every time I was in the graveyard doing my chores, he would be up the house. Lord knows how that house still stands after all that's been done to it."

"I've been told that Elizabeth was pregnant when she died. Do you know anything about that?" I said as I watched Ashta's brow furrowed in wonderment.

"Why I never did hear anything of the sort. Who would say a thing like that?" she asked.

"I was also told that Elizabeth was quite forward with Dr. Hyde, and wanted him to abort her. It was also said that he caught Elizabeth and one of the help in a compromising position the night she had him thrown out."

"You mean James, don't you?"

I watched the expression on Ashta's face change to one of disbelief that anyone would even think such a thing about her ancestor. Sly reached over and took her hand.

"Vince I'm sure would like to know who told you all these slanderous things," Sly said.

"I'm not saying any of it is true, but I've heard different renditions of the same story since I've been here.

"Ashta, maybe I can shed some light on the missing graves."

Ashta bolted upright, and asked, "What do you mean?"

"Have you ever been in the crypt on the plantation?" I asked.

"I've never seen a crypt anywhere on the property. I don't know what you're talking about," she related earnestly.

"There is a vault under the cross. From there, heading toward the house, are the catacombs. We found them the other night. There are graves, more like ledges, that line the walls along the passage. The skeletons we saw were of Negro descent."

"Can you take us there? I would like to see them. Lord, this may be where they are buried. Please, will you take us?" she begged as she stood up.

Sam and Jenny went to her side as she stood trembling with tears in her eyes. Sam looked at me and turned back to Ashta and said, "Yes, we will." So it was settled. Sly stood there lost, not knowing which way to turn.

We stepped outside to the darkness. No streetlights to light the path, just an old gas lamp at the foot of the porch that waited for the "Old lamplighter of years ago." The night held a chill from the breeze coming across the Sound road not far behind the house.

I went to the trunk of the car where I had put the package that was delivered to me at the motel and took out my trusty army issue Colt .45. Sam came around the back of the car as I inserted the clip.

"What's that?" she asked more out of surprise than ignorance.

"It's a forty-five caliber Colt, Model 1911A1 semi-automatic pistol. I had it delivered to the motel. I thought it might ward off evil spirits," I said as Sam just stood staring in disbelief.

Willy, Jenny, and Sly got in the back, while Ashta and Sam got in the front. Sly had one of those battery-operated spotlights with him, knowing how dark it could be on the plantation. With everyone ready, we were off to see the . . . anyway, we were off.

CHAPTER 32

As we pulled up the drive to the Barrette house, Ashta pointed to a road off to the right of a large sycamore tree that led straight to the cemetery. It was overgrown with weeds but still had the outline of a once heavily used path.

On the way over, everything seemed calm, no lights at the house, no flashing lights at the cemetery, and no rain, thunder, or lightning. The sky was clear with thousands of stars twinkling, and the moon shone brightly, emphasizing the eeriness of the graveyard as we approached.

We all got out of the car. Sly lit the way with his "search light"; I was sure it could be seen for miles. The whole area lit up chasing the darkness to tomorrow. With the sun being held by Sly, we headed to the cross monument.

When we arrived at the cross, I said, "This is where we came out. Someplace around here is a way to open the door to the crypt." I started feeling around the edges of the slab affixed to the cross.

Sam tripped over a small pillar, set a few inches from the base of the bottom-most slab of the monument and fell into the cross, striking a small indented shield symbol on the stone. The stone door opened slightly. The look on Ashta's and Sly's face was one of astonishment. I wondered how many times she must have come up here and never even thought this was possible.

Sly was anxious to get inside as he pulled the door open and started to step inside when I grabbed his arm and told him to take a good look at the steep stairway before leaping. He shone the light into the opening and stepped inside.

Ashta hurried behind him followed by the rest of the procession. I pulled up behind with my gun ready in the belt of my trousers.

We assembled in the main chamber and lit the lanterns, watching the room light up from the mirrored shields placed for best effect by the lighting master of yore.

Ashta asked, "Where are the graves?"

I pointed to the opening and directed her to the stairs. "Be careful, you start going down from there. I think you better let me lead." I took the lead and Sly was behind me with the floodlight.

As we approached the catacombs, Ashta was trembling more out of anticipation than fright. Sly put his arm around her as they approached the ledges and started looking at the remains that lay on the ledges.

"Look! Sly, there are names under their heads," she said excitedly. She was able to see the name because the skull had become dislodged from the neck and was off to one side.

Sly and Willy started to move the skulls carefully and read the names. They had gone through five or six when Ashta yelled out with excitement.

"Over here, over here, come quick! I found James!" she shrieked, her voice near breaking with excitement.

James was laid to rest in a black riding coat, white ruffled shirt, with a preacher's bow tie, black trousers, and black riding boots. This wasn't the normal dress of a slave during that time. Edward Barrette made good on his promise to give James a proper burial. The head was disjointed from the body and lay slightly to the right of where it belonged exposing a stone pillow wedge shaped with an inscription chiseled in it.

JAMES
SLAVE OF BARRETTE FAMILY
HUSBAND OF RAINY
FATHER-TO-BE
BORN 1799 DIED 1826

The doctor reached Ashta first; he started looking over the body and did a preliminary examination on the remains. As he leaned over the remains, he started talking to himself but everyone was watching and listening. "There is a hole in the head that indicates a possible entry by a . . . yes here it is . . . a small musket ball. Yes, he was definitely shot in the head, and by the fracture marks here on the skull, it indicates that it was done at close range. Obviously a small caliber as not to exit the skull."

The doctor just kept talking not paying attention to us standing there while he probed and twisted and turned different parts of the body without disturbing it too much. He finally turned and saw us standing and watching.

"Oh! forgive me I got caught up in the examination. I have always been fascinated by forensics and I—"

He was interrupted by Jenny. "That's okay, sugar, we understand. Now can we move on? This place is a little creepy."

"Jenny, just a little longer. I know Grandmother Rainy is here somewhere."

"Sure 'nuff, Ashta, I didn't mean any disrespect," Jenny said sincerely.

Ashta put her arms around Sly and lay her head on his chest not saying a word.

As she recovered from her emotional state she wiped her eyes and started toward the shelves to see if she could find her long, lost grandmother. Sam walked over to her and took her arm as they walked to another ledge.

It wasn't long before a cry filled the catacomb. "I found her, I found her," Ashta called out with words being choked by tears and heavy sighs.

We all gathered and looked at the remains that lay undisturbed for almost two hundred years. Ashta held onto Sly; she didn't say anything, just stood there looking with a loving smile across her face as tears ran down her cheeks.

The doctor was looking over the figure lying on the ledge adorned in what had once been a white-laced gown ornate with colored buttons and embroidered patterns across the bodice and down the center of the gown to the midsection where it was met by a silken rope belt with the ends running down to the hem that lay at the top of the instep, covering the laces of what had been white, high-top shoes.

Around the head was a silken scarf that had been tied to support the face muscles from falling, as was the practice in those days.

"Look here," the doctor said, more to himself than for us. "There's a book of sorts under her right shoulder." He reached over and removed it carefully so as not to disturb the skeletal structure. The book was leather bound and ragtagged from the passage of time.

"Give it to me," Ashta said as she reached out to the doctor. She took it into her hands assiduously, as if it would crumble to dust if moved too quickly.

"This is her diary. They buried her with her diary. Oh . . . Mr. Falco, thank you, thank you," she kept repeating as she put her arms around me and kissed my cheek.

"It's okay. I'm glad to have helped," I said as Sly came and removed her from me. He just smiled, tears in his eyes, as he nodded his head as a thank you gesture.

"I think we should go now," I said as I directed everyone to the exit.

I led the way with the doctor taking up the rear carrying the floodlight, my pistol drawn anticipating someone or something waiting as we left the crypt. I stepped outside, one hand embracing the Colt the other ready to parry a blow as I looked around the graveyard. Everything seemed okay as we stepped clear of the tomb.

After we closed up the crypt we headed back to the car. In the car I stated, "Ashta, in fact everyone, I think it is important that we keep this little trip and the diary to ourselves until this whole affair is settled. Ashta, you do understand that this diary may or may not contain information that would dispel the credibility of the Barrette reputation as well as provide information on the alleged treasure and its location?

"It's possible that you would be in danger if someone thought having it would help their cause. They may even kill for it," I said as a warning.

"Vince, you're not telling us all of what's going on. I think under the circumstances, you owe it to tell us if we're in danger," Sly requested.

"I can't really tell you much, but there appears to be at least three deaths in the last two or three years, and one attempted kidnapping, and they all have something to do with the Barrette plantation, buried treasure, and . . . Conrad Johnston." I hesitated to let it sink in. There was an eerie calm in the car as silence engulfed the mood. It remained all the way back to the Weavers.

When we arrived, Sly and Ashta got out, everyone bid their goodbyes. Ashta stood holding the diary cradled in her arms against her chest.

"Ashta, I would appreciate any information you may find that would be helpful, but please remember what I said about the danger surrounding that diary. I'll let you know when it's safe, okay?"

"I'll keep it quiet until I hear from you, but it won't be easy. There are others living around here who had family that worked the Barrette plantation and don't know the whereabouts of their ancestors." She looked to Sly. "There's the Wilsons, and Ricers down the road, not to mention the Watts," she said with a slight tremble in her voice.

We remained silent on the way back to the motel—Sam holding my arm and staring out the window not really seeing anything, Jenny doing the same in the back seat with Willy, sitting there detached from the real world.

CHAPTER 33

It was early morning as I sat in the restaurant having coffee and watching two birds battle over territorial rights of a bird feeder hanging from a tree near the road. I didn't bother Sam or the doc when I got up; it was late when we got back to the motel so I let them sleep. As I lifted my cup, I heard a familiar voice getting louder as it came closer.

"Good morning, Vince. I declare it's a beautiful day to be alive," the voice was almost singing as she sat down.

"Jenny, what a surprise this early in the morning," I said tipping my cup to her. "Let me get you some coffee, or something."

"Thanks, Vince, by the way Wilhelm is coming down so we might as well order one for him."

"So what brings you here so early after such a late night?"

"Why, Mr. Falco, I stayed the night with Wilhelm," she said as she cocked her head, and blinked her eyes in a shy, didn't-you-know expression.

Well, I thought, I was right. The doc's got himself a Southern belle.

Willy walked in with Sam at his side as the coffee arrived. He had lost his three-piece suit and was wearing casuals. They looked new, but where could he have bought them this early, I wondered.

"Now don't you feel more relaxed in this outfit?" Jenny asked as he approached the table.

"I . . . I think I do," Willy replied with some hesitation to determine if he did or not. "Yes, I do!" he exclaimed, and then continued, "I wouldn't have dared to be out in public like this. My family was rather, well . . . stuff shirt, if you know what I mean."

I held back saying anything out loud, but I certainly knew what he meant about being a "stuff shirt." Sam just looked at me waiting for a quick, smart remark, but none came as I just smiled and winked at her.

"Good morning, sunshine," I said as Sam sat down. "Would you like coffee or breakfast?"

"Just coffee, thanks," she said to the waitress as she was putting cups on the table, and pouring coffee from the pot she brought with her.

"I declare I had a wonderful time last night. Never thought I could be at that graveyard. It was sort of, well . . . scary, like the haunted houses at the carnival. Didn't you think so, Samantha?" Jenny asked.

"It certainly had an eerie aspect to it. I nearly left my skin when Ashta let out that scream. However, I have to admit that when I first saw those remains earlier, I nearly died. They just appeared out of nowhere," Sam went on.

"I bet Ashta could write a bestseller from what she already knows and what's in that diary. We should call her and see if she found out anything new," Jenny said.

"Well, why don't we all go on to Ashta's place and see what she has learned?" asked Jenny.

"Yes, let's do that," commented Sam.

"I guess the yeas have it." I looked over to the doctor and waited for his comment.

He stammered a little before Jenny spoke up. "You look great in those clothes, so don't get all fretted over noth'n."

I paid the tab and we headed out. Just before I reached the door, there was a page for me. I went back to the counter. "Mr. Falco?" the waitress asked.

"Yes," I answered as she handed me the phone.

"Hello, Falco here," I said on to the receiver.

"Vince, this is Ashta. I tried your room first, I'm glad I caught you. Could you come over here? I think I may have found something in the diary that you would find interesting."

"We were just leaving as you called. We'll be there in about twenty minutes, okay?" I hung up and went to the car.

When we pulled up to the house, Sly came out to the car in his best bib overalls, wearing a shirt that was given to him by that green monster of the comic book sect. He was about ready to bust out of it.

"Glad y'all could come," he said cheerfully. "Ashta was up all night reading that book and every so often waking me to hear parts of it. It sure gives you a different look at those times."

We entered the house to smells of bacon, biscuits, and freshly brewed coffee. It brought back memories of my childhood.

"Come in, come in," Ashta said repeating herself. She directed us to a breakfast nook off the kitchen just inside the sunroom.

"Please sit down. I'll get some coffee for y'all, and please help yourself," she said, pointing to the food.

She had a breakfast spread set up on the table that made your mouth water. There were eggs, bacon, sausage, biscuits, gravy, and some funny-looking white gruel, almost looked like fish eggs. I helped myself to everything but the gruel. The others followed behind. Sly just stood there with a big grin on his face, and said, "You don't much care for the grits, Vince?"

"That's what that is? I never saw any before, but I've heard of it. I don't think I'm ready to try any yet though," I remarked as I took a seat.

We were all seated when Ashta sat down with the diary in front of her. She looked around the table and finally said, "I read this last night and it certainly fills in some of the blanks. I tried reading it to my momma. She seemed to understand most of it, more so than she understands what's go'n on now."

"You were almost right, Vince, about James and Elizabeth. He was in her room that night but it wasn't for the reason you stated. It seems that he overheard the doctor talking to one of the other boys about 'sacking' Miss Elizabeth and taking her away. It seems Elizabeth rejected the doctor for many years. He had once asked Edward for her hand, and was nearly granted the request, but Elizabeth knew how to handle her daddy, and he rejected Dr. Hyde's request.

"Grandmother Rainy went on to say how infuriated he was, and that he would tell the townsfolk that you couldn't trust the Barettes' word. But he made a formal apology so as he could stay on the good side of Edward.

"It seems this Dr. Hyde was into voodoo medicine. He made his own potions. Grandmother Rainy thought that he caused the illnesses of the two suitors of Elizabeth. She mentioned that the doctor had spent many years in the West Indies when he was a ship surgeon and learned the ways of black magic. He would burn colored candles, incense, and was heard chanting late at night." Ashta stopped and opened the diary to a marked page.

"It was true to a point that Miss Elizabeth was with child as you heard. It seemed that the doctor had his way with Elizabeth while she was in his care. When she had realized what had happened, she asked Grandmother Rainy what to do. She told Elizabeth to tell her father, but Miss Elizabeth went to Hyde first, and told him she was going to tell her father and have him whipped till his flesh fell off. This made the doctor furious, and he attacked Elizabeth in the graveyard. Grandfather James saw what was happening and ran to help her. He picked up the doctor and threw him to the ground. He had caused serious injury to the doctor, leaving him there to tend to his wounds. He then took Elizabeth to her room."

"Later that night is when Grandmother Rainy overheard Hyde arrange to have Elizabeth kidnapped. She told James and that is why he was at the house when Hyde went to Elizabeth's room. What he didn't know was that Hyde had his friends tell Edward that they saw Elizabeth and James together, in the biblical sense." She dropped her gaze as she continued.

"Edward was out looking for James when the trouble started in the house with Hyde. James overheard Hyde telling Elizabeth what he had done, and that he was the only one who could fix it, so if she didn't want James to be killed, then she had better go with him. She wouldn't have anything to do with him and was sure that her daddy would believe her. That's when Hyde tried to force her out the window, but James came busting in and knocked him down.

"Edward had returned and came running to the room in time to see James going out the window and Hyde lying on the floor. He whipped Hyde out of the room to the waiting arms of his servants in the hall, and had him beat down the road until he was off the property. Edward was furious, and wouldn't listen to a word Elizabeth had to say."

"James had returned to Grandmother Rainy and told her everything that had happened, and they both agreed that he had to run away until everything was made better.

"It was a few days later when one of the plantation boys came to Grandmother Rainy and said sorrowfully that he had found James lying by the Sound road and was very sorry to have to tell her of her grief.

"It appeared that James had been cut all over and shot in the head as well.

"Grandmother Rainy was beside herself, but she was a strong woman and had the boys bring back her James for a proper burial. She went on to say how she blamed Mr. Edward for killing her man and did confront him for the crime. Mr. Edward was choked up with grief and told her that he was upset enough to kill James but after listening to his daughter's story of the deception of Mr. Hyde, he repented and was going to tell James as soon as he saw him." Grandmother Rainy felt he was telling the truth, and they both set out to give James the proper Christian burial he deserved.

"A few days later, Elizabeth was found dead in the graveyard from wounds in her wrists. It was said that her father wept every day for doubting her, and that on his deathbed he asked Elizabeth to forgive him, staring at the wall as though someone was there.

"It also seems that there was a treasure of sorts because while Edward was alive they never wanted for anything, but after his death, Emily, Elizabeth's mother, couldn't keep the plantation running and had to sell off everything. She died before she had to sell the plantation. Grandmother Rainy saw that she had a proper burial.

"Most of the servants stayed on the plantation and farmed to stay alive. Little by little, they left to go their separate ways. It seems that none of the folks in the area took in any of the Barrette slaves but left them to fend on their own. I guess I have to rely on the stories from there because, as you saw, the diary was buried with Grandmother Rainy. If anyone else kept one after she died, maybe we could learn more. But I don't know of anyone who has one in these parts.

"I can't understand why they all forgot where she was laid to rest." Ashta closed the diary, and looked out to the distance.

I didn't have anything to say. It seemed that the diary was the best source of information. I thought for a minute, then said, "Ashta, I would bet that you could write about your ancestors and their relations with the Barrette family based on that diary. In fact, I would bet that the Historical Society trying to get the Barrette place, would help you get it published. After all it would help their cause as well."

"I would have to think 'bout that for a while, Vince. I would have to think 'bout that," she repeated as her voice trailed off.

CHAPTER 34

The doctor and Jenny went off to see the sights. Sam and I were back at the motel just watching the leaves turn colors. I didn't have anything to say, just needed some time to put the pieces together. Sam on the other hand needed to be busy. She had to have something to do or say, didn't just want to sit and stare.

Finally the silence was broken, it took almost twenty seconds, as Sam said, "Vince, let's go in town and take in the sights."

Where is Willy when you need him, I thought to myself, as the waitress approached the table and said I had a call. Sam looked at me like I planned it. I just shrugged my shoulders and went to the phone.

"Falco," I said.

"I know you have what I've been looking for, Mr. Falco. If you value your friends, I suggest you give me the information and take your friends back to your world and leave mine alone."

"Is this Conrad, the elusive cowardly woman killer, or his bestest buddy Smitty?" I said in my best sarcastic voice.

"I wouldn't be funny if I were in your shoes, Mr. Falco. You see, I know where you are, and you still have to find me. I expect the location of the treasure written down and left with the clerk at the front desk. I expect it there within the hour." Then he hung up.

This Conrad was a cool cookie. He kept an even tone on the phone, didn't give in to the digs, and honestly believes I have all the answers for him. Boy, is he in for a real surprise.

As I approached the table, Sam got up and came toward me. She had a way to make a man think of only one thing whenever she moved, and she knew it.

"Vince, you have that look in your eye," she said with a seductive and devilish smile.

"You sure look good right now, but I think we better leave for now," I said as I dropped a five on the table and headed toward the car.

"What's the matter, Vince? Who was on the phone?" she asked.

"That was our infamous Conrad Johnston on the phone. He thinks I know where his lost treasure is and wants me to leave the info with the clerk by high noon or he's com'in a gunn'in fer me partner." I could see she was worried now that the snake has raised its ugly head and the hissing has begun.

"What are we going to do now?"

"First, 'we' aren't going to do anything. I'm going to give Conrad a note just as he asked. You are going to find the doc and get out of town. I'll call you in a couple of hours, so make sure you have your phone on."

"Vince, you can't do this alone. Remember what happened the last time."

"I'm not going to be alone. As soon as I know you and the doc are gone, I'm going to get Bill and stake out the motel. I'll be all right."

She had a look that said she didn't believe me but knew it was best to let me do my thing. She hesitated but then took out her phone and called the good doctor. After she explained everything to him, we sat down as I composed my "Dear Conrad" letter.

It didn't take long for the doc to return, still hanging on to Jenny. I felt sorry for him thinking of how he fell for the wilds of this southern vixen and wondering what he was going to do after this was all over.

"Samantha, are you all right?" he asked in his best Austrian accent.

"Samantha, I think it would be best if we went—" Jenny started saying as I interrupted her.

"Sorry to interrupt, however, I don't know how Conrad is keeping tabs on us and just to play it safe let's not talk about where we're going or what we've done or anything until we can be sure it's safe. For right now, just get in the car and head out. I'll call later to find out where you are."

The doc took me to the side and asked, "You are not telling something . . . is this correct?"

"You're right, Doc. Conrad wants a piece of all of us, not just me. So you all need to disappear while he's watching me," I said quietly.

"You think this is wise to separate like this?"

"Yes!"

"Then we will go," he said with authority.

CHAPTER 35

I stood there for a few minutes watching them drive away. I turned my head and glanced toward my room on the second floor terrace. It was a good location because it was visible from the pool, the restaurant, and the parking area. I noticed the curtain moved quickly as I glanced in that direction.

I felt my pocket just to reassure myself that the Colt was resting comfortably. Something about a piece that gives one solace under certain conditions, and this being one of them.

"There will be a person coming here to pick this up," I said to the clerk handing him the note for Conrad, still keeping an eye toward my room. Second floor, one way in and one way out. Their ass belongs to me, I thought with a slight smile on my face.

I took the long way up to the terrace but still leaving only one way out for papa bear, mama bear, baby bear or Goldilocks, whichever was sleeping in my bed.

I approached the door knowing whoever was there could come out running, gunning, or waiting inside just for little 'ol me. I didn't want to disappoint him, her, or them. I slipped the card key in the slot, pushed the handle quickly and flung open the door as I stepped to the side of the door frame waiting for a rush of people, bullets, or whatever. Nothing happened. I slowly looked around the opening, it was clear. I entered quickly, gun raised, surveying the room, everything was out in the open except the bathroom. I knew I left the door open before I left but it was closed now. I grasped the handle slowly and quickly turned it and flung the door open gun raised and ready to fire.

We were both surprised as I stood there looking at this nude woman I've seen before, only then she was dressed in white.

"Beth Franklin, as I live and breathe, I would never have expected to see all of you," I said in amusement.

"Don't move, Ms. Franklin, just stay real still until I get some answers," I said as she started to reach for something to cover up with. I could tell she was embarrassed standing there in the all together, and it was all together, in front of me with all the doors open.

"I would guess that you didn't listen and went to meet Conrad. He put you up to this, didn't he?" I asked, already knowing the answer.

"Yes," she said with tears in her eyes.

"Can I get dressed now? He didn't say anything about guns, he just said it was a joke for a friend."

Normally I'm just an 'ol softy but under these conditions I was going to be a meany, and she could see it as she started to move her hands to cover some of the more private parts of her anatomy. I pulled back on the hammer of the gun, and she quickly dropped her hands to her side as the tears started to flow.

"Ms. Franklin, or since we are so intimate I would say Beth would be more appropriate, wouldn't you?"

"I think we should step in the other room," I said as I directed her with the .45.

She started to sit down but I stopped her. "No, no Beth you don't get to sit, not yet anyway." Then I reached for the phone and dialed the local police and asked for Bill. I didn't tell him anything on the phone just that I had a surprise for him at my place.

"Please, Mr. Falco, please. It was just a joke, that's all, just a joke."

"Beth, I gave you a chance to stay straight. This Conrad is not a very nice guy. He murders little girls like you for breakfast and right now you are his next meal. So for your sake, I suggest you tell me when you saw him last, what he said and where you are to meet him next."

She was sobbing but getting a hold of herself, maybe it was the look on my face that told her she would be all right as long as she did as I said. Or maybe she realized this Conrad wasn't such a good friend like she thought.

"Beth now tell me what Conrad said to you to make you come here like this."

No sooner were the words out of my mouth when there was a knock at the door that could only be a cop. "Bill, is that you?" I yelled out.

"Yeah, Vince, it's me."

I opened the door and watched his expression as he stared at Beth from top to bottom and enjoying it.

"I . . . Wha . . . Vince . . .," he stammered as he kept his gaze on Beth.

"You remember Ms. Franklin? Or for sure you'll remember now," I said jokingly.

"Beth has come here to present herself to me under the direction of Conrad Johnston. I thought you should see what he has turned her into."

"Beth, put your clothes on," Bill instructed as he turned to me. "Vince, what's going on here?"

"I got a call from Conrad and I no sooner hung up when I see someone looking out of my window. What a surprise when I find her in her best birthday suit. I felt I needed to share the moment with a friend. In short, I'm on Conrad's hit list. He's watching me and I'm looking for him. He wants me to tell him where his treasures are at, and I don't know treasure from rocks at this point in time. But I will find him and with the help of Ms. Franklin."

"Beth, what in hell's name are you doing mixed up with this man? I told you to call me if he contacted you again, didn't I?" he asked more to emphasize his point than to expect an answer.

"He called me back after you all left the hospital and asked what you wanted. I told him, and he said it would be best if I did what he said or he would . . .," she stopped lowered her head and began crying again.

"Bill . . . I . . . I did some dancing to get through school and it was . . . it was erotic dancing. I was young, needed the money, my folks helped me all they could but they didn't have much so this job came up and it was far from home, so I didn't think anything of it.

But Conrad happened to be in the area one night and saw me. He took pictures and—"

"Conrad threatened to tell your husband if you didn't do his bidding?" I said as I interrupted her.

"Yes, he said he would make my life miserable if I didn't help him. I wasn't married at the time and it was in Tennessee. I never thought anything would come of it, honestly I didn't do anything wrong, just danced . . . just danced . . .," she said, her voice trailing off into sobs as she held her face in her hands.

I felt like a heal making her stand there nude, I thought. Chalk up one more mistake to my long list of things to improve on.

"It's all right Beth, I'm sure Roger would understand," Bill said trying to calm her down.

I looked out the window as Bill comforted her and noticed the same two mirrored reflections across the street behind some houses that were at the plantation.

"Bill, I think I've found Mr. Johnston."

Bill came over to the window. I grabbed his wrist stopping him from opening the curtain more than it already was.

"Just look, don't touch," I said. "There are two reflections close enough to be binoculars. I believe we are being watched."

"That's Woodard Street. I'm going to have the boys come in from both sides. That should get him," Bill said as he reached for his radio.

"I don't think the radio is safe, he may have a scanner."

"I'll use the phone and set it up," he said as he pushed some buttons on the radio.

"Where's the phone?" I asked as he started to talk.

He smiled and said, "We may be a small community but we do have some of the finest equipment. This radio doubles as a mobile phone with three separate lines, call waiting and all. Clever what they come up with." Then he continued with his call.

"Cleavon, now listen, I want you to come up Woodard from the south, no sirens, and call Carsten on the phone. Don't use the radio, and have him come in from the north. I have information that Conrad Johnston is there. Don't let him slip past you."

"Bill, you'll need to take Beth out with you. Better put the bracelets on to make it look good. You'll have to get her and her family out of town for a while. If Conrad thinks for a minute she crossed him, God only knows what he would do," I said as I walked out with them.

I watched as they drove away then looked over to the peeping Tom as the reflection disappeared. I figured I'd head over to Woodard to see the pickup and have a nice little talk with Conrad.

CHAPTER 36

I drove over to Woodard in time to see a yellow Porsche run over someone's lawn and through the hedges, followed by a black and white car, lights flashing and sirens wailing. Mr. Johnston wasn't going to cooperate and give himself up.

As they came closer to me, I turned my rental into the path of the Porsche and got out quick. All I could hear was a loud squeal, a big bang, glass shattering and metal scraping as the car rolled over down the street. After the dust settled the two officers, guns drawn, ran toward the vehicle, with Bill not far behind. The man inside was still alive but unconscious. Both officers struggled to get the door opened just before the meat wagon arrived.

Bill looked over to me and said, "It's Marvin Fairfax, gumshoe out of Raleigh. No disrespect to you, Vince, but Marvin isn't what you would call the most ethical of PI's. He's the peeping-Tom type, camera in hand and cheap."

"Seems as if our Mr. Johnston has an army to pick from to do his bidding," I said as I approached Fairfax as he was being strapped to a board and slowly gaining consciousness.

"I suppose you'll be going to the hospital with this guy and questioning him, right Bill?" I asked only to have something to say.

"Yeah, want to come along since you don't have a car anymore?"

"I would appreciate your help in that matter. Maybe a phone call to the rental place and have them send a replacement to the hospital while you're at it," I asked Bill.

"Falco, you sure do bring back memories of the big city and why I left. I'm surprised you haven't killed anyone yet," he said smiling as we walked toward the car.

"It's still early, Bill," I said.

As I got in the car, I saw Beth sitting in the back seat, white as a ghost staring out the window as a silver gray Buick headed down the street. I took notice of the large man behind the wheel and a smaller framed individual next to him, head turned looking in our direction. It had to be Smitty and Conrad. I just looked at Beth and didn't say a thing.

At the hospital, I grabbed a coffee and waited with Bill for Fairfax to be admitted. Meanwhile one of the deputies was taking Beth home.

"I sure hope Beth listens a little better this time," Bill said as he lifted his coffee to his lips.

"Doctor," Bill said as he began to stand up, "can I see Fairfax now?" he asked.

"I'm afraid not. He's in and out of consciousness. I'll let you know when I feel it will be safe. He has some serious internal injuries as well as a concussion. Nothing serious enough to kill him, but he will have some problems later on if not treated properly at this time. So if you gentlemen will excuse me, I will attend to Mr. Fairfax," he said as he started to leave.

"Doc, I'll be leaving a guard to watch over Fairfax. He is a key witness at this time," Bill said nonchalantly as the doctor started to leave.

"Lately this place is beginning to look more like the police station than a hospital. Wouldn't you say so, Bill?" the doctor asked with a smile.

As the good doctor left the room in walked the local rental agent with keys in hand.

"Mr. Falco, I am very pleased to see that you are all right. I've brought another car, and I have some papers for you to sign so we can get a police report for the insurance company. I declare you sure are lucky to be unharmed. That car is a mess. How on earth did you ever survive? What with most of the damage on the driver's side and all?"

I could tell he was fishing. Anything I would say that could possibly make me totally responsible for the accident would null and void the insurance agreement and make me pay. This guy was good, real good. Made you think of that TV cop with the old overcoat, always asking questions just to trip you up just by the way he comes at you from the corner, out of the blue.

"I must have had an angel in my corner. Strange as it may sound, I could have sworn a pair of hands reached over and grabbed me pulling me over to the passenger side of the car. But when I looked up no one was there. It was an eerie feeling and calming at the same time," I said in the most spiritual manner.

He just stared at me with that "should I believe him or not" look. Then he said, "Heaven was watching over you. I do declare you are a lucky man indeed."

I signed the papers, took the keys, and watched him walk out the door.

CHAPTER 37

I left the hospital wondering where Sam might be and then thought about the Weavers. She may have gone there, and since it was just down the road from the hospital, I figured I'd head over that way and see.

I was in front of the house turning into the drive and could see the truck and car parked close to the barn, but Sam's rental wasn't there. I figured I would stop in any way to see if she had been by.

There wasn't any answer to my knock, but the door was open so I yelled inside. "Sly, Ashta . . . anyone home?"

No one answered. I had one of those feelings when the hair on the back of your head stand up and your brain tells you to turn around and get out. But I must be brain deaf because I kept going.

As I started up the stairs, I could hear a strange sound almost like a dull hum. I took out my .45 and continued up the stairs. As I got closer to the top the hum became louder from the direction of the door to the right of the stairs. The door was partially open, so I stepped quietly toward it and pushed it all the way open. I was quick to enter, gun raised and ready.

Lying in the bed with his hands and mouth taped was Sly. I rushed over to him and quickly pulled the tape from his mouth as he let out a groan that would make a young man cry. While I was removing the tape from his wrists he was telling me that they had Ashta, and said that as long as she cooperated with them she would be okay and returned home. It was just before dinner when they came.

"They have my Ashta, Vince, they took her like thieves in the night that they are. I didn't see their faces—they were covered—but I know it was that Conrad and some big fella cause his weight took the breath right out of me. Vince, I gotta find them, can't call the police, you gotta help me," he said rushing his words as though that would get us out quicker to find her.

I couldn't help but feel it was too late. Conrad had a busy morning watching his disciples and me and that didn't leave him much time for Ashta.

Sly got dressed and pulled out a 12-gauge shotgun and started my way.

"Whoa, big fella, where you going with that cannon?"

"I'm gonna kill 'em when I find 'em" and rushed passed me.

"Let me take care of the gun before you hurt someone or thing you'll regret later," I said as I reached for the shotgun. Sly hesitated but finally let me have it, showing is good Christian upbringing.

In the car, Sly sat silent, staring out the window as if he would see her walking toward him, never speaking, just staring out the window.

"If I were Conrad looking for answers to the treasure location, I would go back to where it is supposed to be. And that would be the Barrett plantation," I said as we drove away.

The plantation was just ahead. As we followed the curve in the road, a gray Buick came around the curve heading in our direction. It didn't slow down. Although I knew who it was, they didn't know who I was in my new car. I could have given chase but I figured it was best to get to the Barrett house as quickly as possible just in case Ashta was there and still alive.

"Sly, you know it could be—" I started to say when Sly interrupted.

"No . . . she's alive, I can feel it. She's afraid but she's alive."

We ran to the house, up the front porch, and into the house. Sly started up the stairs when I called to him. I figured if they had her here they would conceal her in the catacombs. And the best way was to use their secret entrance, the hole in the floor.

Sly just looked at me as I started moving the debris from the floor, but as the opening started to appear, he jumped in and flung everything hither and yon like it was paper. He wasn't a man I would want to piss off on purpose.

With the hole exposed, Sly was in it quicker than a rabbit. I followed doing my best to keep up. Finally, I reached him, grabbed his arm, and slowed him down. "Easy man, we want to find her not run past her."

Sly started yelling, "Ashta, Ashta, honey! Ashta!"

"Sly, Sly, over here, over here," came the reply.

We hurried to her voice and found her tied and placed on a ledge six feet from the floor. Sly lifted her off and cried as he held her rocking back and forth. I reached over to separate them long enough to get her untied.

Ashta had bruises on her face with dried blood from her nose and mouth. I figured it to be the handy work of Mr. Smith.

"Honey, who did this to you, who did it," he kept asking. Finally, Ashta was able to calm down enough to talk.

"It was Conrad Johnston and he had someone with him. The big man did all the hit'n while Conrad kept ask'n where that damn treasure was. I kept tell'n him I didn't know about no treasure, that it was just a story, but they kept hit'n and yell'n at me."

"Let's get out of here and get Ashta to the hospital. I'll call the police and have them meet us," I said as I directed Sly with Ashta in his arms in the direction we came from.

Ashta was a little faint, but Sly had no trouble carrying her all the way to the car. I covered up the hole and took off for the hospital.

On the way I called Bill and told him to stake out the plantation house and grounds. I filled him in on what has been happening and that Conrad was getting careless in his desire to get out of this town.

CHAPTER 38

Sam was waiting at the hospital with the belle and her beau. I had called her on the way after talking to Bill. They all ran up to the car to see how Ashta was, so I stepped away as not to be ran over.

Waiting at the receiving door was the doctor who just looked at me and shook his head and said; "you must be Falco; Bill said you were bringing in another patient. Mr. Falco you have been here as much as I have, is it your wish to be a doctor or you just like hospitals?"

I found his levity to be hilarious and said, "I try to do my best to give all you young doctors a chance to hone your skills so that in the event I should have to attend one of these find institutions I will feel confident that I may be able to leave as well."

He smiled, nodded his head and stepped aside as we entered the building.

Sam just glared at me, didn't have to say a word I knew what she was thinking. Just then the receptionist asked, "Mr. Falco?"

"That's me," I said as I approached her desk.

"You have a call. Please don't hold up the line to long."

Sam looked at me as to ask who was calling; I just shrugged my shoulders to indicate the surprise.

"Falco," I said boldly, thinking it might be Conrad.

"Falco," the voice on the other end replied.

"Charlie, how did you know I was here?" I said with a little surprise in my voice.

"I called Bill, you know the local sheriff, well, I called him to let him know that Conrad Johnston was back. Said he knew already. So I asked him if he met a fella named Falco, and he said Vince, so then I asked if he knew where you were and he said try the hospital."

"Well I knew you weren't there to see Jonah 'cause he was back here as ornery as ever. So I figure you found Conrad and he done you in, so I called to see."

"I don't think that's the reason you tracked me down, old man. You have something else on your mind, don't you? If it's that Conrad is on the loose, well I already know."

"You young whip'r snappers all jump to conclusions too fast, just run'n your jaws. No wonder the world's turning out the way it is," he said more in jest than sincerity.

"Like I said, Jonah is back here and I overheard him talk'n on the phone, one 'o them speaker types, you know . . . the ones you can hear from without lifting it to your ear. anyhow Conrad's do'n most of the talking and he keeps ask'n if you been here ask'n questions 'bout the treasure. Jonah keeps tell'n him there ain't no treasure and he ain't seen you since the hospital. But Conrad keeps a go'n on and on about you get'n in the way and now everybody knows he's back. Jonah tells him to just get out'a town, there ain't no treasure and if he keeps believe'n there is he's gonna get caught.

"Don't make no never mind to Conrad, he says before he leaves he was gonna get that Falco for mess'n everything up for him. So I figure I better let you know what to look out for.

"That Conrad's a mean and stubborn cuss. You better take care."

"Thanks, Charlie. I appreciate the warning. I guess I got Conrad's attention."

"You better be careful, young fella. This Conrad's not a very nice person, never was, and never will be. Take my word for it," he said very sincerely.

"Charlie, do me one more favor, see if you can pump Jonah about Conrad's friends. It seems he has a big guy hanging on his side. He has a smell about him that I can't describe. But he seems to always be at Conrad's side."

"A smell you say, couldn't be a cross between someth'in sweet and rotten meat, could it?" he asked as if he knew it well.

"Yeah, could be, real pungent, so what do you know?"

"That would be Ed Bullock. He was the local sheriff until he got this real bad B. O. problem. He retired and kinda disappeared. Some say he picked up with Conrad 'cause he was always talk'n 'bout how he was gonna find the treasure before Conrad and then laugh 'bout it when Conrad was around. Only time I seen Conrad laugh is when he told the sheriff he'd have to kill him if he did."

"Real strange sense of humor he has, don't you think Falco? You better be careful, all I gotta say is carry your muskets full and your cutlass high boy."

"Thanks Charlie, I'll do that."

Now I had a name to go with the smell. Ed Bullock, aka Mr. Smith. He's seen the outside of the jail for a long time I plan on him getting his chance to see the inside with his good friend Conrad until death do they part.

I handed the phone back to the receptionist and turned to Sam.

"Well?" she queried, with a look of concern on her face.

"Just a friend telling me to be careful. He said he saw Conrad and he 'was a gun'n fer me'," I said jokingly to ease the already tense atmosphere.

"He certainly was right to warn you. You saw what he has done to poor Ashta. You could be next," Sam said as she got up close and personal to me.

"Conrad is definitely in this and out to get me. I'm the thorn in his side, but why would he kill the girls if he thought they could be the source of information to find this mythical treasure."

"No, there has to be someone else involved, but who and why?"

"No doubt Mr. Smith would kill if he was told to by Conrad or at least do some major bodily harm. He had no problem beating me hung up like a side of beef, and same with Ashta, but the girls, he wanted to know what he could get from them in that altered state he created. If that was even possible, knowing that Shannon was the key having responded as a Barrette. And he could have killed Sly and Ashta but didn't, so why kill Shannon and the girls? More questions still no answers." I said more for myself trying to figure out the why's.

Maybe it was the way she looked up to me with those green eyes shining and the curvature of her mouth while it was slightly opened, all together with a smell of desire, the softness of her body against mine in a nonchalant manner making it even more provocative.

I pushed it out of my mind the best I could as I stepped back and said, "Sam if it is all right with Sly and Ashta, if she gets released, I would like you and the doc to stay at their house tonight. There's safety in numbers."

Sam smiled as I stepped back, knowing what I was thinking by the way I looked at her. But her expression changed when I suggested she stay with the Weavers.

"Where are you going to stay if we stay at the farm?" she asked.

"I'll be close. Don't worry about me, I'll be all right."

As I turned Sly was coming through the doors moving his hands in rhythm with his mouth. "She's gonna be fine, just fine. The doctor said she can come home but to take it easy for a while. Yes, my Ashta's gonna be all right, but I won't rest until I have that Conrad in my hands."

I mentioned the fact that it would be a benefit to all concerned if they were able to stay with him and Ashta until this was all resolved. He smiled and said with sincerity, "Sure . . . y'all can stay as long as you like. Good friends like you come once in a life time and Jesus works in many ways to get people together."

Sly sounded more and more like a preacher with his hands gesturing and his voice rising with excitement. You couldn't help but like him with his sincerity and warm accepting mannerism. He and Ashta were the friendliest people I've met in a long time.

Behind him being wheeled out by a nurse was Ashta. She was wearing a bandage over her nose and under her chin. Both eyes were bruised and her lip was cut.

Both women rushed to her side and the doctor followed behind.

After seeing her in the wheelchair, I felt pretty much like Sly. Conrad wasn't going to walk away this time and Smitty was mine, all mine.

I turned to Sam and said, "I'm going to meet Bill. I'll call you later but be careful and stay together in the house."

"Sly, you want to come with me and get your cannon from my car. You may need it later," I said. Sly came over and went to the car with me.

"Vince, do you really think he'll come back to my place tonight?" he asked with worry in his words.

"I don't know but he wasn't done with Ashta. He doesn't know of the diary or he would have asked for it. So all he has is the thought that Ashta knows where the treasure is because of me, and he won't rest until he has it or he is dead. So be careful. Don't open the door for anyone you don't know."

I picked up the shotgun and checked the chamber for a round but to my surprise there weren't any shells in it. I looked at Sly and he just grinned.

"I forgot to grab the shells when we left. I suppose I was too upset worrying about Ashta and all. But as soon as we get back to the house, I'll load right away," he said.

CHAPTER 39

It was a short drive to the Barrette place, and I hoped Bill had arrived ahead of me just in case there was a reception party waiting.

I wasn't driving very long when out from the field came a pickup that looked like a semi from where I was sitting. It came up fast and rammed the rear end of the little car that should, but couldn't at this moment.

I swerved to avoid a second hit, but the truck caught the right rear quarter panel and swung me around. I recovered and ended up behind the monster truck. When he saw me he stepped on the brakes but I swung out and around him picking up speed. We entered a curve as I was doing seventy miles per hour, almost losing control as the tail end of the car started to swing around and kiss the front end. I recovered thinking I may want to change my shorts after getting out of here.

I looked into the rearview mirror to see were the truck was and I saw it as it rounded the curve on two wheels and then continued turning as it rolled over and over and over coming to an abrupt stop against a mighty oak that wasn't ready to fall.

The truck was belly up with smoke coming from the engine compartment. I stopped the car and headed to the truck seeing the driver struggle to get out. He was a huge man but he wasn't Smitty. As I neared the vehicle, the door swung open and then it burst into flame as the front end blew out, causing me to be thrown to the ground. I could hear the cries from the truck and saw his arms flaying wildly to put out the fires then they just fell as he was engulfed in the fire.

Bill pulled up behind me and scurried to the truck, extinguisher in hand. I got up and went over to help, actually to see what was left.

As I reached Bill, he had just put out the fire and looked at me quizzically and asked, "You all right? What happened here?"

I told him and then said "I thought this was Conrad at first when the truck came out of nowhere, but then I saw this was a big man and knew it had to be Smitty. Wrong again. I never saw this guy before and haven't a clue why he was after me."

"He is Ed Bullock," Bill replied.

"The ex-chief?" I asked. Now I had more questions, as if I needed them, and still no answers. Why was the ex-sheriff after me and since this wasn't Smitty, who the hell was?

"Yeah, any idea why he would be after you?" Bill asked as he continued, "I think there may be a little more you should tell me seeing as how we now have a body. With you around it seems more and more like New York, the place I left. You do remember me telling you that, don't you?

"What do you think, Vince?"

"Bill, I really don't know this guy from Adam. And I haven't a clue as to why he was after me. I told you about Conrad and this big fellow who was his shadow, but this isn't the same guy.

"Bill, you said the sheriff retired after twenty years, but he was still a young man, so what pushed him to retire?"

"It was pride, I think. It seems he, well . . . I'm not sure how to put it, but well he just began to stink."

"He went to all the doctors about the odor, took all kinds of medicines, but it just kept getting worse. And to top it off, he started putting on powders, perfume, anything to mask the smell, but it only made it worse. Finally, he decided to just pack it up and leave. Never heard from him again."

"Bill, I remember you saying that he retired because of a thyroid problem? Which was it?"

"Well, he said it was thyroid, but like I said I think it was the pride thing because of the odor. Don't know if I'd say I'm quitting because I stink. Would you, Vince?"

"You got a point.

"You know, Bill, Charlie told me that Bullock and Conrad were friends. Just how close were they?"

"When I got here they weren't exactly friendly toward each other. The sheriff had us watch him, not to the point of a stakeout, just as he would say, 'Sort a keep an eye on him, and let me know what he's doing,' you know, watch him close."

"Well, we followed orders but one day Conrad caught Franklin, he's one of us, and wanted to know why he was watching him. Well Franklin told him."

"This sent Conrad into a rage. He shoved Franklin knocking him over. This didn't go well with Franklin as he is six feet four and weighed two hundred twenty pounds, no slouch by any means. Conrad was all of six feet and a hundred pounds soaking wet. So pushing Franklin was not a good thing to do.

"Franklin got up and slapped Conrad a couple of times, to put it nicely, and then cuffed him and made a scene for everyone to see as he put him in the squad car and brought him in for assaulting a police officer.

"I tell you, Vince, the station was like a teenager's boom-box. Conrad no sooner got in the door and he started yelling at Ed for having him tailed and kept yelling about how he was going to sue the sheriff, the department, the mayor, and on and on.

"Ed didn't take to him shouting and just pushed him down the hall and into a cell where he took the cuffs off him and made the rest of us leave. It quieted down awfully quick."

"When Ed came out he pulled Franklin into his office and how the roof stayed on the station house, I'll never know. But when Franklin came out he dropped his badge and gun on the desk, said nothing and just walked out. We all thought he was canned, but Ed came out behind him and said he was suspended, and if any of us breached the confidentiality of his orders, he said, 'I declare I will fire the whole damn bunch of you,' then he went back in his office and nearly knocked the hinges off the door as he slammed it shut.

"Later we saw Conrad with black eyes."

"What happened to Conrad?" I asked.

"Ed had us release him a couple of hours later. And believe me he was mad as hell when we opened the cell. But before he left, Ed called him in his office and when Conrad came out, he and Ed shook hands and bid their goodbyes but the look in Conrad's eyes said it wasn't over."

"After that we didn't see much of Conrad, and then the incident came up with the girls, and Conrad was gone.

"It wasn't always like that with Conrad and Ed. The boys said they used to be thick as thieves. Don't know what changed between them, just one of those things, I guess.

"Anyway, Vince, I'll need a statement from you since you were the only one on the scene. I'll be back as soon as we get this cleaned up and give you a call to come down to the station."

I shook my head as I got in the car. This wasn't going to make it easy trying to get Conrad without some backup but you do what you have to do and I had to get Conrad.

CHAPTER 40

I remembered what Charlie told me about how Ed Bullock was the person I ran into with the foul smell, but it wasn't Ed Bullock. I needed to talk to Charlie again.

"Balmorial, Ben speaking, how may I help you?"

"I'd like to speak with Charlie Hands, tell him Falco's calling."

"One moment, please, I'll page him."

Balmorial seemed like a good place to retire to—clean, polite, and full of dames, I mean hens. If I live long enough to retire that is.

"Falco, still kicking, I see. What can I do for you?"

"Charlie, you gave some wrong information, it wasn't Ed Bullock that I ran into with the foul odor, it was someone else. You got any idea who it might be?"

"Now how do you know it wasn't ol' Ed since you didn't see him, only smelled him?" said Charlie.

"Let's say I met him at a barbecue and it wasn't the same fellow. Anyone else you might know that had a peculiar odor around here that would be a friend of Conrad's?"

"You remember me tell'n you about Ed always hanging out with Conrad, but I didn't tell you about Ed's little," Charlie chuckled at the little part, "brother. He left to live with his mother somewhere around Elizabeth City, not sure where. Ed, he stayed here with his father, became sheriff, well you know all that.

"Seems his little brother had a bad odor problem too, started early for him. But a mother's love and all, you know.

"Well, Ed and Conrad had a fall'n out and Ed left shortly after Conrad disappeared. But Ed's little brother it seems signed articles with Conrad, and they be shipmates from then on. Strange relationship, if you ask me. Didn't know Conrad knew Barney, that's Ed's brother, Barney Smith, same mother different fathers. Like I said, he left here when he was thirteen, fourteen years old. Ed and Conrad were a few years older, didn't hang around together as kids, it was after Ed became sheriff that Conrad and him became friends. Anyway, the father and mother split, Ed became a deputy at eighteen and thought he was the cat's pajamas. Conrad had the same attitude, so I guess it drew them together."

"So if it wasn't Ed, good chance it was his little brother Barney. So how's ol' Ed doin' these days?"

"Not so good, Charlie, he was the barbecue, seems he had an accident and went up in smoke. Too bad for the lad, but we all gotta go sometime, some sooner than others."

"Charlie, nice talking with you."

So now I have a name and some background on Smitty. Maybe his mother is still around and knows how to contact him. Sam might be able to find her.

I still have questions without answers, but some of the answers are beginning to form, like this Conrad's obsession with the lost treasure. The doc said once that Shannan must have been prepared to accept this alter personality. That's where Conrad comes in. He was the accepted "guru." But why would he kill the golden goose or for this case "geese" if he wanted the phantom treasure.

Something sticks in my gut that there is or was someone else involved. Now that's where Mr. Toasty, the ex-sheriff, comes in. But how do I tie a nice ribbon around him and Conrad?

I turned into the drive to the plantation. It was twilight time, and I knew Conrad wasn't here since I saw him going the other way in a hurry obviously upset that Ashta was gone from "his" special place.

Knowing that Bill had men at the Weavers, and I had my trusty .45 with me, all would be good with the world. Or so I hoped.

I slowly walked around the graveyard looking for anything out of the ordinary, only guessing what would be ordinary in a graveyard. After all it was the time for ghost and goblins to appear, maybe just the Barrettes would come out to play and give me an end to the "Mystery of The Lost Treasure."

But since I was here, one more look inside the crypt wouldn't hurt, I thought.

I descended into the crypt, flashlight in hand. It was enough light to get around, but I needed a little more to see everything again. So I lit the four lanterns again and the room opened up with light.

As I looked around, the four etchings caught my eye but this time I noticed that the coat of arms was sitting on a boat with two sails and what appeared to be cannons. It was a work of art, the stone work was neat with clean chiseled lines and a depth to it that made it look alive.; a little color would really emphasize the lines.

There were names at three different locations: one was Elizabeth Anne Barrette, 1800–1826; the second was Edward Hardie Barrette II, 1750–1827; and the third was Edward Hardie Barrette, Died . . . There was a fourth one started but not finished, it was Emily Maye Barker-Barrette 1760–. She died after the plantation was going broke so where was she put to rest. I can only guess that this Rainy Daye took care of her but where did she put her?

Right then a cold breeze went up the back of my neck and the smell of jasmine filled the air. I thought I heard a whisper faint as it was, "Look to the sloop, Falco." Then the cold was gone and the goose bumps remained.

It was time to leave. I wasn't dreaming. I wasn't imagining, and there wasn't anyone around but little 'ole me. Now what was a sloop that I had to look into?

CHAPTER 41

All I have are questions and speculations. What I needed were some answers. Or at least a small connection, something, anything would help.

I called Mike to get the results of Shannan's autopsy and how it fits in with the two girls here.

"Mike Cavenaugh here, how can I help you?"

"Mike, Vince—" he interrupted.

"Vince, where are you and what have you got on the Shannan case?"

"I'm just fine, thank you for asking," I said with a little sarcasm. I continued. "I need a little info on the autopsy report of Shannan. What drug was in her system that caused the paralysis, and was there any sign of blunt force trauma and was there any bruising around the puncture wound?"

"What's going on, Vince, and don't tell me nothing."

"The two girls here that were close to Shannan had their wrists slit and had the same puncture wounds as Shannan. Can't just be a coincidence. Also there was evidence of blunt force trauma.

"There wasn't an autopsy performed per the then sheriff and junior M.E., but the local mortician's assistant found the marks and notified one of the local deputies. He wanted to take it further but his boss said no, for reasons of his own, claimed he didn't want their families to go through more pain and suffering. The case is still open, a warrant has been issue for person of interest, his name is Conrad Johnston, you should be able to pull it up."

"I'll see what I can do. I'll get back to you. It sounds like you're in deep as usual, so take care, buddy. I'm not there to watch your back. Send what you have and I'll try to work it here. Oh, and make it in my lifetime please," he added as he hung up.

Still reaching for that brass ring, I remembered something Bill had said about what the late sheriff said to Conrad, "If you find that treasure first I would have to kill you." So how did Mr. Toasty fit in with Conrad's quest.

Somewhere in this triangle is the answer that could pull this whole thing together or at least set the wheels in motion to find the answers.

I still had to find out where this sloop was and I knew just the man to ask.

"Charlie, Falco, I need some information. I was told to look to the sloop, any idea of what this sloop is?"

"Sure do, it's a sailing boat, there was the 'Sloop-of-War' known in the 1800s. It was a small sailing warship with a single gun deck with up to eighteen cannons, and most were two-masted usually carrying a ketch or a snow rig. The ketch had a main and mizzen mast while the snow, a main and foremast. Of course the sailing boat sloop was a single mast with a fore-and-aft rig. It had one head sail if it had more sails then it would be a cutter."

I interrupted Charlie and thanked him for his help. But he wasn't done talking.

"Falco, what's going on, you buying a boat or something?"

"Charlie, you are without doubt the best source of information I know, and when I find out what's going on, you will be the next person to know. Thanks again. I'll get back to you."

So now all I have to do is find a boat in a town with all kinds of boats in the bay. "Look to the sloop"—what does it really mean? It has to do with the Barrette plantation, but how?

What's wrong with just getting "here's the killer and the treasure," not look for some boat. And where would they have put this boat anyway? The ocean is at least five miles away.

I've had some really weird cases but this one goes on the very top of the list. If there is a saint for PI's then give me the divine inspiration to get the answers I need.

My cell started buzzing like a beehive that had been disturbed. Could my divine request be answered so soon and on my earthly communication device?

"Hello," I answered in my best angelic tone.

"Vince, Mike, what's wrong with your voice you sick or something?"

"No, just, let's say tired for now. Do have the report from the M.E. because I really need something from this time period, the past is something else," I said in the most sincere way.

"What's that?" he asked.

"Nothing, nothing at all, just a little frustrated with all the questions, that's all. So what've you got?"

"The postmortem shows signs of Amytal Sodium, bruising at the base of the skull, and redness around the puncture wound. No defensive wounds found."

"Hope this helps, as for this Conrad, he is a slippery fellow. Seems he is wanted in Texas and Michigan, both states had him but he managed to escape."

"So what now, Sherlock?"

"Mike, all I have is one massive migraine. Thanks for the info. I'll add it to my questions list."

"Give me something, Vince. Anything would be nice."

I filled him in on Conrad, Smitty, and the late sheriff.

"Should have known someone would end up dead with you on the case. Vince, take care and try to keep me informed. This still is an open case here."

I hung up, thinking how all this added up. Still needed a connection besides this reincarnation thing. Just more to think about.

CHAPTER 42

I went back to Ashta's, tried the door. It was locked. I knocked and heard Sly bellow, "Who's there?"

"Vince," I replied.

He pulled back the curtains enough to see it was me. He opened the door cradling the cannon just in case I brought someone with me that wasn't wanted.

"Sly, you can put the hardware down I'm alone. So has anything happened while I was gone?" I asked.

"No, just sit'n an' talk'n," he replied.

The phone rang while we started walking into the living room. Ashta answered it, and with a quizzical look she handed it to me.

"Hello," I said waiting for an answer.

There was a slight hesitation then a familiar voice said, "Mr. Falco—"

I interrupted. "Is this my old pal Conrad? We're so close you can call me plain 'ol Falco. I sure would like to see you face to face, after all I do owe you one. So what can I do for you?"

"Mr. Falco," he repeated, "I obviously underestimated you. I know you have information I want and since you eliminated a thorn in my side I'm willing to give you and your friends a chance for a long peaceful life. If not, well Mr. Smith is very upset with the death of his brother and would like very much to lend his talents to inflicting some pain and suffering of the kind that would make a statue scream, if you get my meaning."

He continued, "Now what you can do to have peace of mind is simply to put on paper all the information concerning the Barrette treasure and leave it at the Tea Pot. Have it there no later than 10:00 p.m. this evening, and no cops. I won't be able to restrain Mr. Smith after that. He will get you and your friends, you do understand me, Mr. Falco."

"And 'my little dog too,' Conrad. I'll think your proposition over and by ten tonight I'll give you my answer." Must have said something to upset him because he slammed the phone down. Oh, well can't make everybody happy.

I turned around and the whole gang was standing there, waiting for my summary of the conversation with Conrad.

"Well, I had a nice chat with my good buddy Conrad. He said if I gave him everything I know about the Barrette treasure, he would spare me any inconvenience and would not bother any of you again. All I have to do is leave this information at the 'Tea Pot' by 10:00 p.m. He failed to give direction for the tea party, so I guess that's that."

Ashta spoke up. "He must mean the Edenton Tea Pot, It's down on Colonial Avenue. It represents the Edenton Tea Party back in 1774. Penelope Barker and fifty-one ladies petitioned not to buy taxed British tea or any other items taxed by the Crown. In its day it raised some eyebrows in England."

"So what are you going to do, Falco?" Sam asked.

"I'm going to see Bill and put together a noose for Conrad and Smitty. I would like all of you to stay here and keep everything locked, don't answer the door, just be ready for anything, that means make sure that cannon of yours, Sly, is locked and loaded."

"Why don't ya'all come stay at my place till this is all over. I have plenty of room," Jenny said.

"You know that's not a bad idea, but wait awhile after I leave, Conrad obviously knows I'm here and is watching to see what I'd do next. He'll follow me and with him will be Smitty."

"Doc, before I go, I need a little help from you."

"Well, yes, anything, anything at all."

"Shannan's postmortem said she was drugged with Amytal Sodium. I know it's a so-called truth serum, but how does it work?"

"Amytal Sodium is one of the intermediate-acting barbiturates. It takes a little longer to act, whereas Scopolamine, Sodium Thiopental are classified as short-acting barbiturates which act in as little as one minute. Amytal Sodium usually takes an hour give or take a few minutes. It lasts ten to twelve hours. It acts on the central nervous system and normally used as a sedative, hypnotic, anti-convulsive, and for narcoanalysis."

"You once said ideas or beliefs could be implanted in a person's mind when in a hypnotic state. Would this drug be an agent that would manipulate a person's behavior?" I asked.

"Yes, it is as I stated a hypnosis-inducing drug. Depending on the individual, it is given to aid in altering their memories or even inserting a false memory," the doctor said while stroking his beard, looking upward as in deep thought.

"Thanks, Doc, it helps a lot," I said as I started out the door.

CHAPTER 42

I drove away watching to see if Conrad was on my tail. I was a mile down the road when I noticed a car about two hundred yards behind me. I picked up speed, just enough to see if they were following me but not enough to look like I was trying to get away. It was them. I could see two in the car. I called Bill, apprised him of the situation, and told him I would keep them both on my tail as long as I could.

"Look, Vince, I have a man out that way. I could have him up in Conrad's face in no time."

"Bill, if you could box him in I would say do it, but if not then let's set a solid trap at the Tea Pot."

"Okay, Vince, we'll play it your way, but in that area there is no guarantee. It isn't the 'easiest area' to set a trap, but we'll do our best. I don't want them to escape."

"Thanks, Bill. I'll take Conrad and his Tin Man for a trip down the yellow brick road."

After driving awhile, I stopped at a coffee shop, parking on S. Broad Street near E. Water. Conrad turned onto W. Water Street, making a U-turn facing east so as to give him a better view of my movements.

I made sure I could be seen by sitting next to a window. I took out a pen and notebook I carry all the time making sure it could be seen, and began to write. After all, he wanted to know all that I knew, so it wasn't difficult to put it all down in my little book.

I made sure to write in big bold letters:

I DON'T KNOW ANYTHING. NOW WE BOTH KNOW EVERYTHING I KNOW. So don't forget your promise to leave us alone.

Love and kisses, Falco.

I just can't help antagonizing this guy. It seems so easy with him.

I could see they had the engine running, probably thinking I wasn't going to stay long. I'm sure Conrad feels he has the upper hand with full control of the situation, after all I wouldn't want anything happening to my friends. We'll see just how much control he has at this Tea Pot.

I ordered a sandwich, ham, and cheese on rye to go along with my coffee. Just as I was about to take a bite, my phone interrupts me by buzzing like a busy little bee. Good thing I had it on vibrate or I would be entertaining the guest of this fine establishment a little ditty of "The Twilight Zone," a personal favorite.

"Bill, what a surprise, what ya got? I've got Conrad watching me so you've got time to do your thing. Make sure it's tight, he has a way of getting out of tight situations. He may have set up a dummy pick up just to see what I would do. He did escape custody in two states."

"I thought of that. I got some extra help from the state police. I've set up posts on E. Water, King and Court streets. I've covered the yards off Colonial Avenue, both sides. I have a couple of ex-military good with camouflage. If they show up, we'll have them. You better be careful they may not be planning to let you walk away."

"Don't worry, Mom. Conrad wants to feed my hide to Smitty. He's saving the last dance for me. See you around ten tonight," I said as I hung up

CHAPTER 43

Back in my room I started thinking about this boat, "look to the sloop," what did this mean? Then the burial stones, unlike the grave stones on the surface, these were ore ornate with decorative carvings not just the usual born, died as on the ones in the graveyard. These were done by a very good stone mason, with care.

They were more monuments than grave markers. There was Elizabeth Barrette, her father Edward Hardie Barrette II, but the one unfinished, Emily Maye Barker-Barrette, she died after Edward and when the plantation was in the decline. Does this mean she was buried elsewhere because this part of the family burial place wasn't known to this Rainy Daye and her people?

The opening to the underground crypt from the catacombs looked to be dug out sometime in the last year, but nothing appeared to be disturbed in the crypt. Still something about it keeps me going back to it.

I shook it off, it was getting close to ten and I was sure Conrad was outside waiting for me to leave for the drop zone. I wasn't going to disappoint him.

I stepped out the door with my trusty .45 in hand under the package for Conrad just in case he changed his plans and wanted to get it here and not at the drop.

Nothing happened so I continued cautiously to my car and drove off. Not too far down the road, lights came on all of a sudden. It had to be Conrad. "The Games afoot" as the well-known sleuth, "Sherlock," would say. I sure hope my "Dr. Watson" is set up and ready to net the fish down at the harbor.

CHAPTER 44

I turned off S. Broad Street onto E. Water heading to Colonial Avenue. I could see the headlights turn off as the car behind me started its turn. The light from the moon still outlined the car stopped at a safe distance.

I stopped at Colonial, waited to see if Conrad was following, but he just stayed where he was. I turned left onto Colonial and drove to E. King Street. As I neared King, I could see Conrad stopped at the corner of Water and Colonial. I continued to King, stopped at the corner, grabbed the envelope with all the answers to Conrad's questions and proceeded down Colonial toward the drop zone.

When I arrived at the Tea Pot, I looked around then sat the envelope on the fence, turned and jogged back to the car. I drove off toward Broad St., stopped when I was out of sight and walked back to Colonial. I saw this hulk lumbering toward the drop, it obviously wasn't Conrad but for sure it was Smitty.

When he reached down for the package, lights came on, police rushed toward Smitty. He started to run, for a big man he could move, the police caught up with him and started to wrestle him to the ground. He put up a fight, broke free, and started running toward King. I couldn't let this go; I owed him some of what he gave me. I started toward him, when we were close, he started to throw a punch. I stepped into it and sing his weight I threw him to the ground. He hit the ground with a loud thud, and I could swear the seismometers in the area would register a big ten. As he hit the ground three cops were on him like flies on. They cuffed him, picked him up and while he was still struggling they shoved him in the car. I looked down the street toward Water and saw Conrad starting to drive away only to be stopped by two cars one at Colonial and one at Court.

I walked over to Bill standing next to the car with Smitty in it. Smitty glared at me with fire in his eyes I just looked at him and smiled. I turned to Bill, "Good job, I'll see you," and looking into Smitty's eyes, "and you at the station."

Smitty couldn't take it—he lunged at me banging his head against the window. I just smiled.

I could see over at Colonial Street where they were putting Conrad in their car. Well that was the last of it; the scene was secured and all the players drove away.

Satisfaction was close, all I needed now were the answers to my many questions.

I just stood by my car and wondered, was it all worth it? A mystical treasure, three young lives whose only fault was believing they lived in a time before now that was implanted in their minds by Conrad Johnston's insatiable drive to find this treasure spawned by the devil.

It was over now. Conrad and Smitty were in custody. All that was needed was a confession and conviction. I pulled out and headed for the police station. I wanted in on the interrogation.

CHAPTER 45

When I arrived at the police station Bill was waiting for me at the door.

"What took you so long? We have Conrad and Barny in separate rooms. I figured you might like to have a chat with Conrad. It seems you and him have some unresolved issues."

"Thanks Bill, I have more than some issues."

Looking through the glass, Conrad was sitting at the table, hands cuffed to it, with a smug look on his face as if to say, "You can't keep me."

When I entered the room, his demeanor changed quickly. His eyes glared at me, his jaw tightened. If looks could kill, I would be a pile of dust waiting for someone to vacuum me up.

"Conrad, Conrad, we finally get to meet face to face and you not standing in the shadows. So how does it feel sitting here where it all started? A bit like running in a circle."

"You think you're smart setting me up. You were just lucky I didn't figure on outside help," he said staring at me.

"We have you for three murders, kidnapping, and God knows how many other charges. So why kill the two girls and hunt down Shannan? They were your reincarnate believers."

"I didn't kill anyone. Why would I, you even said they were my inside help to get me the information I needed to find the Barrette treasure. So what do I get if they're dead?"

"Fifty to life," I said.

He continued, "I'll tell you what happened. Sure, I arranged to meet with Betty Jean and Katherine at the Barrette plantation, but it all changed. I was on my way when Barny caught up with me and told me we had to leave town and quick. He said Ed told him the girls were dead and that the whole town would know I did it."

"I went up anyway and saw them lying there—their wrists cut, blood around them. They appeared to be asleep, so peaceful-looking, they couldn't have been awake when he killed them. That was the only saving grace. I liked those girls. I could never do anything to hurt them."

I knew this Ed was involved some way. After all, he was the one that insisted on not pursuing it as a homicide. I was thinking almost out loud.

"Why did you run?"

"This town never really cared for my family, mostly me. So who would you believe, me or the town sheriff?" he said.

He had a good point but none of this would have happened if wasn't for him.

"So why Shannan, she was gone from this town. She had a life far from here, so why her?"

"I found out where she was living and made arrangements to meet with her. I went to her apartment, she was glad to see me.

"We talked, a little about old times, about her employment, and then she brought up that she was seeing a psychiatrist because of some strange dreams, her words. I asked her to describe these dreams. They were beyond what I would expect. She told of having a struggle with a Jonah Hyde, strange that his name would come up, he was a long past relation, one whom my grandfather was named. As she went on about the struggle and something about him being banished, it didn't make any sense.

"The things she said were so real I had no doubt she really was Elizabeth Barrette in her past life.

"I asked her if she would be willing to be regressed as we did before, she said yes, anything to end the nightmares. I injected a sedative and began questioning, as she was answering there was a knock at the door. I went to answer it. I asked who was there, then the outer door slammed shut. I looked out the door window and saw Ed running away. I told Barny Ed was around, so he went outside to look for him. When he returned, he said all he saw was a car speeding down the street.

"I went back to Shannan but couldn't get her to talk. I waited awhile, still no response. I checked her pulse, it was normal, her breathing was as if she were asleep. I reasoned that I may have given her a bit too much of the sedative—"

I interrupted him. "You gave her Amytal Sodium," I said.

"What, no, that would take too long to work. I used sodium thiopental, it's a short-acting drug, doesn't last more than fifteen minutes depending on the subject. I figured I gave her little more than usual and the reaction acted like a sleeping pill.

"I decided to leave and would come back in the morning. I set the door lock so we would be able to get in in case she was still asleep.

"When we returned, she was lying there, wrist cut, blood all around her. I knew it was Ed, it was just like Betty Jean and Katherine were left at the plantation. He has a temper and if he couldn't get her to talk, he would end it so I wouldn't be able to get any information from her. We left but stayed in the area to see if Ed was in the area."

"What time did you return?" I asked.

"It was around five-thirty, six, I figured the drug had to be worn off by then and I wanted to get to her before she went to work. By getting to her early could increase the chance of getting her in a hypnotic state."

"So why would Ed want her dead when he was after the same information as you?"

"Ed always said if he didn't get the treasure, he'd make damn sure I wouldn't."

"You weren't in the crypt."

Conrad interrupted. "What crypt?"

I continued, "The one at the end of the catacombs where the Barrettes are buried."

He had a quizzical look and asked, "What, I didn't find a crypt, what was in there? Were there any angels, sloops, cannons, what was in there?"

Obviously he didn't get that far. I didn't want to share any information so I told him, "Just stone coffins with some names of the occupants."

"Nothing like I described?" he asked. And then talking to himself quietly, "I didn't bother going any farther after I saw the empty coffin hanging down from the grave. I didn't see any crypt. It could have had all the answers."

I looked toward the mirror window to let Bill know I had nothing else.

"I wanted to hear what Smitty had to say."

As I started to leave the room, Conrad said, "You know where it's at, don't you?"

I didn't reply, I just kept walking. "Falco," Conrad yelled out, "don't you?"

CHAPTER 46

I arrived at the interrogation room. I stayed on the outside watching and listening to Bill as he was asking Barny what happened to the girls at the plantation. Barny just sat there mouth shut and staring into space.

"Barny, you're up for murder—"

Barny interrupted, "I didn't murder anyone." Then he just stopped talking and continued to stare.

Bill just went on. "Barny you may want to cooperate as it seems Conrad has already confessed to his and your involvement. It would go a lot easier for you if you cooperated." Bill stopped talking, giving him a chance to reconsider.

You could hear the wheels turning in Barny's head as his eyes started moving, slightly but noticeably. Then he looked up at Bill and started talking.

"All right I'll tell you what happened. My brother had it in for Conrad, he wanted the treasure and really believed Conrad was getting closer by using these girls . . . how wrong he was."

Barny continued, "Conrad was good at getting the girls to believe they lived during the Barrette time, even that they were friends of this Elizabeth, the clincher was that he had Shannan believing she was this Elizabeth Barrette. He was so sure of it that he believed she was the reincarnation of this woman."

Bill said, "You don't seem to share Conrad's belief."

"He believed in reincarnation, he is my friend, so I just went along with him, but we didn't kill anyone. Like I said, Ed wasn't going to let Conrad find the treasure so he did whatever he could to keep it from him.

"Ed came to me and told me he heard Conrad making arrangements to meet Betty Jean and Katherine at the Barrette plantation, so he went there to meet them. He said they told him they had nothing to say to him and started to walk away. Ed said he picked up a board and hit them with it and while they were unconscious he used one of Conrad's methods and injected both of them with a drug he picked up at Conrad's place. Conrad never locked his apartment. Ed knew that so it wasn't difficult to get."

"Ed said they didn't respond, they just lay there out cold. He couldn't let them wake up and tell everyone what he had done or let them continue helping Conrad, so he made it look like a double suicide."

"I stopped Conrad on his way up the drive and told him what Ed had done and told him we had to leave town because Ed said he would make sure Conrad got the blame. He told me to stay away from Conrad or I would be considered an accomplice.

"At Shannan's, she was alive when we left, dead when we returned. Earlier that night, Ed was prowling the area. Since she was in the same state as the girls, we knew it had to be Ed. He was watching us all this time waiting for Conrad to make a break in this treasure hunt."

Barny said, "I asked Conrad on more than one occasion to let it go, there wasn't any treasure, all the stories told of the plantation going broke.

"Conrad just laughed and said that's what we are supposed to believe."

Barny stopped talking and went back to looking into nowhere. He wasn't a puppet on a string, he was a good friend to Conrad, probably the only friend he had since he had a serious health issue. In a way, you had to feel for him.

Bill came out shaking his head. "I don't doubt that Ed did it. How to put it all together, well, that's another thing."

"We know Ed wanted this supposed treasure, and he wasn't exactly best of friends with Conrad. Also he, for what reason, came after me, probably thinking as did Conrad, that I had the answers," I said.

"It all seems circumstantial. One had a deep belief in a treasure and reincarnation, the other just believed in a treasure and that he was entitled to it and wasn't going to let anyone have it. So who would you believe had a stronger drive to murder and had the mind-set to do it? Most people consider cops have that mind-set, shoot and ask questions later," Bill said more to himself than to me.

"Bill, you still have him on other counts, assaulting an officer, kidnapping and assault on Ashta, and who knows what else you have them both on, but I don't think murder is one of them," I said giving him something to think about.

"You're right, Vince, no one said this job was easy. Well, we have him now. It's up to the prosecutor to figure it out."

I nodded and turned to walk away, hesitated and said, "No one said a cop's life was easy—win some and be pissed when you lose some. Good luck, Bill, but one thing is in our favor, he is still wanted back in my town."

CHAPTER 47

I sat in my car going over everything that has happened. Still eating at me was this sloop thing, hallowed ground, and then there is this unknown crypt built under the graveyard. Talk about not wanting to push up daisies, this certainly would do it.

Something Jonah said about Conrad running around singing a made up song was nipping away at my brain. I went back inside just as they were taking Conrad to his cell.

"Bill," I called out, "I need a moment with Conrad, okay?"

"Sure, Vince, what's up?"

"Just something his grandfather said that's just nagging at me. If Conrad remembers this poem, or song he made up, it may help me satisfy Shannan's request."

Bill looked at me as though I was keeping something from him.

"Don't worry, I'm not hiding anything. Jonah said Conrad ran all over the place singing this weird song about the Barrette treasure. I need to know what it was. It just may help me get the answers I need to satisfy the last request Shannan hired me for."

"That's the girl whose death brought you here, right, Vince?"

"Yeah, never dreamed it was so involved."

"Okay, Vince, he's all yours. Enjoy the serenade," he said shaking his and laughing under his breath.

I walked over to Conrad and asked out right, "What was that poem or song your grandfather said you were always repeating, or was it something he just imagined," I asked.

"You must mean the grave etching in the Barrette cemetery. Yeah I know it, why do you want to know?"

"It's been eating at me since he told me about it. Just want to get it right so I can rest easy, close up this case, and finally go back where I belong," I said as sincerely as I could hoping Conrad would buy it.

He looked at me for what seemed forever but was only a few seconds, then all at once he started to sing: "Beneath ye badge of Christian charge, Lies ye consequence of ancestry, Legion will ye cenotaph be, Whilst Cherub ye isthmus implies. Is that all you wanted? It won't help, I analyzed it every way possible. I took it to a Professor of Old English Literature at Duke University. He said it was just a poem celebrating the death of someone special. He said it wasn't unusual in those days to use this type of epitaph to have closure with the dead.

"Is that all you want?" he asked as expecting more.

"That's all." I knotted and turned to leave, turned my head back and said thanks and walked away.

So much to think about even though Conrad and Smitty were in custody; Ed Bullock, dead and accused of being the killer. I needed to rest and let it all go.

I drove back to the motel. Not a soul in sight, so I headed back to my room figured on a nice hot shower and maybe a little sleep. It was a very long night.

CHAPTER 48

All of a sudden bells went off shaking me from a most deserved sleep. This was one those of times I really wished there was such a thing as time travel. I would go back and see to it that Mr. Bell never made the phone.

I reached over and grabbed the phone, "Hello," at the other end on the phone was Sam.

"Vince, where are you?" She was all concerned about lil 'ol me.

"Check the number you called and it will be a dead giveaway. You called the motel, any hint there?"

"Okay, now what happened last night, did you get him, are you all right?"

I interrupted. "Put a hold on the twenty questions. Where are you?"

"We are at Jenny Lee's. So come on tell me what happened. Don't leave us all hanging."

"Conrad and his pal are safely tucked away at the local police station. I'll give a blow-by-blow rundown when I see you. Right now since I'm awake, I'm going to call Mike let him know all that happened and let him handle it from there."

"We're coming back to the motel, see you then." She hung up.

I sat for a while as that damn poem kept banging in my head. Conrad was in jail, the alleged killer identified, reason for the murders were answered, so why this nagging pressure in my head? I guess I may have caught that "treasure fever."

Maybe talking to Mike will get my head back on track.

"Mike Cavanaugh, can I help you?"

"Mike, how's everything at your end? Murders, theft, all the really good normal stuff."

"Vince, nice hearing from you. See you're still alive. So what's up?"

I told him everything that had happened, and if he needed more information he should get a hold of Bill Lexter acting chief of police for the official report.

"Thanks, Vince, when are you coming home? It sounds like you got a little too close on this case. I've said it before I'll say it again, take a real vacation. No crime of any kind. You may surprise yourself and actually like it."

"Mike, when did you become my mother? Okay, I'll take a little time while here in the sunny south."

"You do that, sonny. Take care," he said as he hung.

What the hell. I might as well enjoy a few days here and walk around the town with Sam. I know she would like that, I thought to myself as I lay back in the bed, letting everything go, just relaxing, and for me, that would be something new.

CHAPTER 49

I woke up from what was a sound sleep, the first I've had in a very long time. Then that boom, boom happened again. It was the door being attacked by that legendary guerilla that swats planes on top of high buildings.

"Who is it?" I asked knowing it had to be Sam.

"It's me, Samantha, open the door."

"How do I know it is you and not a stripper hired to cheer me up?" I asked with a grin.

"So why don't you open the door and find out, big boy," she said in her best May West voice.

I opened the door and standing there looking like an angel with the morning sunlight shinning behind her, outlining all of her womanly attributes.

"Close your mouth, Falco, nothing here you haven't seen before."

"Maybe I forgot," I said as I pulled her into the room, leading her to the bed.

"Hold it, big fella," she said as she pushed me away. "You owe us a story, and they are all waiting at Ashta's and with a nice big breakfast."

"I can't get a break," I said as I watched her put that "too bad" look on her face.

We drove to Ashta's without a word spoken between us. The silence was actually comforting. Sam just sat there, her dress open from the bottom to mid thigh exposing her smooth tanned thighs. It just made me wish we stayed back at the motel.

We arrived just in time at Ashta's. I was sure I would have stopped the car and parked just like kids at some romantic rendezvous if we had driven a little while longer.

We walked into the house and instantly a smell that made you feel like you arrived at the Pearly Gates filled your senses and made your mouth water.

"Come in, come in, sit down, everything is ready, you came just in time," Ashta said as she pointed to a spread that was fit for a king. And right now I felt like that King and picked up a dish and started toward the buffet. I turned on the way and said, "Ashta you know how to get to a man's heart. Sly is one lucky guy." I turned to Sly, "Fella, don't let this one go."

Sly put on that big grin I've seen before and reached over and put his arm around his wife.

I sat down, picked up my fork, and just before I could put the food in my mouth, I noticed everyone looking at me. I thought maybe I was drooling or had stuff stuck in my teeth.

"What?" I asked looking back at them.

Sam elected to speak for all of them. "Tell us what happened, Vince, you have us all curious."

"You know that curiosity killed the cat, right?" I said with a smile.

Sam didn't hesitate and came back with, "Yes, but satisfaction brought him back, so give, big boy."

"Okay, okay, it all went according to plan. Smitty put up a little fight but it gave me that well-deserved chance to even the score with him, but it didn't last as long as I would have liked.

"Conrad tried to get away but didn't count on outside help. He figured there wasn't enough of the local police to catch him and surprise! Bill was one step ahead of him by arranging for the State police to assist in his capture and still have a patrol unit to watch over the town.

"Conrad and Smitty both caved in and told everything. They didn't admit to the murders but they both pointed the finger at Ed Bullock."

Sly broke in somewhat surprised, "The sheriff?"

"Yes, the ex-town sheriff. He, just like Conrad, had a strong desire to find this mystical Barrette treasure before Conrad and if he couldn't, then he would see to it that Conrad would never have it."

I continued. "Bullock didn't have the reserve that Conrad had and when the girls didn't give the answers he wanted, well he wasn't going let them talk to Conrad or give him up for trying to force them to talk to him.

"He followed Conrad north, and killed Shannan the last girl that may have been the key to this treasure.

"Conrad and Smitty admitted to kidnapping, assault, and a few other charges, but not murder. They put that one on Bullock.

"They will still get to be together in a nice not so comfortable little room locked up for a long, long time.

"The good thing that came out of this affair is you, Ashta, finding your long lost grandmother Rainy Daye and her James, and possibly be able to give some of the families around here closure to some of the stories surrounding their ancestors."

"Amen to that, Vince," Ashta said.

Sly just stood next to her shaking his head in agreement.

We finally got to eat what to me was the best breakfast I ever had. I thought it would be best not to mention this fact to Lilly when I see him.

There were questions and I gave the answers as best I could, still having many questions of my own running through my head.

I must of had a quizzical look on my face as I answered their questions because Sam spoke, "What's wrong, Vince, you solved the case so why the quizzical look?"

"I still have some questions of my own, but no answers." I turned to Ashta, "This breakfast is the best I've had. I'll miss it unless you would consider coming North."

"Thank you, Vince, but Sly and me have a good home and friends here, but it's good to know we now have some very good friends up North."

CHAPTER 50

Sam and I left to go back to the motel, Doc went with Jenny Lee. He definitely, had a schoolboy crush on this southern vixen. It just may turn into something good. After all, he is far from his Austrian birthplace and shouldn't have any trouble leaving the cold, snowy winters of the North, for the milder winters and warm summers of the South. As for me, well I'm a glutton for punishment, and prefer the four seasons and harsh winters of the North.

I looked over to Sam and said, "Sam I want to go back to the Barrette plantation for a last look around. If you want, I can drop you at the motel."

"No, I'd like to go with you. What are you looking for?" she asked.

"The treasure, if it really exists. That poem you heard on the Jonah tape may actually have something to do with this treasure myth. I just don't know how. Maybe the graveyard has the answers."

"If nothing then I can forget all about it and you I can take a couple days and tour the town. That is if you want to," I said knowing the answer.

She threw her arms around my neck almost making me lose control and said, "Oh, Vince, I would love that."

As I was driving I started thinking; "This poem has to have some meaning. It can't just be an epitaph. There has to be more to it.

I started repeating it, "'Beneath ye badge of Christian charge'; a badge, it's a symbol, and Christian charge, could be a relic, holy symbol. The cross monument in the cemetery is a symbol of Christian charge, yes a charge or belief. 'And lies ye consequence of ancestry.' Lies, lays, in a cemetery it could mean at rest. Ancestry, long dead relatives, family. Could it mean that something is buried beneath the cross? We know there is a crypt there, and in it is the tomb of the alleged son of Blackbeard, Edward Thatch Hardie. He could be the 'consequence.' 'Now comes the legion' . . . legion . . . a crowd, mass, a host, someone who greets you, holds a party, commands the affair.

"So what do I have? Under the cross are buried the estranged family of Blackbeard, which could be considered a crowd with the head of the family being the host. The cenotaph is a monument or a commemorative plaque, while the cherub is an angel or cupid, a symbol of one of them. Then there is the isthmus—a land mass, ground, a cape," I said thinking out loud.

I looked over at Sam and she was looking at me like I needed a long rest in a well-guarded padded room.

"No, I'm no nuts. Conrad didn't know about the crypt. He asked me after I mentioned it, if there were any angels, a sloop, cannons. He knew what was there but he didn't know about the crypt.

"What do we have, I'll tell you. We have the cemetery, hallowed ground, the badge of Christian charge, the cross. The consequence of ancestry, Edward Thatch Barrette and his family buried under the cross. The isthmus being the cemetery. Now where does the angel, sloop and cannons come in?

"The answers have to be in that crypt."

Sam looked at me and said, "How did you pull all of that out of those few words, were you a code breaker in your last life?" She asked with a little amazement and a dig at my questioning of the reality of reincarnation.

"Don't know, it just seemed to make sense to me," I said.

"Then let's get going and look in that crypt," she said pointing to the graveyard.

CHAPTER 51

We entered the crypt from under the cross. The door opened easier than before. Must be from all the use it has had in the last few days.

I lit the lamps a little surprised they still had oil in them. They opened the room up with light. We looked at each stone vault, checked each name and date, hoping there would be a hidden message to point the way.

Angels, cannons, sloops, all sticking in my head, when suddenly someone turned the lights on in my head. I looked around again this time reciting the poem.

There in front of me was the coat of arms. In it were the four etchings, a boat with two sails, angels looking to the center were a Jolly Roger looked back at them. A deep chiseled circle surrounded the symbol—it had a diameter close to three, three and half feet, there were four cannons, one on each corner of the skull and cross bones. All of the cannons had extruded barrels; the sloop was set just beneath the Jolly Roger.

Sam looked around and said, "This floor is concrete, they didn't have concrete back then, did they?"

"Some time back I was on a case were a body was found, its hands sticking out of the cement. The foreman of the construction crew pouring the cement gave me a little history of concrete. It seems it was invented in England around 1824. Barrette had connection with English traders and probably knew of this then 'new' cement and had this floor covered. You can see the erosion, little as it is, that happened over time."

"Thanks for the history lesson. What about these burial vaults? They seem to be covered with something," she asked.

"Plaster, it has been around for a long time. I think the pyramids had a substance similar to it, the Italians and Greeks were using it for years. So nothing new here."

We went back to the shield and as I studied the symbols, all at once I said out loud, "Could it be that simple?"

Sam interrupted, "What could be simple, what do you see that I don't?"

"It has been in plain sight all this time. Look here." I reached down and grabbed two of the cannons on opposite corners and tried to lift the plate but it didn't budge. Sam saw what I was doing, and I repositioned my hands grabbing the two cannons on my side and she grabbed the two on the other side.

We pulled, then all of sudden I felt my ribs letting me know I wasn't ready for this. Sam noticed me grimace and asked, "Are you all right, should we get some help?"

"No, this is our find and I want to know what's under this slab."

"Okay, but you need to be careful, let's take it slow," she said with a worried look on her face.

With a groan we pulled and then we felt it move. We pulled harder and all at once it gave way. We set it to one side. We looked at the hole, a vault would best describe it, and there, was a chest. I reached down tried to lift the lid, but my side wouldn't let me do it. Sam saw me pull my body to the side and then reached down and with a strain on her face and a little grunt, she managed to get it open.

We looked at each other like kids in a candy store. There in front of us was what could best described as pirate treasure as seen in movies. There were jewels, gold chains, coins, silver, and more. We could see beneath the chest that there was another chest and on the bottom off to the sides were cloth bags rotted obviously over time, with coins spilled out. This was a classic scene from the old time movies. We couldn't believe our eyes.

"Vince, we found the Barrette treasure, it is real. I wouldn't even guess how much it's worth. What do we do now?" she asked.

I shook my head and started to close it up, when Sam said, "Maybe we should take something to show that we found the Barrette treasure."

Why not, I thought. "Sure, I don't see anything wrong with it, after all we found it. Of course, I'm sure we won't be able to keep it, but maybe, just maybe we'll get the credit for the find and God willing, we may get a finder's fee."

In the car Sam said, "I think it would be only right if Sly and Ashta get the reward for the find or maybe a percentage of the worth."

"Well there goes our reward. Easy come easy go," I said.

"Well I think it is only right, after all Ashta and her family have been taking care of the cemetery and her ancestor Rainy Daye and James actually are buried in that land. That should give ownership to the Weavers."

"It isn't for us to decide. After we see Ashta and Sly, I'll get a hold of Bill and let him contact the State attorney general and they can decide what to do. Of course I'll suggest that they get their own attorney so they won't get shortchanged."

"I guess that is the right way to go," she said with a chuckle and continued, "Or they could just say nothing and use it as they like. In your world, they would find a Fence and dispose of it piece by piece."

"MY WORLD," I said loudly.

"She threw her head back and laughed. "You know what I mean. You deal with . . . how should I say this so as not to upset you . . . some less than honorable people in your daily activities." She looked at me and had this big grin.

I smiled and we drove away. I couldn't help but wonder how good 'ol Conrad will take this. He had the clue to solve the problem and was so close to the crypt.

CHAPTER 52

Back at the Weavers, I told them of the find; Ashta held on to Sly somewhat weak in the knees from what I could tell. Sly just looked at us with total amazement on his face as to say it couldn't really be true.

I told them they should get an attorney before anyone lays claim to the find. Sly, still speechless, shook his head.

Sam and I left the Weavers and went to the police station to tell Bill in person what was found at the Barrette place. When I finished telling him, he stood there in disbelief that there was an actual treasure and found by an outsider after all the locals through the ages couldn't. He said I should be the one to tell Conrad, and I didn't hesitate to accept the offer.

Conrad listened to the tale and just stood there silent and in a daze. He tried to speak but words never came out. I left him standing there satisfied that he wasn't getting a share of the treasure he had searched for most of his life and caused the death of three innocent young women.

All of this going through my mind as the plane with Sam and I headed back to the North, the land of winter and what seems as endless sunless days and cloud-covered nights. And where most people experiencing some form of winter depression giving the doctors and pharmacies a huge hike in their already blotted profits. Too bad I didn't invest stocks in these drug companies.

We hardly spoke on the plane, partly due to all that happened and partly due to the people we left behind. Sam became very close to them in a short period of time.

CHAPTER 53

Back in my office, there was a message on my phone from Bill. He said Conrad kept pacing the floor in his cell, then one day he just ran head first into the block wall. He ended up with a concussion and a few stitches.

As for the treasure, the Historic Society was backing the Weavers for compensation and a piece of the find for their Museum and the Plantation with full rights to the catacombs and crypt.

The state was leaning toward an agreement with all of them, but there was a possible international implication due to the jewels, gold, and what not that possibly was taken by pirates from various countries.

It seemed to just be poly-talk to insert more road blocks. Well, it was their headache. I submitted my report and was through with.

I turned off the machine, and here in my office I stood looking out my window as the sun, just peeking over the horizon, was letting the evening darkness creep in. People walking, cars moving slowly through the snow from stop light to stop light.

Somewhere out there was Sam. Perhaps sharing the sunset with me and thinking of all that has happened these past few weeks. And Lilly leaning on his counter, thinking of the times he carried a little girl named Shannan on his shoulders. The doctor with his Southern belle, still in the south deciding if he would stay or return to the everyday rush of the north.

I stood there with all these thoughts rambling through my head when a strange feeling came over me. A breeze rolled across my face, cool, scented with a trace of jasmine, and then a whisper, very slight yet warm, in my ear. “Thank you, Falco, thank you.”

The end

CPSIA information can be obtained
at www.ICGtesting.com
Printed in the USA
LVHW032201271018
594844LV00002B/43/P